Hemingway's *In Our Time*

Hemingway's *In Our Time*

Lyrical Dimensions

Wendolyn E. Tetlow

Lewisburg
Bucknell University Press
London and Toronto: Associated University Presses

Associated University Presses
440 Forsgate Drive
Cranbury, NJ 08512

Associated University Presses
25 Sicilian Avenue
London WC1A 2QH, England

Associated University Presses
P.O. Box 39, Clarkson Pstl. Stn.
Mississauga, Ontario,
L5J 3X9 Canada

The paper used in this publication meets the requirements
of the American National Standard for Permanence of Paper
for Printed Library Materials Z39.48-1984.

Library of Congress Cataloging-in-Publication Data

Tetlow, Wendolyn E., 1947–
    Hemingway's In our time : lyrical dimensions / Wendolyn E. Tetlow.
        p.   cm.
    Includes bibliographical references and index.
    ISBN 0-8387-5219-5
    1. Hemingway, Ernest, 1899–1961.   In our time.   I. Title.
PS3515.E37I538   1992
823'.912—dc20   91-55092
                                                              CIP

PRINTED IN THE UNITED STATES OF AMERICA

In memory of my mother

Contents

Acknowledgments

THE idea for this work grew out of conversations with Professor M. L. Rosenthal and from his work with Sally M. Gall, *The Modern Poetic Sequence: The Genius of Modern Poetry*. I wish to acknowledge most gratefully Professor Rosenthal's guidance and attentive suggestions, and his fine example.

Appreciation is also due to Bruce Fogelman for comments on parts of this work, and to Philip Cioffari and others at William Paterson College for many years of friendship and encouragement and for pointing me in this direction. Special thanks go to my father for reading and commenting on the final version and for his interest in the production process. And of course I give much gratitude to my family for forebearance and support.

For their assistance in making the Hemingway manuscripts accessible, I wish to thank Megan Floyd Desnoyers and Lisa Middents at the John F. Kennedy Library in Boston. The Interlibrary Loan staff at William Paterson College and Julie McCarthy at Upsala College, Wirths Campus, were also helpful in making available critical works. Thanks to Marsha Labovitz, Judy Gessel, and others at the Sussex County Library for helping me to keep perspective, and to George and Barbara Matrayek for their help at the technical end. In addition, this study would not have been possible without the pioneer scholarship of Hemingway enthusiasts and dedicated members of The Hemingway Society; in particular, thanks to Susan Beegel and Robert Lewis for helping clarify publishing procedures in this field.

Finally, I am grateful to New Directions Publishing Corporation for permission to quote from the following copyrighted works of Ezra Pound: *Personae* (copyright 1926 by Ezra Pound) and *Literary Essays of Ezra Pound* (copyright 1935 by Ezra Pound); and to Charles Scribner's Sons, an imprint of Macmillan Publishing Company, and Hemingway Foreign Rights Trust for permission to quote from the copyrighted works of Ernest Hemingway: *In Our Time* (copyright 1925 Charles Scribner's Sons; copyright renewed 1953 Ernest Hemingway); *A Farewell to Arms* (copyright 1929 Charles Scribner's Sons; copyright renewed 1957 Ernest Hemingway); *Death in the Afternoon* (copyright 1932 Charles Scribner's Sons; copyright renewed 1960 by Ernest Hemingway); *By-Line: Ernest*

Hemingway. Selected Articles and Dispatches of Four Decades (reprinted with permission of Charles Scribner's Sons; copyright 1967 by Mary Hemingway); *Ernest Hemingway: Selected Letters 1917–1961* edited by Carlos Baker (copyright 1981 The Ernest Hemingway Foundation, Inc.); *A Moveable Feast* (reprinted with permission of Charles Scribner's Sons; copyright 1964 by Mary Hemingway); and *The Nick Adams Stories* (copyright 1972 The Ernest Hemingway Foundation).

Hemingway's *In Our Time*

Introduction

The secret is that it is poetry written into prose and it is the hardest of all things to do.[1]

MY object in this study is to demonstrate that *In Our Time*[2] is a coherent and integral work. Hemingway certainly thought so. In an often-quoted letter to Edmund Wilson he wrote:

> Finished the book of 14 stories with a chapter of in our time between each
> . . . to give the picture of the whole between examining it in detail. Like
> looking with your eyes at something, say a passing coastline, and then looking
> at it with 15x binoculars. Or rather, maybe, looking at it and then going in
> and living in it—and then coming out and looking at it again.
> . . . it has a pretty good unity.[3]

Hemingway clearly indicated in this letter that he had the structure of *In Our Time* as a whole much in mind. More than that, he was so sure about what he was doing that when a Liveright editor wanted to cut some material from the book, he wrote to John Dos Passos:

> A Mrs. George Kauffman is here and she claims they want to cut it all cut
> [sic] the Indian Camp story. Cut the In Our Time Chapters. Jesus I feel all
> shot to hell about it. Of course they cant [sic] do it because the stuff is so tight
> and hard and every thing hangs on every thing else and it would all just be
> shot up shit creek.[4]

At Hemingway's insistence, *In Our Time* was published without any of these proposed cuts. Yet ever since its publication, the integrity of its structure has been questioned by numerous critics, including Jackson L. Benson, Clinton S. Burhans, Jr., E. M. Halliday, Robert M. Slabey, Philip Young, and others.[5] It is true that it does not depend on continuous narrative but is made up of the short, epiphanic stories, punctuated by the italicized, imagistic paragraphs of the interchapters.[6] These smaller units, however, embody distinct, ultimately related, emotional sets and build into a clear curve of feeling from the introductory "On the Quai at Smyrna" to "L'Envoi." The relationship among the stories and the interchapters is precisely analogous to that within a modern poetic sequence as characterized by M. L. Rosenthal and Sally M. Gall:

> a grouping of mainly lyric poems and passages, rarely uniform in pattern, which tend to interact as an organic whole. It usually includes narrative and dramatic elements, and ratiocinative ones as well, but its structure is finally lyrical. [7]

On the surface level, we can see that the chapters and stories in *In Our Time* are linked by being numbered, by the presence of the character Nick Adams in eight of the pieces, by recurring images of birth, death, water, fishing, and walls, and by themes of violence and initiation. More deeply, though, the book's structure is lyrical. That is, it progresses by a succession of "tonal centers," "lyric centers," or "affects," to use Rosenthal's and Gall's terms, "centers of specific qualities, and intensities, of emotionally and sensuously charged awareness," [8] which "reside in the *language of a passage* [italics Rosenthal's] rather than in the author's supposed feelings or those of a supposed 'speaker.' "[9] The structuring—or the rhythm of feeling—of *In Our Time*, then, is similar to that of such poetic sequences as Ezra Pound's *Hugh Selwyn Mauberley* and T. S. Eliot's *The Waste Land*, works that progress tonally. [10]

Although my main purpose in this study is not to show the influence of Pound and Eliot on Hemingway, one must take some account of the importance for him of their aesthetics. That Pound influenced Hemingway's writing is well established. [11] Hemingway said in a letter to Arnold Gingrich that he had learned from "Ezra, in conversation principally," and we know that he also received advice by letter. [12] In a letter dated 21 December 1926, for instance, Pound commented on "An Alpine Idyll," a story Hemingway had sent to him for consideration in *Exiles*:

> This is a good story (Idyl) but a leetle litterary and Tennysonian. I wish you wd. keep your eye on the objek MORE, and be less licherary.
>
> Do you onnerstan what I mean about being licherary. Bein licherary mean that the reader (even the interested, and in my case abnormally HOPING reader) has to work to keep his eye on the page during the introductory pages. . . .
>
> ANYTHING put on top of the subject is BAD. Licherchure is mostly blanketing up a subject. Too much MAKINGS. The subject is always interesting enough without blankets. [13]

Hemingway did not take Pound's advice in this instance, but he did when writing *In Our Time*. As he wrote to Pound concerning the *In Our Time* stories:

> I am writing some damn good stories. I wish you were here to tell me so, so

I would believe it or else what is the matter with them. You are the only guy that knows a god damn thing about writing.[14]

In addition to the correspondence, Hemingway's "Homage to Ezra" in *This Quarter* and his comments about Pound in A *Moveable Feast* and the *Paris Review* show Pound's importance for Hemingway. But Hemingway's actual writing is naturally the best evidence. Analysis of the tonal patterns of *In Our Time* demonstrate how Hemingway's prose illustrates methods called for in Pound's criticism. These include "direct treatment of the 'thing,' whether objective or subjective"; a style with "no word that does not contribute to the presentation"; association of images and tones by juxtaposition; and "a rhythm which corresponds exactly to the emotion or shade of emotion to be expressed."[15]

Hemingway was aware of these tenets and the modern movement in poetry that Pound spearheaded. As he wrote to Arnold Gingrich on 13 March 1933:

About Pound I believe I've read almost every line he ever wrote and still believe the best is in the cantos. Matter of opinion. There is also several stale jokes, and quite a lot of crap in the Cantos but there is some Christwonderful poetry that no one can better.[16]

These observations underscore Hemingway's openness to Pound's example. He responded both to Pound's theory of style and to his qualities of sensibility, particularly as they related to World War I. The sensibility in *Hugh Selwyn Mauberley*—whose method, as Rosenthal notes, anticipates that of *The Cantos*[17]—is embittered by the brutality and hypocrisy of the age, particularly as revealed by World War I, and must, to maintain dignity, stave off disorder by asserting personal values.

Hemingway did not have the close relationship with Eliot that he had with Pound; in fact, Hemingway was often openly contemptuous of the man himself. "Mr. and Mrs. Elliot," a satire preoccupied with the failure of adults to connect emotionally and physically, is a direct slap at Eliot. As Kenneth S. Lynn points out:

That he chose not to call it "Mr. and Mrs. Eliot" did not once again, have anything to do with mercy, but stemmed rather from his habitual uncertainty about how to spell T. S. Eliot's name. In his correspondence, he occasionally got the spelling right, but generally he referred to him as "Elliot" or "Elliott."[18]

Furthermore, in a tribute to Conrad in the *transatlantic review,* Hemingway wrote that if he knew that "by grinding Mr. Eliot into a fine dry powder and sprinkling that powder over Mr. Conrad's grave [in Canterbury] Mr. Conrad would shortly appear," he would "leave for London early tomorrow morning with a sausage-grinder."[19] And in a letter to Harvey Breit, 9 July 1950, Hemingway wrote:

> Well I guess, some of us write and some of us pitch but so far there isn't any law a man has to go and see the Cocktail party by T. S. Eliot from St. Louis where Yogi Berra comes from "Royalist, Anglo-Catholic and conservative." A damned good poet and a fair critic; but he can kiss my ass as a man and he never hit a ball out of the infield in his life and he would not have existed for dear old Ezra, the lovely poet and stupid traitor.[20]

Despite Hemingway's acid comments, however, he could not escape Eliot's influence.[21] The "waste land" motif, for example, shows up strongly in In Our Time, The Sun Also Rises, and A Farewell to Arms.[22] Even more important for Hemingway's method is Eliot's idea of the "objective correlative,"[23] as a number of critics note.[24] Thus, he evokes states of feeling through the way he makes scene function as image.[25] In "The End of Something," for example, the opening scene of the ruined milltown with the schooner loaded with the remains of the mill moving out toward the lake is the correlative for a particular complex of loss and disillusionment. Hemingway thought this process of evoking states of feeling essential to the art of writing:

> Find what gave you the emotion; what the action was that gave you the excitement. Then write it down making it clear so the reader will see it and have the same feeling you had.[26]

In Death in the Afternoon Hemingway puts these thoughts in a slightly different way:

> I was trying to write then and I found the greatest difficulty, aside from knowing truly what you really felt, rather than what you were supposed to feel, and had been taught to feel, was to put down what really happened in action; what the actual things were which produced the emotion that you experienced.[27]

And as Hemingway explained to his father in 1925 concerning his work on In Our Time:

> You see I'm trying in all my stories to get the feeling of the actual life across—not to just depict life—or criticize it—but to actually make it alive. So that when you have read something by me you actually experience the thing.[28]

As his letters indicate, then, Hemingway was consciously concerned

with conveying experience as felt life. The present study aims to characterize the emotive structure, or tonal patterns in *In Our Time*, as a means
of demonstrating that it is a coherent, integral work. Chapter one looks at
the six prose pieces in the *Little Review* as Hemingway's first attempt at a
lyrically-interrelated prose sequence. Chapter two looks at the *in our time*
sequence and considers the changes Hemingway made in the interchapters when he alternated them with the stories in the longer sequence.
Chapters three and four of this study focus on the lyrical structure of *In
Our Time*. All four chapters consider the influence and relevance of
Pound's and Eliot's methods on Hemingway's writing. Chapter five briefly
summarizes chapters one through four and discusses how the sequence's
emotive pattern anticipates the movement in *A Farewell to Arms*, a later
work with a more continuous narrative contour.

1
"In Our Time" (1923)

As a writer you should not judge. You should understand.[1]

HEMINGWAY'S early efforts to arrange a sequence of emotively-connected writings appeared in the *Little Review*, Spring 1923.[2] As critics have often pointed out, the six paragraphs in the *Little Review* are preoccupied with violence. Five of them are concerned with war incidents and one with bullfighting. They all show the influence of Hemingway's days as a reporter for the *Kansas City Star, Toronto Daily Star,* and *Toronto Star Weekly*; they are concisely written and pictorial, but they lack climax and plot. Each piece consists of a single paragraph, the shortest, the fourth, having seventy-five words, the longest, the second, having one hundred and eighty-seven words. Separated by a series of three asterisks, they are untitled except the fourth which is titled "Mons (Two)."

Of the six, only the third is based on first hand experience: Hemingway's witnessing the Christians flee from Eastern Thrace in 1922.[3] The source for the first interchapter—I will call them interchapters since they subsequently became interchapters between the stories in *In Our Time*—has been unsatisfactorily identified. It is an image of a drunken battery of men riding off to war in the dark. But the second interchapter, a description of a matador trying to kill five bulls, was imaginatively recreated from conversations with Hemingway's painter friend Mike Strater.[4] The third and fourth interchapters, having to do with wartime fighting in Mons, Belgium, August 1914, were recreated from conversations with Chink Dorman-Smith, a British army officer and friend of Hemingway's.[5] The sixth interchapter, concerning the execution of six Greek cabinet ministers in Athens on 28 November 1922, is a recreation of an article Hemingway read in a newspaper.[6]

Beyond these general observations, I will demonstrate on closer examination that the interchapters are also connected by their lyrical tonalities.[7] As a whole, the sequence of six moves in the first from a mix of humor and anxiety as an artillery unit marches toward death to elemental brutality in the second as the colloquial idiom of an American describes a series of bullfights. The third continues the movement toward disaster in its gloomy depiction of refugees driven from their homes under the most dismal circumstances during wartime. The third and fourth, presented in the chipper idiom of an Englishman, depict respectively the killing of Germans in a garden in Mons, Belgium, and an attempt by soldiers to barricade a bridge for defense. Both move the sequence closer to the catastrophe hinted at in the first. The sixth interchapter closes the sequence on the most miserable note with the grisly image of the assassination of six cabinet ministers—a humiliating death toward which the sequence has been moving.

The first piece (Chapter I in both *in our time* and *In Our Time*)— quoted here in its entirety—opens the selection in the *Little Review* on a comically anecdotal note, but with an undercurrent of anxiety:

> Everybody was drunk. The whole battery was drunk going along the road in the dark. We were going to the Champagne. The lieutenant kept riding his horse out into the fields and saying to him, "I'm drunk, I tell you, mon vieux. Oh I am so soused." We went along the road all night in the dark and the adjutant kept riding up alongside my kitchen and saying, "You must put it out. It is dangerous. It will be observed." We were fifty kilometers from the front but the adjutant worried about the fire in my kitchen. It was funny going along that road. That was when I was a kitchen corporal. [8]

This first-person account of a French kitchen corporal's march toward war in the Champagne in 1915 begins with a suggestion of merriment— "Everybody was drunk." But the picture of an entire artillery unit drunk, going "along the road in the dark," and a "soused" lieutenant talking to his horse riding with the unit is at least subliminally foreboding and unsettling. In fact, much of the tension in the piece derives from the contrast between the speaker's comments—"We were fifty kilometers from the front but the adjutant worried about the fire in my kitchen" and "It was funny going along that road"—and suggestions of a journey to confusion and terror. For instance, the repetition of "dark," "drunk," "road," and "kept riding" (twice each), and words that suggest danger, such as "night," "dangerous," and "front," counter the opening note of revelry. Furthermore, the use of military terms—"lieutenant," "adjutant," "corporal," "battery," and "front"—obviously contradicts the domestic and peacetime associations of the word "kitchen."

Like tightly-written poetry, this opening piece further projects emotive tension by juxtaposing initial consonant sounds. The hard *d* sounds of "drunk," "dark," and "dangerous" in the first few sentences are offset in

the final sentences by the soft *f* sounds of "fifty," "front," "fire," and
"funny," paralleling the contrast in the tonalities of humor and anxiety in
the passage.

The play on the word Champagne, however, is Hemingway's greatest
stroke of irony, for as Hagemann explains:

> The Champagne was not a wine but a frontal assault against an intricate
> German defense. After a terrific artillery preparation on 25 September 1915,
> the French attacked and engaged the enemy until Christmas Day. In three
> months they lost 145,000 men, 120,000 in the first three weeks. The Ger-
> mans suffered heavily. A French tactical victory, military experts call it. This
> depends on one's viewpoint; plainly, the Champagne was mass execution.[9]

The final line of the paragraph, "That was when I was a kitchen
corporal," closes the piece with a clinching understatement that suggests
that the speaker is no longer as innocent in war as a newly-enlisted
kitchen corporal might be.

Through its contradictory elements, then, the first interchapter reflects, on the one hand, denial of a violent world, and on the other,
mildly bitter engagement with it. It also demonstrates the wide gulf
between language and experience, a gulf that paradoxically serves to
intensify the emotional character of the writing. In addition, it reveals the
influence of Pound's and Eliot's methods on Hemingway. It clearly
demonstrates Pound's idea of direct treatment of the subject, for Hemingway renders the image through the language of a soldier who lived the
incident. By using a soldier's first person account, Hemingway achieves
detachment similar to that achieved by Eliot in *The Waste Land* in
adopting varied voices. And like certain tonal centers in the postwar
works *The Waste Land* and *Hugh Selwyn Mauberley*, this interchapter
reflects disgust and anger at the war and other feelings of the times.
Likewise, Hemingway's concise, spare language bears out Pound's idea
that one should use no word that does not contribute to the presentation.
In 112 words, 48 of which are repeated at least once, and only 20 of
which have more than one syllable, Hemingway manages the kind of
compression that was to be his hallmark.[10] The deceptively simple
diction, as well as the simple, almost choppy sentence structure, contribute to the unsettling, disunified view of the world that is also a characteristic of the stories in *In Our Time*. In fact, this version in the *Little
Review* is so tight that Hemingway had only to add a comma after "Oh"
to include it in *in our time* and *In Our Time*.

In addition to its concision, this short dramatic scene—analogous to
Pound's idea of the image[11]—needs no clarification in terms of its
reference to place and time. For what matters is a particular state of

awareness that the sensibility projects, in this case an attempt at denial of fear mingling with a darker knowledge of it. As in lyric poetry of high immediacy, this interchapter and the interchapters that follow it attempt to objectify experience, not merely to present characters or scenes. The experience Chapter I conveys is a journey toward death, a movement that is sustained throughout the sequence in the *Little Review*, as well as in *in our time*, *In Our Time*, and later in *A Farewell to Arms*.

Finally, Chapter I anticipates subsequent interchapters with its technique of moving through a series of juxtaposed images, facts, and sense impressions that are not necessarily sequential, drawing toward a shockingly abrupt, ironic remark or image at the close. And while this interchapter only subtly hints at discouragement with an ideal, the subsequent interchapters fully express disillusionment with ideals of war, love, religion, and youth, imparting a pervasive sense of loss throughout the sequence.

While Chapter I has to do with war, the second piece in the *Little Review* (Chapter II in *in our time*, Chapter IX in *In Our Time*) focuses on bullfighting. But it, too, is characterized by conflicting elements, and it, too, is a self-contained emotional entity. Even though Hemingway had not actually witnessed this bullfighting incident himself, he was able to recreate the incident in such a way that his third-person narration is compelling and immediate. [12] Chapter II, as it was revised for *in our time*, opens with mercilessly violent images:

> The first matador got the horn through his sword hand and the crowd hooted him out. The second matador slipped and the bull caught him through the belly and he hung to the horn with one hand and held the other tight against the place, and the bull rammed him wham against the wall and the horn came out, and he lay in the sand, and then got up like crazy drunk and tried to slug the men carrying him away and yelled for his sword but he fainted. (*iot*, 10)

The absence of any comment upon the action thus far and the use of words that are reminiscent of violent American frontier action, such as "hooted," "rammed," "wham," "crazy drunk," "slug," and "fainted," give the passage a quality that recalls Mark Twain. [13] But this image of the bullfight, in part seen as a grim microcosm of the world, [14] becomes slightly less grim as the third matador bravely struggles to take on the bulls that the other matadors have failed to kill:

> The kid came out and had to kill five bulls because you can't have more than three matadors, and the last bull he was so tired he couldn't get the sword in. He couldn't hardly lift his arm. He tried five times and the crowd was quiet

because it was a good bull and it looked like him or the bull and then he
finally made it. He sat down in the sand and puked and they held a cape over
him while the crowd hollered and threw things down into the ring. (*iot*, 10)

The tension in the passage is heightened by the contrast in the underly-
ing tragedy of the action and the American colloquialisms: "kid,"
"puked," and "hollered." Such ungrammatical phrasing as "the last bull
he" and "couldn't hardly" give the interchapter an anecdotal, con-
versational character that ironically heightens the very serious purpose of
the piece. In an early draft Hemingway wrote that "The first matador got
the horn through his sword hand and the crowd hooted him *on his way to
the infermary*" [*sic*; italics mine].[15] By omitting "on the way to the
infermary" and substituting "the crowd hooted him out," Hemingway
underscores the idea of a hostile universe, one that offers no consolation.
The final sentence with its disturbing presentation of an exhausted
human—"He sat down in the sand and puked and they held a cape over
him while the crowd hollered and threw things"—provides one of the
dominant images in *In Our Time*. It is an image of defeat and degradation. This very powerful image of a prone human, vomiting and con-
cealed from disapproving observers, is a large emotive leap from the last
line of the first piece, "That was when I was a kitchen corporal," with its
subtle indications of horror to come. In other words, Chapter II plunges
rapidly into a world where heroic action is scorned.

The shift from the first piece's mingled denial and awareness of a
dangerous world to the second's frank confrontation with that world is
beautifully handled. It is communicated in simple, understated language
that is revealed in its informal vernacular and the external horror of the
scene. Also, unlike Chapter I, which is composed of eleven choppy
sentences, Chapter II has a breathless, cumulative quality attained by its
six paratactically-phrased sentences. Four of the sentences are run-on;
only one is simple, "He couldn't hardly lift his arm," to emphasize the
heroic nature of the third bullfighter. Although Hemingway subordinates
two phrases, "because you can't have more than three matadors," and
"because it was a good bull," most of the facts are coordinated, giving the
prose an uneasy character, suggesting a chaotic world. Stylistically, Chapter II is more compatible with the other interchapters concerned with
bullfighting, which are also composed of long sentences. This point
might have been a consideration in Hemingway's moving the chapter to
ninth position in *In Our Time*.

Although this juxtaposition of disparate tones and images between the
first two interchapters is an effective technical device, Hemingway must
have felt that it was too abrupt, for his placing Chapter II between "The
Revolutionist" and "Mr. and Mrs. Elliot" in the latter part of *In Our Time*

is aesthetically more satisfying than if he had placed it between "Indian Camp" and "The Doctor and the Doctor's Wife," the first two stories in *In Our Time*. Indeed, the sequence of interchapters and stories in *In Our Time* is characterized by a movement of feeling that progresses by juxtaposition of images and tones, stories and interchapters, a movement that builds gradually in intensity.

In *in our time*, however, Hemingway placed this interchapter second among the eighteen. As he wrote to Pound on 5 August 1923,

> When they are read altogether they all hook up. It seems funny but they do. The bulls start, then reappear and then finish off. The war starts clear and noble just like it did, Mons etc., gets close and blurred and finished with the feller who goes home and gets clap.[16]

At this time, then, Hemingway felt that the position of Chapter II was correct. When he published the six prose pieces in the *Little Review*, however, he had not written the others concerned with bullfighting, so ordering them as written perhaps seemed logical.

"In Our Time" in the *Little Review*, then, was clearly a sequence in progress. In fact, Hemingway's retaining the title of the sequence for the eighteen "chapters" that make up *in our time* and the fourteen stories and interchapters that make up *In Our Time* emphasizes the point that this work was not yet complete.

The third interchapter in the sequence (Chapter III in *in our time*, Chapter II in *In Our Time*) is based on a cable Hemingway sent to Toronto from Adrianople on 20 October 1922 as a result of his involvement in the Greco-Turkish war.[17] Charles Fenton traces Hemingway's compositional process through three drafts: "Newspaper dispatch; publication in the *Little Review* in April 1923; and final revision in the summer of 1923 for *in our time*."[18] He demonstrates how Hemingway's elimination of modifiers and explanatory comments from the dispatch makes it more compressed.[19] The revised version in *in our time* reads:

> Minarets stuck up in the rain out of Adrianople across the mud flats. The carts were jammed for thirty miles along the Karagatch road. Water buffalo and cattle were hauling carts through the mud. No end and no beginning. Just carts loaded with everything they owned. The old men and women, soaked through, walked along keeping the cattle moving. The Maritza was running yellow almost up to the bridge. Carts were jammed solid on the bridge with camels bobbing along through them. Greek cavalry herded along the procession. Women and kids were in the carts crouched with mattresses, mirrors, sewing machines, bundles. There was a woman having a kid with a young girl holding a blanket over and crying. Scared sick looking at it. It rained all through the evacuation. (*iot* 11)

Arthur Waldhorn, like Fenton, notes the compression of the paragraph, pointing out that Hemingway first gives a distant view of the minarets, then a panorama of the people and possessions, then a close up of the terrified girl watching a woman give birth; and then he moves back to the rain and the space. Waldhorn also points out that the three sentence fragments—"No end and no beginning," "Just carts loaded with everything they own," and "Scared sick looking at it"—break the rhythm of the sentences in the interchapter and force the reader to focus on the details of the information. I might also add that the third sentence fragment with its lack of subject and verb, "Scared sick looking at it," lends ambiguity to the passage, implicating emotionally both speaker and reader as well as the girl. [20]

Of the many modifiers Hemingway used in the cable to Adrianople, he kept only four adjectives in the interchapter. Waldhorn notes the specific purpose of each: "old" refers to the people; "yellow" gives the river a sickly appearance and makes it blend with the dismal landscape around it. In addition, the adjective yellow is in the middle of the paragraph where it effects, according to Waldhorn, "a transition from the generalized description of the first half to the concrete details that follow." The remaining two adjectives, "young" and "sick," are used in the dramatic incident involving the girl.

Waldhorn also discusses parts of speech and their importance in conveying emotion and movement:

> Verbs, as always, function to direct emotive response but also to avoid possible misdirection. Thus, the potential exoticism of *minarets* is snuffed out by the harshness of *stuck*. The gerund, however, bears the ultimate responsibility for "moving" the reader literally and emotionally.

Both Waldhorn and Fenton point out that gerunds occur every thirteen words, thus sustaining the movement of the interchapter. [21]

While Fenton's and Waldhorn's observations are valuable, I might also add that, like the first two interchapters, the third also mixes conflicting tonal elements. The image of the minaret—a slender tower from which people are called to worship—rising in the dismal rain above the mud where "old men and women, soaked through" are herded by Greek cavalry, is a bitterly ironic note, for here faith, religion, and church offer no solace. The language of the passage also yields contrasts: "No end and no beginning" sounds biblical as if it were a truncated incantation. This fragment, oddly hyperbolic, buried as it is in the details of the forced evacuation of the Christian people from Thrace, seems more like an understatement. Also, the etymology of the word "procession" suggests a religious or formal movement, when in fact, the population is being herded like animals toward slaughter. That Hemingway intended the people to appear as animals is clear, for the version in the *Little Review* reads, "Greek cavalry rode hard on the procession," Hemingway having changed "rode hard" to "herded" in *in our time* to sustain the feeling in the sequence of a journey to death (*LR*, 4; *iot*, 11).

Further contrasts are created by the use of words that suggest frustration, misery, and powerlessness, such as "stuck," "jammed," "loaded," and "crouched," and words that suggest movement, such as "hauling," "walked," "bobbing," and "herded." Even the Maritza river is "running" faster than the people. Yet the river's yellow color implies a speedy movement toward death. Thus, the emotional progression in this interchapter is a steady dismal march through a series of images that become increasingly grave, from the bleak minarets rising from the mud, a dreary betrayal of hope, to the frightening image of a woman giving birth and a terrified young girl looking on.

The action in Chapter III picks up the forward movement of the artillery unit in Chapter I, thus sustaining the idea of a journey toward disaster. Stasis and motion are counterpointed among the first three interchapters, however, from the movement of the battery in the first, to the static, beaten bullfighters in the second, to the movement of refugees in the third. But the images of defeat and degradation link the second and third. The picture of the "woman having a kid with a young girl holding a blanket over her and crying" recalls the vomiting, cape-concealed bullfighter in the second interchapter. While birth is often associated with new hope and spiritual renewal, Hemingway shows how demoralizing and ugly it can be. This juxtaposition of images suggesting birth and death is prevalent in *In Our Time*, both within stories ("Indian Camp") and interchapters (Chapter XIV, "Maera lay still . . .) and between them (Chapter XV, "They hanged Sam Cardinella . . ." and "Big-Two-Hearted River"). As I will demonstrate in chapter three of this study, this interchapter in *In Our Time*, placed as it is after the first story, "Indian Camp," serves to emphasize the emotional impact of the story with its tonalities of repressed fear and terror.

One final comment about Chapter III: the "rain," which opens and closes the passage, is the objective correlative, as it is in *A Farewell to Arms*, for a desolation of spirit.[22] Even though water and rain are often associated with rebirth or cleansing, in this sequence of six prose pieces there is little hope for renewal of spirit. That optimistic note does not come until later in the interchapters in *in our time*.

The fourth interchapter (Chapter IV in *in our time*, Chapter III in *In Our Time*), the shortest in the sequence, composed of eight brief sentences, focuses on fighting in Mons, Belgium:

We were in a garden at Mons. Young Buckley came in with his patrol from across the river. The first german [*sic*] I saw climbed up over the garden wall. We waited till he got one leg over and then potted him. He had so much equipment on and looked awfully surprised and fell down into the garden. Then three more came over further down the wall. We shot them. They all came just like that. (LR 4)[23]

As in the previous interchapters, irony is the predominant mode of presentation. The first sentence prepares for something pleasant—a garden—but the interchapter becomes nightmarishly horrifying as one image piles on another. The clipped nature of the sentences with their British idiom—for instance, "potted," "awfully surprised," and "just like that"—provide much of the intensity of the conflict between what's being described and the nonchalant, urbane way it's being expressed. This presentation of a British soldier's account of war is a desperate attempt to hold back the ugliness of violence. The short sentence, "We shot them," emphasizes the idea that real men, "surprised" men, men like "young" Buckley, were killed in this garden. The speaker is all the while anxiously trying to keep fear away so as not to appear vulnerable.

Further irony is created in the description of the Germans being shot, or "potted," coming over the wall as if they were ducks in a booth being shot at by fun-seekers at a county fair. But the idea of "potting" the Germans in a garden, or planting them, is a devastating play on words, one that recalls the gruesome line from *The Waste Land*:

"That corpse you planted in your garden,
Has it begun to sprout?"[24]

The words "garden" (repeated three times) and "wall" (repeated twice) become important images in *in our time* and *In Our Time*, for Hemingway's earthly garden is one where men "fell," and where they consistently butted up against physical and emotional walls.[25] Indeed, in a draft of the second interchapter and in the version published in the *Little Review*, Hemingway took out the word "barrera" in "the bull rammed him wham against the barrera," and replaced it with the word "wall," perhaps to emphasize a feeling of futility and failure.[26] Since the garden that Hemingway writes about is historically "unverifiable," as Hagemann explains, we must assume that Hemingway deliberately included the garden motif to heighten the irony in the sequence.[27] Thus far, Hemingway's picture of the world is hardly a paradise, and the people who are expelled from the land are as miserable as those successive generations in the Bible who are expelled from the Garden of Eden.

The tonal pattern in this fourth interchapter, then, begins with an innocent cheerfulness, then moves through a series of increasingly disturbing details that pull up short with a jolly dismissiveness in the line

"They all came just like that," as if this were a bizarre nightmare that can only be held off by the speaker's making light of it. This interchapter is so stripped and spare, and its impact so intense, that for publication in *in our time* and *In Our Time* Hemingway made no revisions except to capitalize "g" on "German" (although this change could have been the publisher's).

The action in the fifth interchapter (Chapter V in *in our time*, Chapter IV in *In Our Time*) also takes place at Mons, Belgium. The date of the incident, as Hagemann indicates, is 23 August 1914, and "The British Expeditionary Force has set up defense along a sixteen-mile stretch of the ruler-straight Mons-Conde Canal, spanned by eighteen bridges."[28] At the barricade across the Mariette Bridge, Dorman-Smith is "frightfully put out" when he has to retreat under the advance of the German commander, Alexander von Kluck.

While these details about the historical incident are interesting, Hemingway actually needs no background information to convey the emotion in the prose. In the voice of a spirited-sounding Englishman, Hemingway relays an occasion that results in disparaged failure. The only difference between the version in the *Little Review* and the version in *in our time* is the addition of the three commas, and the title "Mons (Two)," which was eliminated from the following version as it appeared in *in our time*:

> It was a frightfully hot day. We'd jammed an absolutely perfect barricade across the bridge. It was simply priceless. A big old wrought iron grating from the front of a house. Too heavy to lift and you could shoot through it and they would have to climb over it. It was absolutely topping. They tried to get over it, and we potted them from forty yards. They rushed it, and officers came out alone and worked on it. It was an absolutely perfect obstacle. Their officers were very fine. We were frightfully put out when we heard the flank had gone, and we had to fall back. (*iot*, 13)

As in the fourth interchapter, in the fifth the British speech characteristics serve to intensify disillusionment and anger. In particular, "absolutely perfect obstacle" and "absolutely topping" are funny in the worst kind of way when later the speaker says that "we had to fall back," the word "fall" bringing to mind the "surprised" Germans who fell into the garden. Also, Hemingway's wit is as sharp in this interchapter as in the others. The word "topping" precedes the comment that "they" would have to climb over the top, presumably, of the barricade to engage in battle. This image calls to mind once more the image of the men climbing over a wall only to get shot at. And, too, the word "potted" recalls the Germans in the fourth interchapter who were planted in the garden. Perhaps Hemingway was playing on another American meaning of the word potted—intoxicated—which reaches back to the battery of drunk men in Chapter I who go along the road in the dark toward certain death.

In addition, by repeating the image of the wall from the fourth interchapter, which relates how the Germans "fell" by gunshot into the garden, and by repeating certain words such as "jammed" used in the third interchapter to portray the beaten nature of the Christians, Hemingway sustains the mordant thread that runs through the sequence. To emphasize this thread, Hemingway contrasts an image that suggests domesticity and peacetime with an image that suggests battle and ruin. The image of the iron gate "from the front of a house" used as a "barricade across the bridge" for soldiers to shoot through suggests that there is no haven from war and violence, not even in private homes.[29]

The sixth interchapter, the only one of six to survive from the *Little Review* without changes, brings the sequence to a definite closure. It is based on a story Hemingway had read in a newspaper about the execution in Athens in 1922 of the Greek cabinet ministers who were thought to be responsible for the Greeks' defeat in the Greco-Turkish war.[30] The article describes how one of the men, Gounaris, was brought out of the hospital on a stretcher and

placed in a motor van and driven to a place about one and a half miles outside of the city. He was left lying on his stretcher in a dying condition while the car went back to fetch five others from the prison where they had all been confined in a single room.

To begin the horrors of that morning it was discovered by the guards that one of the five had died in the van on the way out from heart failure.

On the arrival of the van Gounaris was lifted out of stretcher to stand up and face a firing party. It was then that this wretched man, who, after all, had been a figure in the recent history of Europe, was unable to stand at all. He was thereupon given sufficient injections of strychnine to strength the action of his heart to enable him to stand up in front of the firing party. The man who had died on the way out was propped up beside him—a ghastly line of four live men, one half alive and one dead man.

They were then asked—Gounaris, the dead man, and all—if they had anything to say, an appalling instance of mockery. No reply was made, but M. Baltazzis took out his monocle, polished it and put it back again. General Hadjanestis calmly lit a cigarette.

The order to fire was given. The moment the prisoners fell the firing party rushed forward and emptied their revolvers into the corpses, including that of the man who had died on the way from the prison. The bodies were then thrown into a lorry and taken to a public cemetary just outside of the city and were thrown out casually in a heap in the mud which covered the ground.[31]

Employing Pound-like concision, Hemingway strips the article to these eleven, devastatingly blunt sentences:

They shot the six cabinet ministers at half past six in the morning against the wall of a hospital. There were pools of water in the courtyard. It rained hard. All the shutters of the hospital were nailed shut. One of the ministers was sick with typhoid. Two soldiers carried him downstairs and out into the rain. They tried to hold him up against the wall but he sat down in a puddle of water. The other five stood very quietly against the wall. Finally the officer told the soldiers it was no good trying to make him stand up. When they fired the first volley he was sitting down in the water with his head on his knees. (*LR*, 5)

Reynolds, Lynn, and Meyers note the important changes Hemingway made to the newspaper account.[32] He changed the hour of execution to dawn to heighten the drama of the scene. The shuttered windows of the hospital are "nailed shut" to show how helpless the ministers are without medical assistance, and we might add, to carry forward the feeling from the earlier interchapters that civilization with all its supposedly comforting institutions has turned its back on the individual. I might also add that the pronoun "they" needs no antecedent, for what matters in this scene is the feeling of abject misery and utter wretchedness conveyed by the description of the men and the setting.

Also, Hemingway has stripped away telling modifiers, as Reynolds, Lynn, and Meyers note, so that the bald details speak for themselves. Hemingway's image of "wet dead leaves on the paving of the courtyard," shows that Hemingway was familiar with the Imagists, particularly Pound. Although this image does not have the clarity and delicacy of "A wet leaf that clings to the threshold" from Pound's "Liu Ch'e,"[33] it certainly reflects Hemingway's familiarity with the idea that an image is "an intellectual and emotional complex in an instant of time."[34] Having changed from an earlier draft the word "stone," in "wet dead leaves on the stone of the courtyard," to "paving," in "wet dead leaves on the paving of the courtyard," Hemingway juxtaposes a natural element on a manmade surface, so that the rain, like the dead leaves, serves to underscore the inevitability of the natural life and death process and also the feeling of futility and hopelessness that suffuses the interchapter.[35]

The final factual detail Hemingway changed when he used the article for the basis of his interchapter is the inability of the minister to stand at all. Hemingway's picture of the minister "sitting down in the water with his head on his knees" as the firing squad begins to shoot is a fittingly horrid image to close the sequence because it links this interchapter to the second and third interchapters with their closing images of human suffering and failure of ideals and courage. But unlike the preceding five interchapters with their distinctive idioms, this final piece in the *Little Review* yields a feeling of numbness by its simple, matter-of-fact sentences and undistinctive vernacular. Only the last sentence has a dependent phrase which halts the steady rhythm of the parallel sentences and calls attention to the image of the sick minister.

As the concluding piece in the sequence, the sixth draws together a number of tonal threads. The image of a wall (the word "wall" repeated three times) picks up the note of emotional and physical impotence, recalling the fallen bullfighter of the second interchapter and the Germans being shot at as they come over the wall in the fourth interchapter. Likewise, images of "rain," "puddle," and "pools of water" (the word water is also repeated three times for emphasis) carry forward the feeling of desolation and despair from the preceding interchapters.[36] And in its morbidly depressive rhythms and images, which were anticipated in the preceding interchapters, Hemingway condemns war and everything associated with it. In short, the unrelenting oppressiveness of the succession of sentences speaks of a dejected disillusionment with the ideal that a government can rule and protect its people effectively and with the expectation that in the face of death man will act nobly. The sensibility of the sequence is every bit as repelled at the state of the world "in our time" as the sensibility that presides in *Hugh Selwyn Mauberley*. For the "myriad" that die in Hemingway's world also die, as Pound writes in *Hugh Selwyn Mauberley*, "for an old bitch gone in the teeth, / For a botched civilization."[37]

2

in our time (1924)

> Forget your personal tragedy. We are all bitched from the start and you especially have to be hurt like hell before you can write seriously. But when you get the damned hurt use it—don't cheat with it.[1]

HEMINGWAY sustained the bitter, fragmented view of the world that characterizes the six prose pieces in "In Our Time" in the *Little Review* in the twelve pieces he added to them to make *in our time*.[2] In the sequence of eighteen, Hemingway continued to use language to build lyric centers rather than for dramatic or narrative purposes.[3] The tonal pattern in *in our time* takes the shape of a journey, or a voyage, through various states of feeling, reflecting a troubled reaction to the modern world.[4]

While Chapter VI leaves us with a disturbing image of death as six cabinet ministers are assassinated, Chapters VII and VIII focus in closely on individual responses to war and death. Chapter IX moves away from the focus on war in Europe to crime, bigotry, and social corruption in America. Chapter X, the longest interchapter, consisting of seven paragraphs, moves back to Europe and presents the impact of the failure of love upon a wounded soldier who is jilted by his lover, the nurse who cared for him. Chapter XI shows the irony of holding on to political ideals in a debased world as it presents an idealistic revolutionary through the eyes of a politically more experienced speaker. Chapters XII through XVI—forming a short sequence within the longer one—shift to action in the bullring as a way of concentrating more intensely on responses to death and violence. Chapter XVII moves back to America again in its focus on the execution of a criminal. Chapter XVIII ("L'Envoi" in *In Our Time*) closes the sequence with a picture of a Greek king sipping whiskey in his palace garden while hoping to flee from the terror around him.

From the unpleasant picture of death by firing squad in Chapter VI, Chapter VII shifts abruptly to the close-up of two wounded men.[5]

Nick sat against the wall of the church where they had dragged him to be clear
of machine gun fire in the street. Both legs stuck out awkwardly. He had been
hit in the spine. His face was sweaty and dirty. The sun shone on his face. The
day was very hot. Rinaldi, big backed, his equipment sprawling, lay face
downward against the wall. Nick looked straight ahead brilliantly. The pink
wall of the house opposite had fallen out from the roof, and an iron bedstead
hung twisted toward the street. Two Austrian dead lay in the rubble in the
shade of the house. Up the street were other dead. Things were getting
forward in the town. It was going well. Stretcher bearers would be along any
time now. Nick turned his head carefully and looked down at Rinaldi. "Senta
Rinaldi. Senta. You and me we've made a separate peace." Rinaldi lay still in
the sun breathing with difficulty. "Not patriots." Nick turned his head
carefully away smiling sweatily. Rinaldi was a disappointing audience.[6]

The tonal movement in Chapter VII is similar to that of earlier
interchapters in that its simple, staccato-like sentences reveal ugly images
that terminate in dispiritedness and acerbity. Hemingway entitled a typescript of this interchapter "Humour" to intensify the acid tone of the
work.[7] But even without the title, it imparts anger and disillusionment
with an ideal. Images of helplessness and stymied action, in particular the
image of the wall and the wounded men propped in front of it, help
create this feeling. That the wall is around a church unable to help Nick
recalls the failure of the minarets and hospitals to help the evacuees and
sick ministers in Chapters III and VI.

To intensify the feeling of helplessness, Hemingway describes Nick as
dirty and disabled, his legs protruding "awkwardly" while "the sun shone
on his face" as if he were suddenly illuminated by the truth of the
situation. The Austrian dead, in contrast, lie "in the rubble in the shade
of the house." Nick's companion, Rinaldi, lies "face downward against
the wall," so severely wounded he appears dead. In spite of the carnage,
however, "things were getting forward in the town," and "it was going
well"—meaning that the more dead there are, the more successful the
assault.[8] Nick's and Rinaldi's "separate peace" coming in the midst of an
assault where the dead are strewn, and Nick's and Rinaldi's being so
incapacitated that Rinaldi breathes "with difficulty" are perhaps the most
bitter notes of all, for the separate peace has been decided for Nick, and
his disillusionment with patriotism—"Not patriots"—is clear.[9]

In the drafts of this interchapter Hemingway wrote that Rinaldi
breathes "heavily," but he changed the adverb to the prepositional phrase
"with difficulty" to underscore the seriousness of Rinaldi's wound and the
inevitability of Nick's and Rinaldi's making a separate peace.[10] In addition, Hemingway added in his final draft the word "carefully" in "Nick
turned his head carefully" (the second use of this word in the interchapter) to suggest the great pain Nick is in and his stoical attempt to keep

pain and fear away.[11] He also changed "Nick was smiling brilliantly" to Nick was "smiling sweatily," to further emphasize this idea.[12] For the last line of the interchapter Hemingway wrote in one draft, "You're no patriot Rinaldo" [*sic*], and in another, "He was disappointed in his audience but laughed. It was a good joke." But the revised version in *in our time*— "Rinaldi was a disappointing audience"—demonstrates more sardonically Hemingway's idea of "Humour."[13]

Hemingway's painstaking revisions of Chapter VII all reveal the loath-someness of war. The addition of one image in particular evokes the barbarity of war: "The pink wall of the house opposite had fallen out from the roof, and an iron bedstead hung twisted toward the street." In these lines Hemingway not only reveals the extent and severity of the bombing, but also shows how war violates private lives, in this case the privacy of the bedroom. And beyond this implication, the juxtaposition of the image of Nick's legs sticking out awkwardly, followed a few lines later by the image of the "twisted" iron bedstead hanging "toward the street," suggests that Nick's physical and emotional being have been rendered impotent. His impotency and helplessness parallel the predicaments of the murdered cabinet ministers and the beaten refugees and bullfighters in the earlier interchapters.

Additional revisions Hemingway made to Chapter VII also show his concern to convey directly and unflinchingly the harshness of war. Thus the phrase "two Austrian dead" replaces the wordier "two Austrian *cadavre* very crumpled looking" of one version and "two Austrian *cadavre* heavily dead" (italics mine) in another.[14] But in contrast to the images of helplessness are promising images: the sun is shining on Nick, and he bravely makes an effort to hold back physical and emotional pain, anticipating Villalta's noble behavior in Chapter XIV (the most affirma-tive interchapter in the sequence).[15] Nick's determination to make a separate peace, however, parallels a pattern of evasion that threads through *in our time* and *In Our Time*.

This pattern of evasion is obvious in Chapter VIII, another close-up response to war. In one version of this interchapter Hemingway gave it the title "Religion," most likely to demonstrate how ineffective faith and prayer are in the modern world.[16] Counterpointing Nick's attempt at dignity in Chapter VII, the speaker in Chapter VIII tells of a soldier who, wounded and sweating from both pain and fear, breaks down and chants desperately for help:

> . . . oh jesus christ get me out of here. Dear jesus please get me out. Christ please please please christ. If you'll only keep me from getting killed I'll do anything you say. I believe in you and I'll tell every one in the world that you are the only thing that matters. Please dear jesus. (*iot*, 16)

The incantatory, prayerlike quality of the first part of the passage with its repetition—"please" six times, "jesus" four times, and "Christ" three times—and its promise to "tell everyone in the world that you [Christ] are the only thing that matters," is brought up short by "he did not tell the girl he went upstairs with at the Villa Rossa about Jesus." The final, short punchy sentence—"And he never told anybody"—stresses the cynical tone in the piece, and underscores the hypocrisy of turning to prayer only at moments of great weakness and then only ashamedly. It also emphasizes the misguided notion that real comfort can be found in transitory love.[17]

The typescripts of Chapter VIII show the effort Hemingway put into writing uncluttered prose with clear tonal notes. For instance, he omitted from one version that the sun came up "from toward Venice," that "there was no attack" the next day, and that they had "two bottles of Capri at dinner at Mestre."[18] By doing so, he focuses on the protagonist's desperate fear of death and subsequent shame at having broken down and prayed for help. By changing the first person narrator to third in the final version, Hemingway achieves the same kind of aesthetic distancing he accomplished in the other interchapters by employing different speakers. But he retained the first person plural in "We went to work on the trench . . .," thus broadening the scope of the work beyond one speaker's experience and contrasting varied voices as he does in preceding interchapters.[19]

Chapters VII and VIII of *in our time*, then, form a point near the center of the sequence that contrasts bravery and cowardliness. In addition, feelings of disillusionment about religion and ethical values, and their failure to allay suffering, impart meaning, or provide comfort are also conveyed by Hemingway's focusing closely on particular characters and naming one to make him distinctive like the bullfighters in subsequent interchapters. These close-ups reveal more vividly that the loss of manhood and courage are replaced by feelings of fear and evasion. As a unit, the two interchapters anticipate a shift toward control of fear.

Chapter IX departs slightly from the other interchapters with its American setting and its characters' racist attack on Italians. According to Reynolds, this interchapter is based on a story in the *Kansas City Star*, 19 November 1917, concerning the robbery of a cigar store by three men and their subsequent shooting by policemen.[20] Although we are not certain if Hemingway wrote the newspaper account, he did cover the beat and was familiar with the case. He transformed the newspaper story into the following brief account as it appears in *in our time*:

At two o'clock in the morning two Hungarians got into a cigar store at Fifteenth Street and Grand Avenue. Drevitts and Boyle drove up from the

Fifteenth Street police station in a Ford. The Hungarians were backing their wagon out of an alley. Boyle shot one off the seat of the wagon and one out of the wagon box. Drevetts [*sic*] got frightened when he found they were both dead. Hell Jimmy, he said, you oughtn't to have done it. There's liable to be a hell of a lot of trouble.

—They're crooks ain't they? said Boyle. They're wops ain't they? Who the hell is going to make any trouble?

—That's all right maybe this time, said Drevitts, but how did you know they were wops when you bumped them?

Wops, said Boyle, I can tell wops a mile off. (*iot*, 17)[21]

Entitled "Crime" and "Crime and Punishment" in the early typescripts, Chapter IX is every bit as critical of the times as the preceding interchapters, for here crime takes on a two-fold nature: the Irish policeman Boyle, equating "wops" and "crooks," makes race a justification for his murdering the Hungarians.[22] Even though this interchapter concerns "crime" rather than war or bullfighting and employs a slightly different technique—images do not pile up as they do in some of the other interchapters, and dialogue advances the movement more than in the other interchapters—Chapter IX succeeds in conveying through understated speech another scene of violence and failed ideals.

It progresses from a blunt, shocking statement, "Boyle shot one off the seat of the wagon and one out of the wagon box," to the fearful, accusatory speech of Drevitts, "There's liable to be a hell of a lot of trouble." Then it shifts to Boyle's bigoted defensiveness, "They're wops ain't they," and then it moves to Drevitts's conciliatory, "that's all right maybe this time. . . ." It closes with Boyle's savagely condescending remark—"I can tell wops a mile off"—and drives home the point that violence extends to civilian life even in America.

Like a tight poem, the sounds in the interchapter carry the reader forward and focus the feeling. In the first few sentences the *oo* sounds in "two" (twice), and "Avenue," and the long *o* in "drove," "Ford," "store," and "both," parallel the difference in Drevitts's uncomfortable doubts about killing the Hungarians and Boyle's racist confidence in doing so. Likewise, the repetition of words, "Fifteenth Street" (twice), "Hungarians" (twice), "wagon" (three times), "wops" (four times), give Chapter IX coherence and a rhythmic quality that hammers in the characters' hypocrisy. A series of four rhetorical questions increase its pace, but these are pulled up short by Boyle's final self-righteous remark, emphasizing a familiar pattern in the sequence: an abrupt pitiless closure.

Chapter X, the longest in the sequence, relies more than the other interchapters on narration and exposition than on description and dialogue to yield a curve of feeling.[23] Entitled "Love" in an early typescript, to parallel in bitterness the interchapters concerned with "Religion" and

"Crime," the story presents a soldier who is betrayed by his girl and seeks consolation in easy sex.[24] Its direct treatment of the affair, with no authorial comment, conveys the cynicism borne of the breakup of the affair and points up the contrast between the title "Love" and transience of feeling.

Hemingway was aware that Chapter X and Chapter XI break the mode of emotive presentation in *in our time*, for he later gave them titles, "A Very Short Story" and "The Revolutionist," and included them as stories in *In Our Time*. Even though Chapter X does not focus on a single instant or moment as the other interchapters do, but rather covers a number of moments over a period of months, its simplicity of diction and sentence structure, its straightforward presentation, and its tonal movement from deceptive optimism to revulsion and resentment give it some common ground with the other interchapters.

It begins on a satiric once-upon-a-time-in-a-far-away-land note as it describes how a wounded young soldier is carried to the roof (of the hospital supposedly) to look out over the town. His nurse and lover Ag cares for him, and he eventually recovers and returns to the States to get a job and wait for Ag to join him.[25] But Ag stays in Torre di Mosta and makes love to an Italian major and writes back to the young man that theirs was "only a boy and girl affair." The soldier never answers Ag's letter, and "A short time after he contracted gonorrhea from a sales girl from the Fair riding in a taxicab through Lincoln Park" (*iot*, 19).

Keith Carabine notes that the disillusion in the work is "cheaply earned."[26] Likewise, Hemphill says it is "a very bad story" because the only reason given for the breakup of the affair "is quite an accident, excessively naturalistic, dramatically inert, and more cynical than it need be under the circumstances."[27] On the contrary, the cumulative bitterness in the preceding nine interchapters suggests a dissatisfaction with traditional ideals and thus anticipates the failure of love in Chapter X. Also, within the interchapter itself are foreshadowings of this loss of love.

The story's mocking tone mingles a romantic playfulness with a dark foreboding that becomes increasingly intense. These are the opening lines as they appeared in *in our time*:

> One hot evening in Milan they carried him up onto the roof and he could look out over the top of town. There were chimney swifts in the sky. After a while it got dark and the searchlights came out. The others went down and took the bottles with them. He and Ag could hear them below on the balcony. Ag sat on the bed. She was cool and fresh in the hot night. (*iot*, 18)

The image of the chimney swifts is uplifting and romantic. But the image of searchlights scouring a dark sky recalls the realities of the wartime situation and suggests a more unsettling tonal stream in the prose.

Likewise, in the second paragraph Ag's and the soldier's private joke about his operation and his thoughts about their intimacy suggest the intensity of their relationship; yet a darker current is also present in the image of the soldier's holding himself tight, as if he were afraid of something:

> When they operated on him she prepared him for the operating table, and they had a joke about friend or enema. He went under the anaesthetic holding tight on to himself so that he would not blab about anything during the silly, talky time. (*iot*, 18)

The third paragraph also makes ready for the failure of love. Even though Ag and the soldier pray in the Duomo and they want to get married, "there was not enough time for the banns, and neither of them had birth certificates" (*iot*, 18). The following lines most clearly anticipate the end of the relationship: "They wanted everyone to know about it [their love] and to make it so they could not lose it" (*iot*, 18). Hemingway added this sentence to an early typescript and omitted the line, "They loved each other very much," to emphasize that they will most certainly lose their love.[28]

Wartime circumstances then turn against the lovers: the soldier doesn't receive Ag's letters until after the armistice; then he reads all fifteen "straight through" about "how much she loved him" and "how terrible it was missing him at night" (*iot*, 18).[29] After the armistice, the soldier goes home to get "a job so they might be married" because Ag "would not come home until he had a good job," as if their happiness hinged on his ability to get "a good job" (*iot*, 19). One of the most resentful notes comes in the line, "It was understood he would not drink, and he did not want to see his friends or anyone in the States." The repetition of the phrase, "Only to get a job and be married," makes the soldier sound more condemned than committed to their relationship (*iot*, 19).

Finally, Ag's unwillingness "to come at once" looks forward to her capitulation to the Italian major. The paraphrase of her letter brings Chapter X to a crescendo of resentment: "She knew he would have a great career, and believed in him absolutely" (*iot*, 19). The repetition of "theirs had been only a boy and girl affair" and the final line telling of the soldier's contracting gonorrhea from a sales girl from the fair riding in a taxicab through Lincoln Park conclude Chapter X on the most sour note in the sequence.[30]

At first entitled "Youth" in the typescripts, Chapter XI, like Chapter X, subsequently became a separate story—"The Revolutionist"—in *In Our Time*.[31] Its lyrical pattern moves from gentle admiration to muted cynicism with a tension between skepticism and idealism. A politically skeptical speaker tells how a shy, young Hungarian communist travels by train in Fascist Italy in 1919 carrying "a square of oilcloth written in indelible pencil and saying here was a Comrade who had suffered very much under the whites in Budapest and requesting comrades to aid him in any way" (*iot*, 20). The speaker in Chapter XI, unlike the speaker in Chapter X, is not stunned by the course of events; he is sympathetic to the young protagonist's plight.

Based on a piece Hemingway wrote for the *Toronto Daily Star* in 1922,[32] Chapter XI reveals that the Magyar meets the speaker in Bologna and that the two travel together for a while on the rails where the speaker finds out that "Horthy's men had done some bad things to him" [the Magyar].[33] Burhans argues that the Magyar "responds to cruelty, violence, and suffering not with self-pity or bitterness or detachment but with a stronger faith and a deeper joy in the beauty and kindness and love he finds in the world."[34] He rejects the speaker's offers to view the Renaissance painter Mantegna and the speaker's offers of shelter and companionship in Milano because "his mind was already looking forward to walking over the pass." The last time the speaker hears of him "the Swiss had him in jail near Sion" (*iot*, 20–21). To drive home the pointlessness of holding onto political ideals in a violent, chaotic world, Hemingway preceded the final line of this story in *In Our Time* with this addition: "He loved the mountains in the autumn" (*IOT*, 82).

Other ironies abound: the Magyar is jailed in a country traditionally known for freedom and lack of political involvement. As Anthony Hunt explains, the pun on Sion, or the Biblical Zion, the earthly paradise, also contributes to the critical tone of the work.[35] Furthermore, in the context of world events at this time (Italy was about to fall to Mussolini's rule), the youth's comments that Italy, as far as the communist movement goes, is "the one country that everyone is sure of " (*iot*, 21) seems the epitome of political naivete.

Following ten interchapters that focus on death, violence, and misery, the Magyar's believing "altogether in the world revolution" (*iot*, 20) appears all the more foolish, for in the world that Hemingway has drawn there seems little hope for peace through revolution or any other way. Connections to the other interchapters do exist, however. Jackson L. Benson notes the following thematic similarities:

> The policeman, Boyle [in the ninth interchapter], kills them [the cigar store thieves] because although they are Hungarians, he thinks of them as "wops." The two previous sketches have been about Americans on the Italian front during the war, and the story which follows Chapter VIII ["The Revolutionist" in *In Our Time* (1925)] is centered on a Hungarian revolutionary who has been persecuted in Hungary and has fled to Italy for sanctuary.[36]

Keith Carabine also identifies similarities between this interchapter and Chapter IX. He says that the narrator of Chapter XI has a "know-it-all stance" and, though condescendingly recognizing the youth's idealism, rejects his faith. In addition, the Hungarians in Chapter IX receive an "equally dismissive justice" when Boyle calls them "wops."[37]

In another interpretation, Johnston disagrees with Defalco who says in *The Hero in Hemingway's Short Stories* that the youth is innocent and untouched by experience.[38] Johnston gives important political-religious information about the interchapter's historical background to make his point: the youth is a victim of the White Terror, a Catholic uprising against Communism in Hungary, at which time 5,000 men and women were executed, 75,000 jailed, and 100,000 fled the country.[39] The youth's repeated dislike of Mantegna—a ruthlessly realistic Renaissance artist—suggests he has suffered too much. His idealism has been tested. He is, as Johnston explains, Hemingway's initiate, and his dislike of Mantegna implies his recent suffering.[40]

The Magyar's suffering and innocence, as suggested, serve to contrast with the speaker's loss of faith. The youth has survived, as Larry E. Grimes argues, by making his separate peace through commitment to an ideal.[41] From this point on in the sequence, however, a shift in perspective takes place. Chapter XI acts as a transitional piece in that the quiet bravery and idealism of the young communist—anticipated by Nick's stoicism in Chapter VII—connects this interchapter to the brave bull-fighter Villalta in Chapter XIV. The introduction of this lyric center prepares for a way of being—a "code"—or an alternative to despair brought on by loss.[42]

The next five interchapters constitute a small sequence in themselves and pick up on the tones and preoccupations of Chapter II. Briefly, Chapter XII concerns the goring of the picador's horse; Chapters XIII and XIV contrast the wrong way and the right way respectively to fight the bull; Chapters XV and XVI, as Burhans notes, provide a "coda" to the preceding bullfights, one demonstrating an ignoble escape from the bullring and the other a noble approach that nonetheless ends in death.[43] This contrast in behavior parallels Nick's stoical behavior as he sits wounded against the wall of the church in Chapter VII and the unnamed character's fearful praying in the trench in Chapter VIII.

As a whole, in their attempt at reassertion of certain values, Chapters XII through XVI reflect the concerns of the entire sequence: fear, violence, drunkenness, bitterness, disillusionment, and loss. But they also introduce an assertion of artistry, grace, and determination, analogous to Pound's assertion of beauty amid images of a decaying culture in "Envoi" in *Mauberley*.[44]

Chapter XII is the only one of five to focus on the death of the horse, that aspect of the bullfight that Hemingway called "comic":

In the tragedy of the bullfight the horse is the comic character. This may be shocking, but it is true. Therefore the worse the horses are, provided they are high enough off the ground and solid enough so that the picador can perform his mission with the spiked pole, or vara, the more they are a comic element.[45]

Yet Hemingway's description of a horse's death in Chapter XII is grotesque, not comic:

They whack whacked the white horse on the legs and he knee-ed himself up. The picador twisted the stirrups straight and pulled and hauled up into the saddle. The horse's entrails hung down in a blue bunch and swung backward and forward as he began to canter, the *monos* whacking him on the back of his legs with the rods. He cantered jerkily along the barrera. He stopped stiff and one of the *monos* held his bridle and walked him forward. The picador kicked in his spurs, leaned forward and shook his lance at the bull. Blood pumped regularly from between the horse's front legs. He was nervously wobbly. The bull could not make up his mind to charge. (*iot*, 22)

The shortest of the interchapters (119 words) concerned with bullfighting, it progresses from the realistic sight of the gored horse to the anticlimactic statement that the picadors' effort to rally the horse wasn't worth the time because the bull cannot make up its mind to charge. Serving as a blunt introduction to the spectacle of bullfighting, the incident is recorded with pitiless objectivity. The verbs "knee-ed," "twisted," "pulled," "hauled," "hung," "swung," "cantered," "kicked," "leaned," "Pumped," capture the vigorous action. And the words "whack whacked," "cantered jerkily," "stopped stiff," "blood pumped," and "wobbly" suggest the sight, sound, and smell of the horse's wretched death. The contrast in attitude to the horse in this interchapter and the horse in Chapter I, in which the lieutenant confides his drunkenness to his mount, is glaring for it parallels the inhumane actions of man to man in the rest of the sequence.

Chapter XIII concerns the third stage of the bullfight—the kill. Like Chapter II, this one emphasizes the crowd's disapproval; their cutting the bullfighter's pony tail off indicates their contempt for the bullfighter's lack of courage and manliness:

The crowd shouted all the time and threw pieces of bread down into the ring, then cushions and leather wine bottles, keeping up whistling and yelling. Finally the bull was too tired from so much bad sticking and folded his knees and lay down and one of the *cuadrilla* leaned out over his neck and killed him with the *puntillo*. The crowd came over the barrera and around the torero and two men grabbed him and held him and some one cut off his pigtail and was waving it and a kid grabbed it and ran away with it. Afterwards I saw him at the cafe. He was very short with a brown face and quite drunk and he said after all it has happened before like that. I am not really a good bull fighter. (*iot*, 23)

Once again with unmerciful frankness, Hemingway captures the violent ethics of the bullring. Words such as "shouted," "whistling," "yelling," "sticking," "grabbed," and "killed" stress the crowd's demands to see the bullfighter behave according to certain standards. An early typescript draft of this interchapter shows that Hemingway wanted to demonstrate that the torero was cowardly. It begins, "He was simply awful with the cape and he wouldn't fight the bull. He kept dodging back of the little wooden funk boxes along the barerra and the crowd got angrier and angrier."[46] In the revision Hemingway lets the action speak for itself. Except for the words, "Finally the bull was too tired from so much bad sticking," the crowd's response shows us how hostile this microcosm of the world can be.

Chapter XIII is linked to preceding interchapters by its repetition of images and tones. The image of the exhausted bull lying down in the bullring echoes the helplessness in the earlier interchapters. Likewise, the repeated images of the barrero, or wall, and the crowd's coming over it recalls the Germans coming over the wall in the Mons episode with its emphasis on sudden death. And, finally, the drunk bullfighter in this interchapter recalls the image of the drunken soldiers in their journey to death in Chapter I, and the bullfighter stumbling "like crazy drunk" in Chapter II.

The revision of Chapter XIV is a fine example of Hemingway's skill in showing how action is a vehicle for communicating feeling. A typescript draft of this interchapter is short and explanatory:

> There was one great killer and that was Villalta. He always called to the bull just before he was going to kill it. Toro! Toro! And at the moment of killing he became one with the bull. He folded over and became one with the bull and then it was broken and he was standing straight and just the red hilt of the sword stuck out between the bulls [*sic*] shoulders Villalta with his hand up at the crowd and the bull roaring blood like a hydrant looking straight at Villalta and his legs going.[47]

Hemingway fleshes out the first sentences of this version and removes redundant words so that he renders more and tells less, bearing out Pound's ideas of "direct treatment of the 'thing,'"[48] "rigorous selection," and "exclusion of all unnecessary detail":[49]

> If it happened right down close in front of you, you could see Villalta snarl at the bull and curse him, and when the bull charged he swung back firmly like

an oak when the wind hits it, his legs tight together, the muleta trailing and the sword following the curve behind. Then he cursed the bull, flopped the muleta at him, and swung back from the charge his feet firm, the muleta curving and each swing the crowd roaring.

When he started to kill it was all in the same rush. The bull looking at him straight in front, hating. He drew out the sword from the folds of the muleta and sighted with the same movement and called to the bull, Toro! Toro! and the bull charged and Villalta charged and just for a moment they became one. Villalta became one with the bull and then it was over. Villalta standing straight and the red hilt of the sword sticking out dully between the bull's shoulders. Villalta, his hand up at the crowd and the bull roaring blood, looking straight at Villalta and his legs caving. (*iot*, 24)

A graceful, seductive vengeance as the bullfighter incites the bull to action yields to the fluid movement of Villalta's and the bull's becoming one, suggesting a ritualistic union that is both deathly and sexual.[50] In the first paragraph the predominant *l*, *f*, and *w* sounds of "bull," "snarl," "Villalta," "front," "flopped," "feet firmly," and "when," "wind," and "swing," "swung," and the alliterative sound of "tight together," suggest the artistry, strength, and will power of the bullfighter.

In the second paragraph the sound of *l* in "kill," "bull," "Villalta," "called," and "dully" carries forward the intricately woven rhythm to emphasize Villalta's skill. Likewise, the *f* in "front," "from," and "folds" and *s* in "sighted," "sword," and "same," give the prose a movement like the smoothness of the bullfighter's movements. Since this is the only interchapter to end on a triumphant note—Villalta masters death with courage and grace—Hemingway seems to be saying that this is the way to live life: with bravery and purpose. Harmony is achieved at this point in the sequence, a unity of rhythm, sound, and meaning as the bullfighter, crowd, and bull become one. Here death is sought after; unlike other acts of violence in the sequence, this one is not degrading—it is affirmative. Subsequent interchapters, however, reveal that this is a temporary victory.

Chapter XV, the longest in the group concerned with bullfighting, reenforces many of the tones and images in previous interchapters. Told by a matador, Chapter XV describes how Maera must kill Luis' bulls because Luis is too drunk and cowardly to do so himself. It opens with a suggestion of ritual and celebration: "I heard the drums coming down the street and then the fifes and pipes and then they came around the corner, all dancing." Like Chapters X and XI ("A Very Short Story" and "The Revolutionist" in *In Our Time*), it focuses on a series of actions rather than on an imagistic scene. But as in the first interchapters, the emotive pattern begins with a deceptively merry note, almost a Bacchanalian note, with the bullfighter crouching and hunched down in the street with the crowds, then up dancing with them. It shifts to contempt and resentment when the speaker tries to persuade the evasive bullfighter to return to his position: "I said, Don't be a damn fool Luis. Come on back to the hotel" (*iot*, 25). This feeling of contempt intensifies with a racial slur—"Well, I said, after all he's just an ignorant Mexican savage"—that echoes the hostility of the Irish policeman Boyle in Chapter IX who wants to kill "wops." It ends contentiously when Maera says, "who will kill his bulls after he gets *cogida*" (*iot*, 25) and "we kills the savages' bulls, and the drunkards' bulls, and the riau-riau dancers' bulls. Yes. We will kill them. We kill them all right. Yes. Yes. Yes" (*iot*, 26). Maera's ill-humor reaches back to the biliousness in preceding interchapters and anticipates his death in Chapter XVI; but it counterpoints Villalta's courageous "Toro! Toro!" in Chapter XIV.

One would think Maera might receive some reward for having assumed Luis' responsibility to kill the bulls, but instead he experiences a demoralizing death in Chapter XVI. This interchapter reads in part:

> Maera lay still, his head on his arms, his face in the sand. He felt warm and sticky from the bleeding. Each time he felt the horn coming. Sometimes the bull only bumped him with his head. Once the horn went all the way through him and he felt it go into the sand. . . . Maera wanted to say something and found he could not talk. Maera felt everything getting larger and larger and then smaller and smaller. Then it got larger and larger and larger and then smaller and smaller. Then everything commenced to run faster and faster as when they speed up a cinematograph film. Then he was dead. (*iot*, 27)

The prose progresses from the morbid image of Maera's defeat as he lies with his face in the sand to the final frightening suggestions of the recognizable world disappearing. The sudden shock and unreality of the incidents are conveyed in this line: "Then everything commenced to run faster and faster as when they speed up a cinematograph film." Words such as "bleeding," "bumped," "swearing," "flopping," "running," and "shouting" convey the elemental savagery of Maera's death. The short sentences packed into a tight paragraph lead us quickly to the final terse sentence, "Then he was dead."

To pause for a moment, I could say that Chapter XII and Chapter XIII, with their images of brutality and death in the bullring, correspond to the terror and dread that were presented in earlier interchapters, much the same way that the subjective Part II of *Mauberley* serves to demonstrate the failure of a culture that is suggested in Part I.[51] But Chapter XIV, an image of the mastery of a bull with grace, skill, and power suggests that there are alternative ways of being than those presented in the rest of the sequence. This optimistic note, however, is undercut by Chapters XV and XVI in which first Luis' evasion of responsibility and then Maera's self-sacrifice continue to hurl the sequence forward to catastrophe.

Chapter XVII leaves the bullring and shifts back to America where it reenforces the notion of repugnant death, suggested earlier in Chapter IX by Boyle's and Drevitts's behavior, as it centers on the hanging of Sam Cardinella, a notorious Chicago mobster whose execution Hemingway recreated from imagination.[52] The oppressive corridor of the county jail where Cardinella is to be hanged is "high and narrow with tiers of cells on either side" (*iot*, 28) and recalls the oppressive environment in Chapter VI where the cabinet ministers are assassinated. That three of the criminals are blacks calls attention to the disproportionate number of blacks in jail and the racial injustices suggested by this fact. Hemingway again points to racial inequalities in America. The image of "one of the white men" sitting "on his cot with his head in his hands" and the other "flat on his cot with a blanket wrapped around his head" picks up the earlier images in the sequence of beaten humans (*iot*, 28). These images of devastated humans accumulate in the sequence to give it an overwhelming sense of demoralized, defeated humanity, far outweighing the courageous action of Villalta.

Sam Cardinella's fear—obvious in his losing control of his sphincter muscle and the necessity of his being carried to the place of hanging—repeats the image of the sick cabinet minister in Chapter VI who must be carried to his place of execution. Other tonal links among this interchapter and the others include the Italian name Cardinella which recalls the Italian place names referred to in the sequence; the play on the word cardinal, however, emphasizes Hemingway's point that religion has failed to sustain humankind. Likewise, the comment of one of the priests whispering to Cardinella, "Be a man, my son," and the youngest priest's "skipping" back onto the scaffolding "just before the drop fell" again calls attention to the failure of organized religion to comfort the individual; the word "skipping" is too lighthearted for such an event.

The American setting in this interchapter and the focus on criminal life widen the perspective of fear and horror in the sequence to encompass social systems and implicate all of humanity. It is a hideous picture in which prisoners, priests, and guards alike seem contemptible.

The final piece in *in our time* shifts back to Europe and a political arena. Based on an article dated 15 September 1923 that Hemingway wrote concerning European royalty, "King Business in Europe Isn't What It Used to Be," its details were supplied by Hemingway's friend Shorty Wornall, the American movie cameraman he met in Thrace.[53] This is the version as it appears in *in our time*:

> The king was working in the garden. He seemed very glad to see me. We walked through the garden. This is the queen, he said. She was clipping a rose bush. Oh how do you do, she said. We sat down at a table under a big tree and

the king ordered whiskey and soda. We have good whiskey anyway, he said. The revolutionary committee, he told me, would not allow him to go outside the palace grounds. Plastiras is a very good man I believe, he said, but frightfully difficult. I think he did right though shooting those chaps. If Kerensky had shot a few men things might have been altogether different. Of course the great thing in this sort of an affair is not to be shot oneself!

It was very jolly. We talked for a long time. Like all Greeks he wanted to go to America. (*iot*, 30)

Fenton identifies the power of this interchapter by saying that here in the garden the leader of a once highly-cultured nation reveals himself to be "an amiable facsimile of an English gentleman," not one who equates with "the inherited, accepted concepts of divine leadership and the romantic principles of monarchial glory," but one who equates "with any Greek short order cook in Oak Park or Kansas City or Chicago."[54] The mocking nursery tale tone in this interchapter is appropriate, for the image of a puerile Greek king and queen tending their roses in a palace garden—a fallen Adam and Eve in Eden unaware of their own evil—closes a sequence that bitterly condemns the character of the age. This palace garden recalls the garden gone awry at Mons where men were "potted" and fell. Bridgman points out the "planned cross reference" between the two phrases in the two interchapters, "in a garden" and "in the garden," each appearing in the first sentences of the interchapters. In one interchapter, Bridgman notes, bodies thump to the garden floor; in the other, another man is likewise "working" in a garden, yet under very different circumstances. This comparison is "central to Hemingway's understanding of the actual nature of our time."[55] Other links to other interchapters include the speaker's pseudo-British diction, his feeling "very jolly" about the situation, which seems bizarre given the political upheaval of the time. Likewise, the king's saying that Plastiras is a good man, "but frightfully difficult," recalls the British soldier in the Mons episode saying how "frightfully" put out he and his men are for having to "fall" back from their military advances. The "revolutionary committee" and the Russian communist "Kerensky" recall the idealistic Hungarian's yearning for world revolution in Chapter XI. This link to Chapter XI suggests a relationship between victim (the Hungarian) and victimizer (the king) and reenforces the tonal complexes of bravery and cowardice in the sequence.

Hemingway's parting message (titled "L'Envoi" in *In Our Time*), unlike Pound's lyrical assertion of beauty in "Envoi" in *Mauberley*, does not affirm ties with a more harmonious tradition but condemns tradition. The king's wife is clipping the rose—"symbol of the fundamental indestructability of the self" and often associated with beauty, love, and peerless persons—amid social and political chaos; this suggests that there is no hope for peace.[56] In addition, gardening hardly seems an appropriate activity at this time. And the king's dream of the future, his escape to America—the land of freedom where one can supposedly live in peace with one's convictions—is cowardly and irresponsible given his part in leading his people to death.[57] The America that Hemingway presents, however, is a place where crime, violence, racism, and fear thrive. That a politically, and by extension spiritually impotent Greek king who condones violence ("If Kerensky had shot a few men things might have been altogether different" [*iot*, 30]), wants to flee to America seems suitably cynical for a work borne out of the deepest kind of loss and rage.

Hemingway's eighteen imagistic prose pieces, with their pictures of modern despair, are further fragmented by their truncated title *in our time* taken from the *Anglican Book of Prayer*, "Give us peace in our time, O Lord."[58] The very cover of the book itself with its collage of carefully chosen newspaper clippings of current incongruities in four languages ("Comment va-t-on declarer la prochaine guerre," and "General Public barred from film on Obstetrics") suggests not that the "principle of disorder is paramount" in *in our time*, as E. M. Halliday notes, but rather that a precise arrangement of the interchapters yields a pattern of pain, suffering, and death against the backdrop of an absurd universe where there is little room for human dignity and honor.[59]

3
In Our Time (1925):
Before a Separate Peace

I am writing some damn good stories.

The stories are written so tight and so hard that the alteration of a word can throw an entire story out of key.[1]

EVEN though *in our time* stands on its own as a fictional sequence, Hemingway originally intended the interchapters to be interspersed throughout a collection of stories he was working on.[2] By adding nine new stories[3] to the three already published in *Three Stories and Ten Poems*—"Up in Michigan," "Out of Season," and "My Old Man"—and alternating them with the interchapters of *in our time*, Hemingway felt he would have a substantial collection for publication. He had a definite plan for the order of his stories and interchapters, and he was adamant about keeping it. On 12 September 1924, for instance, he wrote Edward J. O'Brien:

> All the stories have a certain unity, the first 5 are in Michigan . . . and in between each one comes bang! the In Our Time. It should be awfully good, I think. I've tried to do it so you get the close up very quietly but absolutely solid and the real thing but very close, and then through it all between every story comes the rhythm of the in our time chapters.[4]

When Horace Liveright, his publisher, rejected "Up in Michigan," however, Hemingway replaced it with "The Battler."[5] He justified the substitution in a 1925 letter to Liveright on structural grounds as well as because of the new story's quality:

> There is nothing in the book that has not a definite place in its organization and if I at any time seem to repeat myself I have had a good reason for doing so. . . . The new story makes the book a good deal better. It's about the best I've ever written and gives additional unity to the book as a whole.[6]

In the 1925 collection, Hemingway emphasized the rhythm of the interchapters from *in our time* by italicizing them, a device that also connected them visually and differentiated them from the stories. As he later wrote to Max Perkins, "The other thing about the In Our Time chapters is that to get the effect I wanted with them (and it was a strange effect, and they made it), I had them set in italics. They need those italics."[7] Hemingway also emphasized the importance of the interchapters by numbering them and by retaining the title of the earlier sequence. Numbering the interchapters does not, as one might expect, make them continuous segments of a book, as some critics suggest,[8] but rather underscores Hemingway's concern for a precise order and placement of them. In addition, the italicized, numbered interchapters act as single images that counterpoint or reinforce the tonal character of the stories, as I will demonstrate.[9]

Hemingway made few stylistic changes in the interchapters when he included them among the stories, but he did change their order. He moved the second interchapter concerned with bullfighting to ninth position, placing it among the rest of the bullfighting interchapters in order to make contrasts and continuities in their tonal qualities more vivid. And he titled and typeset as stories two of the interchapters, "A Very Short Story" and "The Revolutionist," because their emphasis on a series of events rather than on one incident or image relates them more closely to the stories. To Dos Passos on 22 April 1925, Hemingway explained how the sequence would work:

> They made me take out the Up in Michigan story because the girl got yenced and I sent 'em a swell new Nick story about a busted down pug and a coon called The Battler—the next three stories after the Up in Michigan to be moved up one and his to be story no. 5. Its [*sic*] to go like this—Chap (1) Indian Camp. Chap. II The Dr. and the Dr.'s Wife [*sic*] Chap. III The End of Something Chap IV The Three Day Blow Chap. V The Battler Chap. VI A Very Short Story Chap VII Soldier's Home etc. [*sic*].[10]

In the final version of the sequence, as Hemingway explained in the letter to O'Brien quoted earlier, the first five stories are cohesive partly by their setting in Michigan. In addition, they all have a three-part tonal structure and are concerned, in varying degrees, with the difficulty of expressing feelings. Other preoccupations are loveless relationships between men and women and confrontation with danger and violence in an adult world. These stories, only one of which—"The Three-Day Blow"—is longer than five pages, are made ironic and more emotionally intense by the brief interchapters between them. The stories, like the first six interchapters in *in our time*, suggest a movement toward doom. Also, the first five stories, like the interchapters, are objectively presented with spare, carefully selected details; they employ simple diction and uncomplicated sentence patterns; and they make use of T. S. Eliot's idea of the objective correlative and Pound's idea of presenting "things as they are."[11]

For instance, in "The Doctor and the Doctor's Wife" following the doctor's empty threat to Dick Boulton and his frustrating conversation with his sanctimonious wife, Hemingway uses the action of the doctor's sitting on the bed and pumping "heavy yellow shells" out of the magazine of his shotgun as the correlative for displaced fury and sexual frustration (*IOT*, 26). And at the conclusion of "The End of Something" Hemingway presents "things as they are" in the image of Nick with his head down on the blanket after he has driven Marjorie away and Bill appears and asks him if there has been "a scene." Nick replies, "Oh, go away, Bill! Go away for a while" (*IOT*, 35). Hemingway excludes unnecessary comments on the action; he lets the image of Nick and his response to Bill reveal universal feelings of confusion and loss.

The fifth story, "The Battler," is followed by Chapter VI ("Nick sat against the wall . . ."), then "A Very Short Story," and Chapter VII ("While the bombardment . . ."). These four pieces form a unit that focuses on wartime situations and provides the emotional climax of the entire sequence. (Although "Soldier's Home" shares similar preoccupations with the preceding five stories, it concerns a sensibility altered by the effects of violence and thus will be dealt with in chapter four of this study.) While the first five stories and six interchapters function independently, taken as a whole they portray the movement of a sensibility from denial of death to direct engagement with it. Hemingway's use of the character Nick as a cohesive device in the first five stories helps to underscore this movement by grounding it in a concrete set of recognizable emotions. However, Hemingway's decision not to add the later Nick stories to the sequence when new editions appeared[12] demonstrates that Nick's growth and maturity are not meant, as some commentators insist,[13] to be the focus of *In Our Time.*

Hemingway was clearly less concerned with character development and plot than with portraying various states of feeling as embodied in Nick. The repetition and variation of these feelings, as with the repetition and variation of images and other tonal preoccupations, impart structure and meaning to the sequence as a whole. For instance, at the end of "Indian Camp" Nick's denial of death—"he felt quite sure he would never die"—is echoed in "The Three-Day Blow" when Nick tries to convince himself that after breaking up with Marjorie he can always go into town on Saturday night: "There was not anything that was irrevocable" (*IOT*, 48). Hemingway emphasizes not how and why Nick breaks up

with Marjorie, but Nick's overwhelming feelings of loss and how he deals
with loss and hurt.

Hemingway's 1930 addition of an "Introduction by the Author" helps
to clarify his use of character to embody various states of awareness in the
stories and interchapters. His observations demonstrate his central concern with the emotive structuring of *In Our Time*. Later called "On the
Quai at Smyrna," the Introduction resembles the interchapters in length,
technique, and emotive quality.[14] In an offhand tone of confidentiality
and pseudo-toughness that attempts to cover his pain and vulnerability, a
speaker conveys his memories of war to someone else who has had similar
experiences.

The first of seven incidents the speaker tells of involves screaming
refugees on a Greek quay at midnight who are suddenly quieted by the
brightness of a searchlight turned on them. The incident is told in a
quizzically glib way, as if the speaker cannot allow himself to feel the full
impact of the nightmarish scene. A bizarre helplessness conveys the
surreal image of the solution—"the trick"—to the problem:

> The strange thing was, he said, how they screamed every night at midnight. I
> do not know why they screamed at that time. We were in the harbor and they
> were all on the pier and at midnight they started screaming. We used to turn
> the searchlight on them to quiet them. That always did the trick. We'd run the
> searchlight up and down over them two or three times and they stopped it.
> (*IOT,* 11)

Immediately following this memory another is run into it having to do
with misunderstandings among the English and Turkish military person-
nel, the Englishman deceiving the Turk to avoid further conflicts:

> One time I was senior officer on the pier and a Turkish officer came up to me
> in a frightful rage because one of our sailors had been most insulting to him.
> So I told him the fellow would be sent on ship and be most severely punished.
> I asked him to point him out. So he pointed out a gunner's mate, most
> inoffensive chap. Said he'd been most frightfully and repeatedly insulting;
> talking to me through an interpreter. I couldn't imagine how the gunner's
> mate knew enough Turkish to be insulting. I called him over and said, "And
> just in case you should have spoken to any Turkish officers."
>
> "I haven't spoken to any of them, sir."
>
> "I'm quite sure of it," I said, "but you'd best go on board ship and not come
> ashore again for the rest of the day."
>
> Then I told the Turk the man was being sent on board ship and would be
> most severely dealt with. Oh most rigorously. He felt topping about it. Great
> friends we were. (*IOT,* 11)

This incident, too, is told in the most flippant way, and yet the speaker's incredulousness is apparent in his remark about the gunner's mate being a "most inoffensive chap." Much of the irony, or rather the twisted humor, in the anecdote derives from the fact that the "great friends," the English and the Turkish, need an interpreter to understand one another. And the focus on personal insults (especially imaginary ones) amid world war is preposterous in light of the grotesque events presented later in the sequence. The incident also underscores the irrationality and confusion that often predominate in wartime situations.

Louis H. Leiter points out that the introduction traces the "curve of the storyteller's cauterization."[15] The speaker succeeds in categorizing the "worst" experience as not being able to "get the women to give up their dead babies" (*IOT*, 11). But then he shifts to a rapid rush of words that shows his inability to absorb the memory about an old woman "lying on a sort of litter" who suddenly dies and goes "absolutely stiff," "quite rigid," "quite dead," and "absolutely rigid" (*IOT*, 12). The repetition of the image of a stiff corpse emphasizes the speaker's uneasiness with this memory, its intractability, and his need to repeat it in order to find a place for it in his consciousness.

The final memories in the introduction, however, are so horrible they must be told by their opposites:

> You remember the harbor. There were plenty of nice things floating around in it. That was the only time in my life I got so I dreamed about things (*IOT*, 12).

The speaker cannot even articulate the experience of the harbor and can deal with it only in his subconscious. And the memory of the Greeks' breaking the forelegs of their mules is so terrible the speaker says, "It was all a pleasant business. My word yes a most pleasant business" (*IOT*, 12).

As a preface to the sequence, then, the introduction sets up a number of tonal notes that anticipate the direction of the entire work. One is the presentation of a sensibility so shocked by the violence of wartime experience that his expression of these experiences seems at times irreverent. The affected-sounding British idiom—"topping," "quite," "frightful," "extraordinary," and "chaps"—contributes to this feeling of irreverence and calls attention to the speaker's attempt to restrain his emotions. Likewise, the focus on British and Greek citizens also helps round out a sequence that closes with a Greek king who has failed to lead his people from war to peace. In addition, the confusion of pronouns in the Introduction—"he said," "I do not know," "we were," "they were," "you don't"—give a chaotic feeling which is later expanded by the many speakers and characters in the stories and interchapters. The images of death, birth, and war evoke a sense of primal horror and reveal how senseless violence and death emphasize the need for emotional control. Finally, the movement of humans against the dark night looks forward to the movement in the sequence through various states of awareness and to the more literal journeys undertaken in subsequent stories and interchapters.

Following "On the Quai at Smyrna," Chapter I picks up on the speaker's struggles in the Introduction with memories of war. The lieutenant's drinking to blunt his fear and his confessing his drunkenness to his horse as he rides off to war at night effectively parallel the contrast in the Introduction between the ugly reality of the Greek refugees' plight and the speaker's difficulty in controlling his reactions to his experiences of war and violence.

The contrast in the way things are and the way they are conveyed connects Chapter I to the first story in the sequence, "Indian Camp." This story has been the subject of a number of controversial readings.[16] Paul Smith points out that Hemingway cut a twenty-nine page untitled manuscript to a seven-page typescript which he entitled "One Night Last Summer"; this typescript subsequently became a typescript entitled "Indian Camp/Story."[17] Part of the twenty-nine-page untitled manuscript became "Three Shots."[18] This story concerns Nick's firing three shots from a rifle in his tent in the middle of the night to call back his father and Uncle George from fishing to his bedside because, as Nick said to his elders, he heard an animal nearby "like a cross between a fox and a wolf."

This section of the story in its original position in the twenty-nine page manuscript marred the three-part emotive flow of the story that ultimately became "Indian Camp," and did not sustain the intensity and directness of the final version of the story. Rather than trusting in action and dialogue to convey feeling in "Three Shots," Hemingway creates a narrator who tells that Nick "was always a little frightened of the woods at night," and "Nick had realized that some day he must die. It made him feel quite sick. It was the first time he had ever realized that he himself would have to die sometime."[19] In the revised version of "Indian Camp" Hemingway conveys fear and an attempt to repress it in the understated dialogue between Nick and his father as they row across the lake at the end of the story.[20] He offers little comment on their conversation and allows the music of the language to convey feeling.

As it appears in *In Our Time*, "Indian Camp" is a story of how Nick's father tries to introduce Nick to the experience of birth as a way of recognizing Nick's sexual maturity, but ironically, how he introduces him to death instead. To suggest tension between fear and an attempt to repress it, Hemingway introduces an eerie, foreboding gloominess in the third paragraph when he describes two boats shoving off from shore in the dark:

Nick heard the oarlocks of the other boat quite a way ahead of them in the mist. The Indians rowed with quick choppy strokes. Nick lay back with his father's arm around him. It was cold on the water. The Indian who was rowing them was working very hard, but the other boat moved further ahead in the mist all the time. (*IOT,* 15)

This movement forward into the dark, cold misty night sustains the motif in "On the Quai at Smyrna" and Chapter I of a nocturnal quest or journey.[21] The introductory movement in the story also presents other foreboding images, such as the Indian "shanty" where "dogs rushed out at them" and "an old woman stood in the doorway holding a lamp" (*IOT,* 15–16). These stark details and vivid impressions prepare for the following scene in the second movement of the story where the description of the Indians tells of a primitive birth about to take place:

> Inside on a wooden bunk lay a young woman. She had been trying to have her baby for two days. All the old women in the camp had been helping her. The men had moved off up the road to sit in the dark and smoke out of range of the noise she made. She screamed just as Nick and the two Indians followed his father and George into the Shanty. She lay in the lower bunk very big under a quilt. Her head was turned to one side. In the upper bunk was her husband. He had cut his foot very badly with an ax three days before. He was smoking a pipe. The room smelled very bad. (*IOT,* 16)

Like sensuous poetry, this description calls upon all the senses as it moves from one sharply honed detail to the next. The agonized screams of the Indian woman, the feel of the rough wooden bunk, the image of the cut foot, the smell of the Indian's pipe, and possibly the scent of blood and gangrene provide a foreign and frightening backdrop for initiation. Nick's fear is immediately obvious when he says, "I know" to his father's comment that "this lady is going to have a baby" (*IOT,* 16). His eagerness to sound knowledgeable indicates that he does not really want to know more than he has already seen and heard. The doctor then says, "No you don't know," and explains that "All her muscles are trying to get the baby born. That is what is happening when she screams" *IOT,* 16).[22] Even though Nick says, "I see" to his father's explanation, he does not literally see what takes place; he looks away while his father is operating and delivering the baby, and he does not look when his father puts the afterbirth, the "something," into the basin. Nick's turning away creates a current of anxiety that intensifies after he sees "a good view of the upper bunk when his father, the lamp in one hand, tipped the Indian's head back" and reveals the slit-throated Indian (*IOT,* 18).

The power of the story lies not only in the image of the Caesarean section done with a jacknife and cat gut suturing, which is "one for the

medical journal," but also in the silent and bloody death of a terrified
Indian. This butchery-style birth and its companion suicide throw a
fearful and deadly light on the meaning of sex. This scene prepares for
later stories in the sequence that focus on the inability of men and
women to connect with one another physically or emotionally.

In the final movement of the story the tension between fear and denial
of fear in the conversation between Nick and his father indicates that
Nick understands that he, too, will some day die, but he cannot now find
a place for this fact in his design of things and therefore tries to repress it:

> "Do ladies always have such a hard time having babies?" Nick said.
> "No, that was very, very exceptional."
> "Why did he kill himself, Daddy?"
> "I don't know, Nick. He couldn't stand things, I guess."
> "Do many men kill themselves, Daddy?"
> "Not very many, Nick."
> "Do many women?"
> "Hardly ever."
> "Don't they ever?"
> "Oh, yes. They do sometimes."
> "Daddy?"
> "Yes."
> "Where did Uncle George go?"
> "He'll turn up all right."
> "Is dying hard, Daddy?"
> "No, I think it's pretty easy, Nick. It all depends."
> They were seated in the boat, Nick in the stern, his father rowing. The sun
> was coming up over the hills. A bass jumped, making a circle in the water.
> Nick trailed his hand in the water. It felt warm in the sharp chill of the
> morning.
> In the early morning on the lake sitting in the stern of the boat with his
> father rowing, he felt quite sure that he would never die. (*IOT,* 19)

The progression of questions from a specific question about the Indian
to the broader questions about men and women—encompassing all of
humankind—then a question about Uncle George's whereabouts (suggesting that Nick thinks Uncle George may have gone off to kill himself)
point up Nick's fear of his own death and his discomfort in stating
precisely his anxiety about it. Nick's questions come closer and closer to
the mark without his asking outright, "am I going to die?" Hemingway
does not state Nick's fear of dying bluntly as he does in "Three Shots" but
rather renders it subtly through dialogue and action.

The language shifts from the back and forth rhythm of Nick's fear and
his father's attempts at reassurance to the piling up of images that suggest
tranquility and peace—the sun rises over the hills, a bass jumps in the

water, and Nick and his father row quietly across a still morning lake. Although Nick is comforted by the thought that "he would never die," his dragging his hand in the warm water in "the sharp chill of the morning" clearly marks his delusion and anticipates, as Joseph Flora notes, "the shattering of comforting illusions" in subsequent stories (*IOT,* 19).[23]

The first story in the sequence, then, introduces the use of narrative as lyrical progression. Like an image in a poem, the first scene opens the story with an eerie ominousness as two boats move across the lake at night. This image forebodes the second image: the bloody birth and suicide that take place in the Indian Camp—the camp itself the correlative for fear and horror, the results of exposure to the adult world of violence, danger, and death. The third image, the peaceful return trip across the lake at sunrise, stands in contrast to the terror and brutality of the second image. It is charged with warmth and sunlight. Yet, the "chill" of the morning air is present as well, a subtle reminder of the encounter with the realm of death.

"Indian Camp" is made more ironic by the placement of Chapter II ("Minarets stuck up in the rain . . .") following it. This interchapter closes with the image of "a woman having a kid with a young girl holding a blanket over and crying. Scared sick looking at it" (*IOT,* 21). The juxtaposition of this interchapter with "Indian Camp" suggests that Nick's experience is not isolated, that violent births and deaths are universal, and that initiation to an adult world is often forced and unpleasant. Originally third in *in our time,* this interchapter became the second when Hemingway moved the bullfighting interchapter to ninth position. The language of this second interchapter parallels the tonalities of fear and an attempt at emotional control in the sequence. The repetition of "jammed," images of water buffalo and cattle hauling carts through the mud, and old men and women soaked through create a picture of human misery that broadens the scope of the sequence and makes more foolish Nick's self-deceit.

With its introduction to death and refusal to accept awareness of death, "Indian Camp" makes way for the cowardliness in "The Doctor and the Doctor's Wife" as the impulse to escape from danger is embodied in the doctor's actions. Like "Indian Camp," "The Doctor and the Doctor's Wife" is set in Michigan and concerns Doctor Adams, Nick, and Indians. And like "Indian Camp," this story has a three-part tonal movement: an intense fear of confrontation during Boulton's and the doctor's discussion of the logs; this scene yields to supressed fury as the doctor and his wife try to communicate with each other through the walls of separate rooms; and finally this fury is vented through escape as the doctor and Nick head for the woods. The issue in the story is not, as some commen tators note, the effect of events on Nick, but rather Dr. Adams' cowardliness in not being able to follow through on his word.[24]

The story opens with a heated exchange between Dick Boulton, a half-breed who "was a big man" and "liked to get into fights," and Doctor Adams who is defensive and hot-headed. Boulton accuses the doctor of stealing logs that have drifted up on the shore near the doctor's cottage. The doctor is "very uncomfortable" about Dick's accusation and says to him, red-faced: "If you think the logs are stolen, leave them alone and take your tools back to the camp." But Boulton antagonizes the doctor by saying, "Don't go off half cock, Doc" (*IOT*, 24). The pun in the cliche "go off half cock" underscores Boulton's contempt and the doctor's anger. The doctor becomes so outraged at Boulton's hostility, he says, "If you call me Doc once again, I'll knock your eye teeth down your throat." Boulton says, "Oh, no, you won't Doc"; but the doctor's response to this is to chew "the beard on his lower lip" and walk away (*IOT*, 25).[25]

To emphasize the impotent rage that has built in the first movement of the story, Hemingway shifts to another scene involving the doctor and his wife. This scene also demonstrates the doctor's ineffectuality and highlights one of the main concerns of the sequence—the difficulty of expressing feelings. Mrs. Adams, a Christian Scientist, lies on a bed in a separate, darkened room "with the blinds drawn," her physical separation from her husband signifying her emotional detachment from him. Hemingway contrasts the doctor's "pile of medical journals on the floor by the bureau . . . still in their wrappers unopened" with Mrs. Adams' Bible and "her copy of *Science and Health* and her *Quarterly*" to underscore the irony of Mrs. Adams' religious sect denying the doctor's profession and thus calling attention to the emotional and physical distance between husband and wife (*IOT*, 25, 26).

After the doctor tells his wife he had a "row" with Boulton, Mrs. Adams quotes from the scripture: "Remember, that he who ruleth his spirit is greater than he that taketh a city" (*IOT*, 25). But the doctor does not respond to his wife's scripture quoting:

> He was sitting on his bed now, cleaning a shotgun. He pushed the magazine full of the heavy yellow shells and pumped them out again. They were scattered on the bed. (*IOT*, 26)

Coming after the doctor's heated discussion with Boulton and his ineffectual communication with his wife, this passage with its image of the doctor's pumping the shells onto his bed captures the pent up fury that has been building in the story. Unable to carry through on his threat to Boulton or connect with his wife on any significant level, the doctor expresses his emotional and sexual frustration by "cleaning" his gun.[26]

Like Boulton, Mrs. Adams knows how to cow the doctor. She calls him "dear" repeatedly, just as Boulton calls him "Doc," neither treating him with respect nor understanding. This disrespect adds to the sense of stiffled anger:

> "Are you going out, dear?" his wife said.
> "I think I'll go for a walk," the doctor said.
> "If you see Nick, dear, will you tell him his mother wants to see him?" his mother said.
> The doctor went out on the porch. The screen door slammed behind him. He heard his wife catch her breath when the door slammed. (*IOT,* 26)

Too repressed to say exactly what he feels about either Boulton or Mrs. Adams, the doctor finally leaves the cottage and his wife's exaggerated piety and walks "in the heat out the gate," the slam of the door behind him only a minor release of his anger. But his saying "sorry" after he hears his wife catch her breath at the sound of his slamming the door undermines his indirect attempt to express himself.

The tension and the smothered fury that build in the first two movements of the story fizzle out in escape in the last movement. Nick, who is sitting with his back to a tree, is reading a book when his father approaches and says to him, "Your mother wants to see you" (*IOT,* 27). The doctor's referring to Mrs. Adams as "your mother" echoes Mrs. Adams' referring to herself as "his mother," which suggests her own self-disjunction and their mutual uncommunicativeness. But Nick, taking his father's side like a sympathetic son, says, "I know where there's black squirrels, Daddy." "'All right,' said his father, 'Let's go there.'" (*IOT,* 27).

This escape to nature, however, is only a temporary relief from the suggestion of impending disaster toward which the sequence moves (just as Nick's escape to nature in "Big Two-Hearted River" is only a temporary relief). The impotent passion that intensifies in "The Doctor and the Doctor's Wife" does not find relief in confrontation with its cause—fear of violence, ultimately death. Later these negative tonalities—the doctor's cowardliness and attempt to repress it—are countered by their opposites, bravery and direct engagement with death, in the interchapters concerned with bullfighting.

Immediately following "The Doctor and the Doctor's Wife," however, comes an interchapter (Chapter II: "We were in the garden . . .") that resonates stunned amazement at the ease with which death can take place—a sharp contrast to the sheer dread of death in "The Doctor and the Doctor's Wife." This shortest interchapter in the book with its clipped British idiom and image of men suddenly shot as they climb over the garden wall foreshadows the surprise ending in the next story, "The End of Something."

Like the first two stories in the sequence, "The End of Something" has a three-part tonal structure. It moves from an elegiac tone to a more clearly defined tension between resoluteness and confusion and then to remorse and grief. The story has to do with Nick's and Marjorie's breakup while they are fishing on Hortons Bay in Michigan. A description of Hortons Bay opens the story:

> The lumber schooners came into the bay and were loaded with the cut of the mill that stood stacked in the yard. All the piles of lumber were carried away. The big mill building had all its machinery that was removable taken out and hoisted on board one of the schooners by the men who had worked in the mill. The schooner moved out of the bay toward the open lake carrying the two great saws, the travelling carriage that hurled the logs against the revolving, circular saws and all the rollers, wheels, belts and iron piled on a hull-deep load of lumber. Its open hold covered with canvas and lashed tight, the sails of the schooner filled and it moved out into the open lake, carrying with it everything that had made the mill a mill and Hortons Bay a town. (*IOT*, 31)

The image of the schooner with its sails filled and hull piled high with what was once a mill town is a graceful, romantic image suggesting nostalgia and loss. The *l* and *oo* sounds in "mill," "lumber," "load," "schooner," and "removable" add to the haunting musical quality of the passage. And the -ing sounds and trilling *l*'s in the penultimate sentence make the passage lyrical and flowing. But the next image is one of barrenness and sterility:

> The one-story bunk houses, the eating-house, the company store, the mill offices, and big mill itself stood deserted in the acres of sawdust that covered the swampy meadow by the shore of the bay.
> Ten years later there was nothing of the mill left except the broken white limestone of its foundations showing through the swampy second growth as Nick and Marjorie rowed along the shore. (*IOT*, 31)

Taken as a whole, the images in the three paragraphs are the objective correlative for Nick's and Marjorie's relationship, the picture of the schooner piled high with the remains of the town anticipating their separation; but the "second growth" suggests that perhaps there is a cyclical nature to things and both Marjorie and Nick will survive the loss.[27]

The elegiac tone of the introductory section shifts to Nick's and Marjorie's strained conversation. Marjorie's simple happiness counters Nick's complex, confused feelings about his loss of love. When Marjorie equates the ruined mill to a "castle" and remarks that the trout are feeding, Nick is recalcitrant and negative and says, "But they [the fish] won't strike." And when Nick and Marjorie cut up the perch for bait,

Nick says to her after she cuts up and skins her perch, "You don't want to take the ventral fin out" (*IOT*, 32). This reference to the ventral fin, taken with Nick's later accusation that "You know everything," suggests that what Marjorie has learned from Nick besides fishing includes sex.[28] Marjorie's knowledge, then, appears to be the source of Nick's unhappiness, yet he is not able to identify the problem himself.

After Nick and Marjorie set the fishing lines, Marjorie says, "What's the matter Nick?" But Nick doesn't know; ironically he says, "There's going to be a moon tonight" (*IOT*, 34). Then Marjorie undermines Nick by saying "happily," "I know it." Hemingway's play on the verb "to know" points out Nick's not understanding or being able to articulate what is bothering him: "You know everything," he says in response to Marjorie's having the edge; "I can't help it," he repeats. "You do. You know everything. That's the trouble. You know you do." And then he says, "I've taught you everything. You know you do. What don't you know, anyway?" (*IOT*, 34) As Dennis Welland notes, "She may not, as Nick aggressively says, 'know everything,' but she certainly knows a great deal more about what is going on than he gives her credit for, and it is Marjorie, not Nick, who really determines when the time has come for the end of something."[29] Before Marjorie leaves, she tries to draw out the reason for his sullenness, their conversation reflecting Marjorie's stoical insistence and Nick's stubborn resentment:

> "You don't have to talk silly," Marjorie said. "What's really the matter."
> "I don't know."
> "Of course you know."
> "No I don't."
> "Go on and say it."
> Nick looked on at the moon, coming up over the hills.
> "It isn't fun any more." (*IOT*, 34)

What isn't fun any more, of course, is their love.[30] But Nick can't explain this and says, "I feel as though everything was gone to hell inside of me. I don't know, Marge" (*IOT*, 24). This is the first time Nick addresses Marjorie and his doing so exonerates her from blame.[31]

Marjorie leaves Nick and pushes the boat off herself, saying to him, "You can walk back around the point" (*IOT*, 35). Her decisiveness and self-assurance emphasize Nick's inability to act at all. Nick appears the more devastated of the two after Marjorie leaves, for he "sat there, his head in his hands" (*IOT*, 35). Hemingway intensifies the feeling of defeat with another image of Nick "lying down with his face in the blanket by the fire" (*IOT*, 35). These images of a man with his head bowed recur many times in *In Our Time*, as I have noted in chapters one and two of this study, creating a pattern of loss and demoralization.

The tone shifts again when Bill enters the story. Hemingway's purpose in introducing Bill is not, as Joseph Whitt writes, to show that Nick is "a man torn by the contradictions of unexpressed homosexual tendencies."[32] Rather, Bill's insensitivity ("have a scene?") and preoccupation with food and fishing ("Bill selected a sandwich from the lunch basket and walked over to have a look at the rods" [*IOT*, 35]) contrast with Nick's gloominess and depression: "Oh, go away, Bill! Go away for a while" (*IOT*, 35). Also, this section of the story makes clear that Nick had planned the breakup with Marjorie but is too confused and cowardly to face her openly. Instead he is reluctant and mean and forces Marjorie to pull his feelings from him.

Like "Indian Camp," "The End of Something" takes the form of a journey that leads not to a positive experience but to one of pain. And like "The Doctor and the Doctor's Wife," the story concerns a loveless relationship between a man and a woman. The tension in Nick's and Marjorie's dialogue between the desire "to know" and the inability to express feelings picks up on the strained dialogue in "The Doctor and the Doctor's Wife" between Dr. Adams and his wife and echoes Nick's telling his father in "Indian Camp" that he "knows" the Indian woman is having a baby. This difficulty of saying exactly how things really are, as opposed to the way they are understated, is reinforced in the first seven interchapters in the presentation of various war scenes.

As in "Indian Camp" and "The Doctor and the Doctor's Wife," Hemingway uses character in "The End of Something" to structure the story lyrically. Later in the sequence Marjorie's stoicism and Nick's confusion will be contrasted with other characters such as Villalta and Krebs, thus giving the sequence coherence. Another connection between this story and the rest of the sequence is the image of the deteriorating mill town used as a correlative for the decay of feeling, which anticipates the bitter loss in Chapter VI ("Nick sat against the wall . . .) and in "A Very Short Story," where the "something" that disappears in a relationship is clearly love.

Although Nick's and Marjorie's failure to catch fish in "The End of Something" correlates with their physical and emotional failures, later in "Big Two-Hearted River" Nick's fishing will take on other meanings.[33] Nick's and Marjorie's failure in fishing and in love, however, anticipates the relationship between the young gentleman and Tiny in "Out of Season" who fail to connect with one another and who set out to fish but never do.

"The End of Something" is bracketed by Chapters III ("We were in a garden . . .") and IV ("It was a frightfully hot day . . ."). In both interchapters the British-sounding idiom and the incredulous tone are analogous to Nick's predicament. In Chapter IV the speaker's comments about jamming "an absolutely perfect barricade across the bridge" parallel Nick's previous discussion with Bill about ending his relationship with Marjorie. In Chapter IV, despite the "simply priceless" obstacle that the speaker and his men put up, they were "frightfully put out" when they heard the flank had gone, and they had to "fall back" (*IOT*, 37). Likewise, despite Nick's anticipation of the breakup with Marjorie, he experiences the "end" with less dignity than Marjorie, who calmly pushes off the boat herself and tells Nick that he can "walk back around the point" (*IOT*, 35). It is Nick, then, who falls back, not Marjorie, just as it is the English who fall back, not the Germans. Although it is not likely that Hemingway is drawing an analogy between love and war, he is emphasizing in the story and the interchapter disappointment and bitterness caused by failure because things have not turned out the way they were supposed to. While the surprise reversal at the end of Chapter IV of the soldiers' having to fall back resembles Nick's defeat at the end of "The End of Something," it also reveals the ridiculousness of Nick's self-deceit at the end of the next story, "The Three-Day Blow."

Although "The Three-Day Blow" is a sequel to "The End of Something," each story is complete itself.[34] The three-part tonal structure of "The Three-Day Blow," however, is more subtle than that of "The End of Something" because of its more dramatic form (there is very little exposition and narration).[35] But its preoccupations with the difficulty of understanding and expressing feelings, the focus on the loss of love, and on the relationships between men and women (as well as between men) connect the story to the former part of the sequence. The comic effects in "Three-Day Blow" make it unique, however, as does the predominance of dialogue to produce emotional flow.

Like "The End of Something," the story opens with an elegiac tone, but instead of a mill town it presents an autumn scene as the objective correlative for Nick's feelings about the end of his relationship with Marjorie:[36]

> The rain stopped as Nick turned into the road that went up through the orchard. The fruit had been picked and the fall wind blew through the bare trees. Nick stopped and picked up a Wagner apple from beside the road, shiny in the brown grass from the rain. He put the apple in the pocket of his Mackinaw coat.
>
> The road came out of the orchard on to the top of the hill. There was the cottage, the porch bare, smoke coming from the chimney. In back was the garage, the chicken coup and the second-growth timber like a hedge against the woods behind. The big trees swayed far over in the wind as he watched. It was the first of the autumn storms. (*IOT*, 39)

The details of a season's end—the picked fruit, the bare trees, the fall wind, and the brown grass—give the scene a sense of something having passed away, something over or lost. In particular, the fallen apple in the grass, though "shiny," suggests an innocence that is no more.[37] Likewise, the bare porch and the "smoke coming from the chimney" suggest a kind of winter seclusion and barrenness (*IOT*, 39). But the "second timber growth" keeps the danger of the "woods" beyond it from taking over. The storm Hemingway speaks of is "Only the first of the Autumn storms," and it anticipates other losses in the latter half of the sequence (*IOT*, 39).

A long section of dialogue between Nick and Bill then follows; it begins with a solemnity that suggests something is troubling them:

> "Well, Wemedge," he said.
> "Hey, Bill," Nick said, coming up the steps.
> They stood together, looking out across the country, down over the orchard, beyond the road, across the lower fields and the woods of the point to the lake. They could see the surf along Ten Mile point.
> "She's blowing," Nick said.
> "She'll blow like that for three days," Bill said.
> "Is your dad in?" Nick said.
> "No. He's out with the gun. Come on in."
> Nick went inside the cottage. There was a big fire in the fireplace. The wind made it roar. Bill shut the door.
> "Have a drink?" he said. (*IOT*, 39–40)

Even though Nick and Bill address each other informally by nickname, the slow, deliberate salutations, the remarks about the weather, Nick's asking about Bill's father, and Bill's invitation into the cabin and offering Nick a drink make their exchange seem more a ritual than the casual greeting of two old friends.[38] After their salutations, Nick's disagreements about McGraw's purchase of Heinie Zim, about the books *Richard Feveral* and *Forest Lovers*, and about Walpole and Chesterton reveal that Nick is the one who is troubled by something.[39]

After each of Nick's disagreements, however, he comes around to Bill's point of view. This rhythm of conflict and reconciliation in the second movement of the story builds to a point of revelry as the two men proceed to get drunk. Thus, after the disagreement about McGraw's purchasing Heinie Zim, Nick concludes that "There's always more to it than we know about," as if this drinking rite must be closed with a formal propitiation (*IOT*, 41). And following their disagreement about Walpole and Chesterton, Nick says, "I wish we had them both here. . . . We'd take them both fishing to the 'Voix tomorrow" (*IOT*, 43).

The more Nick and Bill drink, the more personal their conversations become. In their disagreement about their fathers, Nick insists his father has "missed a lot" because "He claims he's never taken a drink in his life"

(*IOT,* 48). But Bill defends Nick's father, the doctor, and says, "You can't tell. . . . Everything's got its compensations" (*IOT,* 44). To smooth out this difference in opinion, Nick says, "It all evens up" (*IOT,* 44).

This second movement of the story builds comically on waves of reconciliation to the point where Nick and Bill are so drunk that Nick has difficulty being "practical," a word Hemingway repeats four times (three times in the passage below) to emphasize the contrast between Nick's intention and his actions. Earlier, Nick did not think Hewlett's lovers in *Forest Lovers* terribly "practical" for having a naked sword between them in bed at night to keep them apart. In the following passage, however, Hemingway uses the scene of the spilled apricots to counterpoint Nick's opinion about the *Forest Lovers* and to parallel Nick's later self-deluded conclusion that he can always mend his relationship with Marjorie:

> "I'll get a chunk [of wood] from the back porch," Nick said. He had noticed while looking into the fire that the fire was dying down. Also he wished to show he could hold his liquor and be practical. Even if his father had never touched a drop Bill was not going to get him drunk before he himself was drunk.
> "Bring one of the big beech chunks," Bill said. He was also being consciously practical.
> Nick came in with the log through the kitchen and in passing knocked a pan off the kitchen table. He laid the log down and picked up the pan. It had contained dried apricots, soaking in water. He carefully picked up all the apricots off the foor, some of them had gone under the stove, and put them back in the pan. He dipped some more water onto them from the pail by the table. He felt quite proud of himself. He had been thoroughly practical. (*IOT,* 44–45)

Part of the humor of this section is the deadpan tone in which Hemingway relates the incident, and part of the humor derives from the point of view—third person limited through Nick's inebriated consciousness. The repetition of the words "fire," "drunk," "apricots," "water," "practical," "log," and "table" among others, give the section a simple rhythmical quality which reflects Nick's state of mind. He is exaggeratedly deliberate and aware of his actions because he is trying to keep control while drunk, just as he tries to control his emotions elsewhere in the sequence, particularly in "Indian Camp," "The End of Something," and later in "Big Two-Hearted River." The central irony in the story is that Nick's primary practicality—his breaking up with Marjorie—has made him miserable. But for the time being, Nick feels only the pleasure alcohol has provided; both men drink to Chesterton and Walpole, Bill saying, "Gentlemen . . . I give you Chesterton and Walpole." "Exactly, gentlemen," Nick agrees (*IOT,* 46).

A sudden shift in tone from a drink-induced loquaciousness to sober gravity comes as Bill tells Nick he was "very wise" (i.e. practical) "To bust off that Marge business" (*IOT,* 46). Nick's noncommittal responses to Bill's comments that Nick would be working now if he were married to Marjorie, that he would be fat, and that he would be struggling to cope with Marjorie's mother suggest that he agrees with Bill's point of view.[40] Even when Bill says Marjorie is not of his class, Nick assents in silence. While Nick may agree on these points, they are not causes for his breaking up with Marjorie. Nick's problem is that his love for Marjorie has disappeared "suddenly" and for no comprehensible (at least to him) reason.

The second movement of the story reaches a crescendo of disappointment after Bill says Marjorie is now able to marry someone "of her own sort and settle down and be happy" (*IOT,* 47):

> Nick said nothing. The liquor had all died out of him and left him alone. Bill wasn't there. He wasn't sitting in front of the fire or going fishing tomorrow with Bill and his dad or anything. He wasn't drunk. It was all gone. All he knew was that he had once had Marjorie and that he had lost her. She was gone and he had sent her away. That was all that mattered. He might never see her again. Probably he never would. It was all gone, finished. (*IOT,* 47)

The short, staccato sentences and the repetition of negatives such as "wasn't" and "never," and words that suggest loss such as "gone," "finished," "alone," and "lost" provide a somber contrast to earlier notes of revelry. But the closest Nick comes to understanding and articulating his loss is his analogy of his feelings to a three-day blow: "I couldn't help it. Just like when the three-day blows come now and rip all the leaves off the trees" (*IOT,* 47). Hemingway's use of this simile for Nick suggests the capriciousness of love and its devastating effects. The inexplicability of Nick's loss of love parallels the suddenness and irrationality of death at other points in the sequence.

As in "Indian Camp," the story closes with self-deception. After Nick says, "I oughtn't talk about it," Bill says, "You don't want to think about it. You might get back into it again" (*IOT,* 48). But this thought triggers another response in Nick and pulls him out of depression, for suddenly he feels happy:

> Nothing was finished. Nothing was ever lost. He would go into town on Saturday. He felt lighter, as he had felt before Bill started to talk about it. There was always a way out. . . . It was not even very important. The wind blew everything like that away. (*IOT,* 48–49)

Drinking plays a large part in the way Nick perceives his loss, for when he goes outside he feels that "the Marge business was no longer so tragic. It was not even very important. The wind blew everything like that away. . . . Still he could always go into town Saturday night. It was a good thing to have in reserve" (*IOT,* 49).

"The Three-Day Blow," like "Indian Camp," "The Doctor and the Doctor's Wife," and "The End of Something," is less concerned with character development and plot than it is with a progression of tonal centers that build toward a moment of heightened awareness. Characters are not developed; as embodiments of feelings, characters present certain sets of feelings, often very limited. Thus, in "The Three-Day Blow," as in "Indian Camp," Nick denies his awareness of evil in the world. In "Indian Camp" the evil is death. In "The Three-Day Blow" Nick denies his loss of love for Marjorie. Nick's loss is treated in the same way that the awareness of death is treated in the rest of the sequence—as casual, unimportant, often comic.

While the first three stories move toward a shattering of a self-deceived sensibility, Chapter V ("They shot the six cabinet ministers . . ." [*IOT,* 51]) makes clear the irony of Nick's thinking he still has something "in reserve." For the image of the execution of the six cabinet ministers against the shuttered hospital in the rain undercuts any movement in the sequence toward affirmation. The closing image in Chapter V of the minister with typhoid "sitting down in the water with his head on his knees" (*IOT,* 51) links this chapter with "The End of Something" in which Nick lies with his head down on a blanket in remorse and defeat. The grimness and utter degradation of human spirit in Chapter V also anticipates the complex and frightening experience Nick faces in "The Battler." For Nick's first view of Ad Francis, the battered prize fighter, is an image that identifies Nick and Ad as fellow sufferers: Ad "was sitting there with his head in his hands looking at the fire" (*IOT,* 54). These repeated images of defeat emphasize the movement in the sequence toward complete dispiritedness.

"The Battler,"[41] like the first three stories, has a three-part tonal movement that suggests imminent catastrophe. It is set in Michigan, and its preoccupations are, in part, the difficulty of expressing feelings, the loss of love, and initiation to the adult world of danger and death. The story opens with Nick's having been thrown off the train he was hitching on:

> Nick stood up. He was all right. . . . He felt of his knee. The pants were torn and the skin was barked. His hands were scraped and there were sand and cinders driven up under his nails. He went over to the edge of the track down the little slope to the water and washed his hands. He washed them carefully

in the cold water, getting the dirt out from the nails. He squatted down and bathed his knee. (*IOT,* 53)

Nick's physical injuries—his barked knee, scraped hands, and the bump coming up on his eye—are symbolic of a greater beating he experienced when "The lousy crut of a brakeman" said to him, "I got something for you" and punched him off the train (*IOT,* 53). This emotional buffeting recalls the violent scene in "Indian Camp" and the potentially violent scene in "The Doctor and the Doctor's Wife," and it portends Nick's confrontation with Ad, and a more intense conflict in the subsequent stories. But Nick's trying to make light of this experience—"it was only a black eye" (IOT, 53)—suggests that, as in previous stories, the experience has not been assimilated.

The night journey that Nick makes on foot indicates that he has more ahead of him than a black eye from the brakeman:

> Three or four miles of swamp. He stepped along the track, walking so he kept on the ballast between the ties, the swamp ghostly in the rising mist. His eye ached and he was hungry. He kept on hiking, putting the miles of track back of him. The swamp was all the same on both sides of the track. (*IOT,* 54)

The details of Nick's painful journey along the tracks as he puts the miles behind him are an analogue for his journey from innocence to experience. The "swamp ghostly in the rising mist" on all sides accentuates the perilous journey he is taking (*IOT,* 54).[42] When Nick crosses the bridge, his boots ring "hollow on the iron," making a lonely sound that foreshadows his strange and solitary initiation by the fire in "a beechwood forest" where "fallen beechnut burrs were under his shoes (*IOT,* 54). The juxtaposition of a fire and its potential for warmth, light, and companionship, with the burrs and their potential for discomfort indicates that Nick's experience by the fire will be painful but instructive.

The tone of "The Battler" shifts from a mysterious ominousness to a disturbing hostility when Nick meets Ad, who immediately remarks about Nick's "shiner." The hostility becomes more apparent when Ad says, "You're a tough one, aren't you?" Ironically, Nick replies, "You got to be tough," for when he does have a chance to be tough and defend himself against Ad's physical aggressiveness, he can only say, "cut it out"—certainly Nick is no battler. The combination of Ad's reply to Nick's comment about being tough—"That's what I said"—and the ugly image of Ad's face heightens the story's disturbing current:

> The man looked at Nick and smiled. In the firelight Nick saw that his face was misshapen. His nose was sunken, his eyes were slits, he had queer-shaped lips. Nick did not perceive all this at once, he only saw the man's face was

queerly formed and mutiliated. It was like putty in color. Dead looking in the firelight. (*IOT,* 55)

Ad's misshapen face, the outward manifestation of his troubled soul, makes Nick feel "a little sick." Yet when Ad admits he's "not quite right," that he's "crazy," "Nick felt like laughing" (*IOT,* 56). As in the previous stories, the movement toward a breakdown of illusions is counterpointed by denial and rejection. Nick doesn't want to believe that Ad is crazy. Hemingway is playing with the meaning of the word "crazy," however, because Ad calls his friend Bugs "crazy," yet these two "crazy" characters have a greater bond of compassion and friendship than any two in the sequence. But Ad's irrationality parallels the irrational happenings in the rest of the sequence, such as the war scenes in the interchapters, Nick's sudden loss of love, and his viewing the bloody suicide of an Indian.

In the section that introduces Bugs, a shift in tone takes place from the mingled hostility and naivete in Nick's and Ad's conversation to gentleness and anger when Bugs and Ad speak. When Bugs instructs Nick to "Hang onto your knife, Mister Adams" (*IOT,* 58), after seeing Nick cut the bread with it, Nick misses Bugs' warning. His unsuspecting nature contrasts with Ad's antagonistic attempt to get Nick to hit him and Bugs' kindness ("Just close that sandwich, will you, please, and give it to Mister Francis" [*IOT,*58]).

After Bugs gently taps Ad at the base of the skull with a blackjack to keep Ad from hurting Nick, Bugs explains the reason for Ad's aggressiveness. The beatings Ad took in the ring only "made him sort of simple" (*IOT,* 60), but the hurt that makes Ad suffer so is that his wife, who "looks enough like him to be his own twin," left him because "there was a lot of people didn't like it . . . and they commenced to have a lot of disagreements" (*IOT,* 61). Ad's inability to deal with loss echoes Nick's confusion at the loss of Marjorie in "The End of Something" and "The Three-Day Blow," and it anticipates the bitter loss in "A Very Short Story" when a soldier is jilted by his girl.

In the warmth of the firelight, however, Nick finds both companionship and danger. That he has been stirred by this scene is clear because after he leaves the fire,

He found he had a ham sandwich in his hand and put it in his pocket. Looking back from the mounting grade before the track curved into the hills he could see the firelight in the clearing. (*IOT,* 62)

Although Nick and Ad have suffered similar experiences—physical and emotional beatings—later in the sequence in "Big Two-Hearted River" Nick weathers the trauma in his life better than Ad does his.

"The Battler" does not end with an illusion as do the previous stories.

Even though Nick is affected by what he sees, he still remains psychically unharmed by violence. He comes to the brink of violence when he comes face to face with Ad, but Bugs intervenes and spares him. While Nick remains unharmed in "The Battler," the threatening quality of this experience prepares for a far more upsetting confrontation in the next chapter.

Following "The Battler," three units—Chapter VI ("Nick sat against the wall . . ."), "A Very Short Story," and Chapter VIII ("While the bombardment . . .")—concentrate at the center of the sequence the most bitter feelings of loss and disillusionment. Once again employing Nick to structure the sequence lyrically, Hemingway focuses in Chapter VI on the image of a young wounded man surrounded by dead and dying men and a destroyed village. By using the name Nick in Chapter VI (this is the only interchapter in which he does so), Hemingway links Chapter VI to the first five stories, making clear a shifting state of awareness. The anticipation of a shattered psyche in the preceding stories is fully realized in this interchapter. In the close-up of a wounded individual who declares his disillusionment with an ideal—"Not patriots"—Hemingway brings the sequence to direct apprehension of death. Nick sits stoically against a church that cannot console him. He looks "straight ahead brilliantly" (*IOT,* 63). Hemingway's use of the adverb "brilliantly"—one of the few places in the book where he uses an adverb—implies Nick's assimilation of the experience and his attempt to turn to inner strength. Nick's stoicism and his rejection of his role in the war, therefore, provide a turning point in the sequence.

From disillusionment with war in Chapter VI, the sequence moves to disillusionment in love in "A Very Short Story." This seven-paragraph narrative of a soldier's betrayal by his love brings the book to its most cynical note. The mocking nursery tale tone, the direct treatment of the affair, and the absence of dialogue and dramatic technique make this story unique in the book. Its title, taken with its use of understatement, indicates that this is not a "short" story at all, but one that is so emotionally distressing that only through rigorous selection and emotional restraint can feeling be conveyed. It is framed on either side by images of wartime situations that parallel in bitterness the loss of love in the story; indeed the group of three create a stark vision of a joyless world.

The irony of the soldier's seeking comfort in cheap physicality after he has been jilted by his lover anticipates Chapter VII ("While the bombardment . . .") in which the speaker, terrified of death, turns to prayer in a moment of weakness but later finds comfort with a girl upstairs at the Villa Rossa. This soldier's fear of death—he "lay very flat and sweated and prayed oh jesus christ get me out of here" (*IOT,* 56)—parallels Nick's and his father's fleeing in the preceding story, but contrasts with Nick's stoicism in Chapter VI.

Additional connections among Chapters VI and VII and "A Very Short Story" are the effects of violence on a number of characters, and the emphasis on concerns of the spirit: heroism, love, and faith. The sequence has moved steadily to confrontation with death and destruction of ideals. In "The Battler" Nick's sensibility is affected by what he experiences, but he is not altered; in Chapter VI a similar sensibility, Nick again, is affected by what he experiences and consequently alters his perceptions of his illusions by deciding to be a patriot no longer. In "A Very Short Story" the unnamed wounded soldier picks up where Chapter VI left off with injured Nick against a wall, substituting the failure of love for the failure of heroism in war. The emotionally wounded soldier in "A Very Short Story" recalls Ad in "The Battler" who is broken hearted about his wife's leaving him. And the behavior of the soldier who "prayed oh jesus christ get me out of here" (*IOT*, 67) in Chapter VII parallels the current of fear that moves through the former part of the book. In the next story, "Soldier's Home," Krebs' refusal to pray, his lying about his war experience, and his inability to seek comfort in women, carry forward with a new twist the sequence's concerns.

What is revealed at the center of the book, then, is the awareness of the failure of traditional virtues: the belief in god, the fellowship of men, fidelity and fulfillment in relationships between men and women, and the ability to feel dignity and self worth. This awareness of the absence of traditional virtues discloses the truth: at the core of existence is death—a kind of nothingness. The emphasis in the latter half of the sequence becomes the struggle to reassess life given this fact. Since war offers no opportunity for an expression of dignity, and love offers no consolation, nor does faith in god, the characters must seek alternatives to create purpose and meaning in life.

4

In Our Time, Part Two: After a Separate Peace

> Sometimes you know the story. Sometimes you make it up as you go along and have no idea how it will come out. Everything changes as it moves. That is what makes the movement which makes the story. Sometimes the movement is so slow it does not seem to be moving. But there is always change and always movement. [1]

IF the former part of the sequence progresses toward a painful awareness of senseless death and the failure of traditional virtues—love, honor in war, self-respect—the latter shows the attempt at coping with this knowledge with stoicism and an assertion of personal values. The eight stories (considering "Big Two-Hearted River" one story) and eight interchapters and "L'Envoi" in the latter part of the book progress from shocked awareness at the brutality and ultimate nothingness of existence to a quiet, shaky effort at keeping the pain of this awareness under control. The tension in the latter portion of *In Our Time* derives from the conflict between the way the world is and the degree to which this state of the world is accepted and assimilated. [2]

Like the concerns of the stories and interchapters in the first half of the work, those in the second are diverse. "Soldier's Home" focuses on a World War I veteran's alienation from his family and society, Chapter VIII on racism in America, "The Revolutionist" on political idealism, and Chapters IX–XIV on bullfighting as a way of asserting personal values. Three stories—"Mr. and Mrs. Elliot," "Cat in the Rain," and "Out of Season"—have to do, in part, with bad marriages. "Cross-Country Snow" concerns skiing as an emotional escape from responsibility. "My Old Man" focuses on a young boy's discovery—through the death of his father—of adults' dishonesty and cynicism. Finally, the two parts of "Big Two-Hearted River" concern Nick's solitary fishing trip in Michigan as a way of coping with the uncomfortable awareness of the dangers of life.

In many ways, the first story in this group, "Soldier's Home,"[3] continues the preoccupations of the former part of the sequence: strained family relationships; the setting in the Midwest; the impact of war on an ex-soldier's psyche; and the need for a protagonist to learn to cope with unpleasant situations. It also intensifies the tones of bitterness, disillusionment, and loss in the former part of the book. And it emphasizes a conflict between a character's reluctance to accept pointless violence and shocking deaths and the pressure on his part to deal with these realities. Specifically, "Soldier's Home" presents Krebs's need to disengage himself for self-protection from anyone and anything, and his family's—in particular his mother's—insistence that "God has some work for every one to do" (*IOT*, 75).

The story opens with a spiritless matter-of-factness:

> Krebs went to war from a Methodist college in Kansas. There is a picture which shows him among his fraternity brothers, all of them wearing exactly the same height and style collar. He enlisted in the marines in 1917 and did not return to the United States until the second division returned from the Rhine in the summer of 1919.
>
> There is a picture which shows him on the Rhine with two German girls and another corporal. Krebs and the corporal look too big for their uniforms. The German girls are not beautiful. The Rhine does not show in the picture. (*IOT*, 69)

The passage rings with a sense of disillusionment and failed expectations as it reveals the protagonist's alienation. Krebs "did not return" from the war until 1919; Krebs and the corporal were "too big" for their uniforms. To heighten the effect of Krebs's disconnectedness, Hemingway subtly contrasts a picture of Krebs "among his fraternity brothers, all of them wearing exactly the same height and style collar" with another picture which "shows him on the Rhine with two German girls and another corporal" (*IOT*, 69). And to emphasize that Krebs's experience in the war sets him apart from other men and that upon his return from war he is an altered man no longer like those wearing the identical collars in his fraternity photo, Hemingway indicates that Krebs has outgrown his uniform, literally and figuratively. Also, the German girls are not beautiful, as one might expect, and the proof of Krebs's actually being in Germany—the image of the Rhine—is not visible in the photograph. In short, the three "not's," the "too big," and the image of the contrasting photographs convey a strong sense of loss in the passage.

In subsequent paragraphs Hemingway sharpens this tone of disillusionment and the idea that Krebs's life is out of step with the rest of humankind by explaining that upon his return, Krebs, who probably has been at such sights of massacre as the Champagne, does not want to talk about the war, and when he does, no one wants to listen; in fact, Krebs finds out "that to be listened to at all he had to lie" (*IOT*, 69). But after he lies, he has "a reaction against the war and against talking about it" (*IOT*, 69).[4] He doesn't like lying:

All of the times that had been able to make him feel cool and clear inside himself when he thought of them; the times so long back when he had done the one thing, the only thing for a man to do, easily and naturally, when he might have done something else, now lost their cool, valuable quality and then were lost themselves. (*IOT*, 69–70)[5]

This feeling of loss is also carried forward in the following lines:

His lies were quite unimportant lies and consisted in attributing to himself things other men had seen, done or heard of, and stating as facts certain apocryphal incidents familiar to all soldiers. Even his lies were not sensational at the pool room. His acquaintances, who had heard detailed accounts of German women found chained to machine guns in the Argonne forest and who could not comprehend, or were barred by their patriotism from interest in, any German machine gunners who were not chained, were not thrilled by his stories. (*IOT*, 70)

The preponderance of negatives (there are four not's) suggest that Krebs's real war experiences have been trivialized, and that his lies not only remove him from the community, but also emasculate him. As John J. Roberts notes:

What disorients him is not the truth of war but the lie of the Midwestern view of war, not the truth of death but the lie of life. Krebs cannot reconcile the two, and in trying he loses even the truth he had had, so he stops trying for a time.[6]

Yet Krebs feels he "had been a good soldier," and as a result of this feeling he acquires "the nausea in regard to experience that is the result of untruth or exaggeration" (*IOT*, 70). Krebs's nausea is a kind of emptiness or living death.[7] Because of this feeling of nothingness, Krebs cannot cope with relationships that have consequences. He does not want a girl because he cannot deal with "all the talking" he would have to do to get one (*IOT*, 71).

To further emphasize a tension between fear of engagement with life and a strong pressure to do so, as well as Krebs's inability to cope with life around him, Hemingway uses the rhythm of the repetition of "he liked" and "he did not want" in the following passage:

When he went away only little girls wore their hair like that or girls that were fast. They all wore sweaters and shirt waists with round Dutch collars. It was a pattern. He liked to look at them from the front porch as they walked on the other side of the street. He liked to watch them walking under the shade of the trees. He liked the round Dutch collars above their sweaters. He liked their silk stockings and flat shoes. He liked their bobbed hair and the way they walked.

When he was in town their appeal to him was not very strong. He did not like them when he saw them in the Greek's ice cream parlor. He did not want them themselves really. They were too complicated. There was something else. Vaguely he wanted a girl but he did not want to have to work to get her. He would have liked to have a girl but he did not want to have to spend a long time getting her. He did not want to get into the intrigue and the politics. He did not want to have to do any courting. He did not want to tell any more lies. It wasn't worth it. (*IOT*, 71)

In the first paragraph the presentation of the girls evokes a subtly inviting sensuality: the suggestive smoothness and sheen of silk stockings, the soft sweaters, and "the way they walked." These impressions are enhanced by the rhythm of the simple sentences and the repetition of certain words and phrases. Thus, in the second paragraph the recurrence six times of "he did not like" and "he did not want" counterpointing "he liked" in the first paragraph, creates a rhythm of "yes-no" that parallels the tension in the story between reluctance and persistence.[8] This rhythm makes clear the conflict between Krebs's desires and what he is able to deal with, or rather, life as it is, and the degree to which he can accept it. That Krebs admires the girls from the porch, where he is safe from involvement and risk, underscores his fear. Just as "he had been badly, sickeningly frightened all the time during the war," so he is now. He has "lost everything" and must find a way to live with the feeling of nothingness (*IOT*, 70).

In sustaining the tension between a reluctance to cope with the way things are as represented by the midwest values of Krebs's family, and the difficulty of accepting these values, as represented by Krebs's disillusionment and loss, Hemingway shows how Krebs must struggle against the insensitive way he is treated by his family. When he talks to his mother about the war, "her attention always wandered" and "His father was non-committal" (*IOT*, 70). His mother tells him that his father is willing to let him "take out the car in the evenings" as if this were an enormous concession his parents are making to integrate their son back into their home and into the civilian community (*IOT*, 73). And yet the restrictions placed on Krebs are petty and stifling: " 'Harold, please don't muss up the paper. Your father can't read his *Star* if it's been mussed' " (*IOT*, 73).

Krebs's mother, like Mrs. Adams in "The Doctor and the Doctor's

Wife," is manipulative and sanctimonious, and she uses religion to blackmail her son: "God has some work for everyone to do . . . there can be no idle hands in His Kingdom" (*IOT*, 75). Making her lack of empathy and understanding more apparent, Krebs's mother tells him that she knows about "the Civil War and I have prayed for you. I pray for you all day long, Harold" (*IOT*, 75). Hemingway underscores Krebs's resentment of his mother, his hardening himself against her, by juxtaposing the language of Krebs's mother's false piety with an image of Krebs looking "at the bacon fat hardening on his plate" (*IOT*, 75).[9] His mother's demands for his love—"don't you love your mother, dear boy?" (*IOT*, 75)—and her insistence that he pray demonstrate the religious oppressiveness Krebs faces. He responds that he doesn't love anybody, and of course this includes his mother. But her tears make him feel contrite, and he apologizes: "'I didn't mean it,' he said. 'I was just angry at something. I didn't mean I didn't love you'" (*IOT*, 76). The "something" that he is angry at is his family's treatment of him and his acute disappointment in his war experiences. Even the title of the story suggests that Krebs's home is more of a mental institution for soldiers recovering from the war than a family-centered home.

Krebs feels "sick and vaguely nauseated" when his mother tries to coerce him into expressing his feelings: "I'm your mother . . . I held you next to my heart when you were a tiny baby" (*IOT*, 76). To appease her, Krebs regresses to a child's state by calling her "Mummy" and saying, "I'll try to be a good boy for you" (*IOT*, 76). But he cannot follow through in deed; he cannot pray.

In the "yes-no" rhythm of the following passage Hemingway intensifies the conflict between Krebs and his mother:

> They knelt down beside the dining-room table and Krebs's mother prayed.
> "Now, you pray, Harold," she said.
> "I can't," Krebs said.
> "Try, Harold."
> "I can't."
> "Do you want me to pray for you?"
> "Yes." (*IOT*, 76)

Like Nick in "Indian Camp," "The End of Something," and "Three-Day Blow," Krebs has difficulty explaining just what he feels. And like Nick and Mr. Adams in "The Doctor and the Doctor's Wife," Krebs tries to escape from an uncomfortable situation. He tries to convince himself that he's not bothered by this scene with his mother ("He had felt sorry for his mother . . ." [*IOT*, 77]), and then he flees from his mother to go "watch Helen play indoor baseball" (*IOT*, 77).

Earlier in the story, however, Helen, who affectionately calls Krebs Hare (in contrast to his mother who stiffly calls him Harold), also tries to manipulate Krebs in her way:

> "I tell them all you're my beau. Aren't you my beau, Hare?"
>
> "You bet."
>
> "Couldn't your brother really be your beau just because he's your brother?"
>
> "I don't know."
>
> "Sure you know. Couldn't you be my beau, Hare, if I was old enough and if you wanted to?"
>
> "Sure. You're my girl now."
>
> "Am I really your girl?"
>
> "Sure."
>
> "Do you love me?"
>
> "Uh, huh."
>
> "Will you love me always?"
>
> "Sure."
>
> "Will you come over and watch me play indoor?"
>
> "Maybe."
>
> "Aw, Hare, you don't love me. If you loved me, you'd want to come over and watch me play indoor." (*IOT*, 74)

Anticipating Krebs's inability to confess his love for his mother, this passage also reveals the difficulty Krebs has in committing himself. The "yes-no" rhythm in the passage encapsulates the movement of the entire story: an obstinate, fearful aversion to a cloying demand for commitment which ultimately yields to resigned acceptance. Krebs does go to watch Helen play indoor baseball, but not because he loves her so much, but because he is trying to strike a balance between complete rejection of his family's demands and a partial acceptance of what he must do to live his life. At the end of the story Krebs decides "to go to Kansas City and get a job and she [his mother] would feel alright about it" (*IOT*, 77).

Clearly, Hemingway employs Krebs as he does Nick in earlier stories as a vehicle for providing the tonal structure of the story. In "Soldier's Home" Krebs's avoidance of commitment reveals a sensibility that cannot quite accept what he must do to get on in life. But while Nick refuses to accept his mortality in "The Doctor and the Doctor's Wife" and rejects love in "The End of Something," Krebs makes an effort to deal with events and people in his life. Krebs's lack of illusions points toward Nick's self-renewal and acknowlegement of the dangers of the swamp at the end of "Big Two-Hearted River."[10]

Chapter VIII which follows "Soldier's Home" serves to emphasize the corruptness of the America to which Krebs has returned. The violence and the racist remarks about "wops" in this interchapter parallel Krebs's private war with his family and by extension emphasize the terrible consequences of individuals and whole nations failing to get along with one another.

Following Chapter VIII, "The Revolutionist" plunges back into the arena of war in Europe. This story, like "Indian Camp" and "The Battler," presents with irony a tale of an innocent individual oddly untouched by violence. Also, the idea of a man "very shy and quite young," "travelling on the railroads" links this story to Nick of "The Battler" who is also an inexperienced young man riding the rails (*IOT*, 81). Like Nick who is fed and protected by Bugs, the young Revolutionist passes "on from one crew to another" (*IOT*, 81); and since he has no money, "They fed him behind the counter in railway eating houses" (*IOT*, 81). The focus on an idealistic, but persecuted and tortured Hungarian, links this story to the preceding interchapter in which the cigar store thieves become victims of an Irish policeman who cannot recognize the difference between Hungarians and "Wops," Italians in whose country the idealistic Hungarian in "The Revolutionist" seeks refuge. In "The Revolutionist," then, Hemingway is once again pointing to the difficulty of human compatibility. In contrast to Krebs in "Soldier's Home" who wants to live without consequences, however, the tortured Revolutionist advocates a unified people as implied by his socialistic politics.

Chapter IX which follows "The Revolutionist" is one of six interchapters in the book concerned with bullfighting. It prefaces a sequence of three stories—"Mr. and Mrs. Elliot," "Cat in the Rain," and "Out of Season"—that focus on joyless liaisons between man and wife. These three stories, like the preceding stories in the sequence, reveal in varying degrees impotence, spiritual vacuity, and repressed anger. The interchapters between them counterpoint and parallel the stories by emphasizing deliberate confrontation with violence.

Chapter IX, formerly Chapter II in *in our time*, tells about the "kid" who "had to kill five bulls because you can't have more than three matadors, and the last bull he was so tired he couldn't get the sword in" (*IOT*, 83). The informal and ungrammatical vernacular of the American relating how this "kid" bravely tries to kill the bull and the crowd's jeering disapproval of his human limitations effectively follow the story about Krebs's unsuccessful attempt to resist completely his mother, and her partial triumph in keeping him submissive. Chapter IX, then, parallels the movement in the sequence toward an attempt to find a way to cope with life after an unhappy awareness of what it offers. Hemingway's moving this interchapter to this position in the sequence, as a result, intensifies and makes more coherent the tonal structure of the work.

The next story in the sequence, "Mr. and Mrs. Elliot," is a condescendingly satirical presentation of the failure of love between man and wife.[11] In its focus on physical and spiritual impotence, "Mr. and Mrs.

Elliot" was prepared for in "The Doctor and the Doctor's Wife," "The End of Something," and "A Very Short Story."

The story concerns Hubert Elliot's marriage to a forty-year-old sickly southern woman with whom he tries "very hard to have a baby" (*IOT*, 88), but ultimately he takes to "drinking white wine" and living "apart in his own room," while his wife Cornelia sleeps with her girl friend in "the big medieval bed" (*IOT*, 88). It opens abruptly with this mocking nursery tale tone:

> Mr. and Mrs. Elliot tried very hard to have a baby. They tried as often as Mrs. Elliot could stand it. They tried in Boston after they were married and they tried coming over on the boat. They did not try very often on the boat because Mrs. Elliot was quite sick. She was sick and when she was sick she was sick as Southern women are sick. That is women from the Southern part of the United States. Like all Southern women Mrs. Elliot disintegrated very quickly under sea sickness, traveling at night, and getting up too early in the morning. Many of the people on the boat took her for Elliot's mother. Other people who knew they were married believed she was going to have a baby. In reality she was forty years old. Her years had been precipitated suddenly when she started traveling. (*IOT*, 85)

As in many passages in *In Our Time*, Hemingway repeats a single word to draw attention to it, and, as in the case in this passage, to intensify the dissonant elements in the prose. The repetition of "sick" emphasizes that Mrs. Elliot is not only physically, but emotionally sick. In addition, Hemingway's use of the titles Mr. and Mrs. suggests not respect, but disrespect. Hemingway is mocking Hubert's notion of "living straight" and loveless relationships like Hubert's and Cornelia's. Hubert at first had no intention of marrying Cornelia: "He could never remember just when it was decided that they were to be married. But they were married" (*IOT*, 86). Following their marriage, however, Mr. and Mrs. Elliot try "very hard to have a baby" in Paris, Dijon, and Tourain, but they are unsuccessful (*IOT*, 88). In time, Mrs. Elliot's girlfriend, Honey—the only one of the three characters for whom Hemingway gives a name that suggests sensuousness and affection—eventually joins the couple and takes over Mrs. Elliots' job of typing her husband's manuscripts.

Hemingway's allusion to T. S. Eliot's sexually bored typist in "The Fire Sermon" draws attention to the conflicting particulars in the story, for the typist in this story does not join the Elliots to please Mr. Elliot, but rather Mrs. Elliot, even to the point of assuming Mrs. Elliot's wifely support of her husband in typing his manuscripts. This allusion to T. S. Eliot's "waste land" typist underscores the Elliots' failure to join in a meaningful union and the implications of this failure—spiritual malaise. The story ends with all three characters "quite happy" (Elliot drinking white wine) sitting in a garden "under a plane tree and the hot evening wind" blowing around them (*IOT,* 88). This final image anticipates "L'Envoi" in which a powerless Greek king sips whiskey in his palace garden and dreams of escape to America.

The sensuous language that pictures the violent disembowelling of a picador's horse in Chapter X is a jolting contrast to the satire of "Mr. and Mrs. Elliot." The "blue bunch" of entrails that "swung backward and forward as he began to canter" is a disturbing image coming after a story about Mr. and Mrs. Elliot who never connect with each other in "the big hot bedroom on the big, hard bed" (*IOT,* 89, 88). The final line of Chapter X—"The bull could not make up his mind to charge" (*IOT,* 89)—parallels Hubert's and Cornelia's failure, for the picador has spurred the horse forward, but the bull will not charge.

In "Cat in the Rain," the next story, as in "The End of Something," the curve of feeling is conveyed predominantly through dialogue and imagistic setting rather than through exposition or narration. And like "The Doctor and the Doctor's Wife" and "Mr. and Mrs. Elliot," the story is concerned with the difficulty of man and wife communicating with each other. In this case, the man and wife are American expatriates staying in a hotel in Italy after the war.

Although the story concerns sterility and boredom between a man and his wife, as a number of critics have implied,[12] it is less concerned with the failure of a particular marriage than it is with presenting emotional states of unhappiness and discontent. Thus, a tension in the story between the wife's unease and longing and George's refusal to respond satisfactorily to his wife's desires creates a back and forth, "yes-no" rhythm similar to that in "Soldier's Home." To prepare for this conflict, Hemingway opens the story on a melancholy note with the view from the American couple's hotel room:

> There were only two Americans stopping at the hotel. They did not know any of the people they passed on the stairs on their way to and from their room. Their room was on the second floor facing the sea. It also faced the public garden and the war monument. There were big palms and green benches in the public garden. In the good weather there was always an artist with his easel. Artists liked the way the palms grew and the bright colors of the hotels facing the gardens and the sea. Italians came from a long way off to look up at the war monument. It was made of bronze and glistened in the rain. It was raining. The rain dripped from the palm trees. Water stood in pools on the gravel paths. The sea broke in a long line in the rain and slipped back down the beach to come up and break again in a long line in the rain. The motor cars were gone from the square by the war monument. Across the square in the doorway of the cafe the waiter stood looking out at the empty square. (*IOT,* 91)

The vivid details in the description of the square capture a quality of dreariness and loneliness. The monument's glistening "in the rain" makes it a focal point in the empty square; and its presence suggests that this is a postwar scene, a scene that connects this story to previous interchapters and stories concerned with war and its terrible effects. For instance, the water that "stood in pools on the gravel paths" recalls the image in Chapter V of the pools of water that stand in the courtyard when the six cabinet ministers are shot (*IOT*, 91).

Perhaps the most melancholy note in the scene is achieved in the following lines when Hemingway captures the rhythm of the waves by repeating a number of monosyllabic words: "The sea broke in a long line in the rain and slipped back and down the beach to come up and break again in a long line in the rain" (*IOT*, 91). Lacking the philosophical quality of Matthew Arnold's "Dover Beach," Hemingway's lines, nevertheless, recall the feelings of yearning and loss in Arnold's poem:

Listen! you hear the grating roar
Of pebbles which the waves draw back, and fling,
At their return, up the strand,
Begin, and cease, and then again begin,
With tremulous cadence slow, and bring
The eternal note of sadness in.

The actions and dialogue of the characters in this story of disillusionment also reveal the rhythm of "yes-no." The unnamed American wife—she is unnamed because she is the "poor kitty in the rain," or rather, an alienated expatriate (Hemingway calls her "Kitty" in the draft[13])—looks from the hotel window and sees a "kitty" in the rain that she wants, and she tells her husband George that she's going to go down and get it. Her husband says, "I'll do it," but the wife insists, "No, I'll get it. The poor kitty out trying to keep dry under a table" (*IOT*, 91). As Ronald Carter argues, the cat represents "something in her experience which cannot be fulfilled—something which is present but is characterized here by its absence" (*IOT*, 88).[14] What the wife wants is complete sexual, and by extension, spiritual fulfillment. This becomes obvious when she notices the hotel-keeper as she goes downstairs. The parallel sentence structure and the repetition of "she liked" in the following paragraph point to the wife's modest admiration of the padrone's mature characteristics:

He stood behind his desk in the far end of the dim room. The wife liked him. She liked the deadly serious way he received any complaints. She liked his dignity. She liked the way he wanted to serve her. She liked the way he felt about being a hotel-keeper. She liked his old, heavy face and big hands. (*IOT*, 92)

Even though the repetition of "she liked" implies the wife's childlike, playful characteristics, her observations are those of a fully grown woman, in particular her noting his dignity and his "heavy face" and "big hands." And after the padrone sends out a maid with an umbrella to protect the wife from the rain, the American wife feels "very small and at the same time really important" (*IOT,* 93).

Warren Bennett points out that "the wife's recognition of the padrone's extraordinary character suggests that her husband, George, lacks the qualities which the wife finds so attractive in the padrone."[15] Hemingway emphasizes the idea of the wife's dissatisfaction with George by the tension in the dialogue once the wife returns to the room after an unsuccessful attempt to get the kitty: "Don't you think it would be a good idea if I let my hair grow out" (*IOT,* 93). George resists this comment and its threatening implications (she will no longer be a child if she lets her hair grow out) by saying, "I like it the way it is." This is countered with, "I get so tired of it . . . I get so tired of looking like a boy" (*IOT,* 93). But, George, seemingly sincere, says, "You look pretty darn nice" (*IOT,* 93).

The pitch of this "yes-no" tension is heightened when the wife responds to this with a series of wants that reveal her sexual longings:

> I want to pull my hair back tight and smooth and make a big knot at the back that I can feel . . . I want to have a kitty to sit on my lap and purr when I stroke her. (*IOT,* 93)

But George responds with a disinterested "Yeah," and this further exacerbates the wife to express her yearnings like a woman whose empty life desperately needs focus:

> And I want to eat at a table with my own silver and I want candles. And I want it to be spring and I want to brush my hair out in front of a mirror and I want a kitty and I want some new clothes. (*IOT,* 94)

Although this passage suggests the impatience of a child who wants what she wants immediately, the sensuous language of the American wife's desires clearly underscores her mature physical and emotional needs. She wants to "feel" her hair "tight and smooth" in a "knot" at the back of her head.[16] She wants to hear the kitty "purr" when she strokes it. She wants "to eat at a table" using her own "silver," the whole scene to be romantically illuminated by "candles." In short, the wife longs for a kind of rebirth. She wants to begin again in "spring" when the world is just awakening and giving birth; she wants a kitty in her lap, as if it were an infant or a child; and she also wants to see and feel her transformation into a fully replete woman when she releases her hair in front of the mirror and fixes on the new identity that will come with the "new clothes."

The dynamics in the story have been building to this lyrically intoned longing for sexual and spiritual fulfillment. This moment of sensuously charged awareness prepares for Chapter XII, a point in the sequence where in one fluid gesture, Villalta kills the bull, and in doing so becomes master of his own fate. The wife's longings also prepare for the tones of satisfaction in "Big Two-Hearted River." But this longing for fulfillment in "Cat in the Rain" is met with an irritable impatience by George, who, fed up with the wife's insistence, says, "Oh, shut up and get something to read" (*IOT,* 94). This abrupt change in tone elicits a more serious note from the wife: "Anyway, I want a cat . . . . I want a cat. I want a cat now. If I can't have long hair or any fun, I can have a cat" (*IOT,* 94). Hemingway drops the childlike tone of the wife's earlier wants and with the word "cat" emphasizes the seriousness of the wife's adult needs.

The wife gets a cat, but not the kitty she saw outside, the one she could cuddle. Rather, the padrone with the "old, heavy face and big hands" who "wants to serve her" sends up with the maid a "big tortoise-shell cat that pressed tight against her and swung down against her body" (*IOT,* 94). The wife, who has been resisting the conditions of life, as represented by her inattentive husband, must settle for reality. Therefore, although she will not be fulfilled by George's complacence, she will accept the offering of an older man who has "dignity" and who is "deadly serious" in the way he receives complaints.

Chapter XI, the third interchapter of the six concerned with bullfighting, is an effective commentary on "Cat in the Rain." The crowd's lack of sympathy for the bullfighter—its disapproval of his "bad sticking"— parallels George's disapproval of his wife's desires. Also, the bullfighter's feeling of failure ("I am not really a very good bull fighter" [*IOT,* 95]) complements the wife's failure to have her desires fulfilled. A further parallel in both story and interchapter lies in their association of hair with self-regard and personal identity. The bullfighter is symbolically emasculated when his pigtail is cut off by someone in the crowd; the wife feels like a boy with her short hair and therefore wants to grow it out to feel like a woman.

Chapter XI also prepares for the next story, "Out of Season," with its focus on an ineffective adult male. [17] This story echoes preoccupations rendered earlier in the sequence: the lack of sympathy between man and wife, a returning soldier, fishing, and characters who drink to blunt their fear. More importantly, the story concerns the frustration of understanding and articulating feelings, as well as the difficulty of understanding and accepting individuals and whole peoples for who and what they are.

The story opens with a mix of sullenness, forced cheerfulness, and comic drunkenness as three people set out to go fishing: the young gentleman[18] (he is unnamed like the unnamed American wife in "Cat in the Rain," to give the feeling of alienation in the story), his wife Tiny, and their guide Peduzzi[19] (who has schemed the outing). It shifts to the ameloriative tone of the young gentleman and the churlishness and anger of his wife in the second movement of the story as they struggle to overcome their misunderstandings in the Concordia. The third movement begins with a guilty uneasiness mingling with relief and a desperate pleading from Peduzzi after Tiny returns to the village and the young gentleman cancels the next day's fishing trip with Peduzzi.

As the title suggests, something is not in season:[20]

> On the four lire Peduzzi had earned by spading the hotel garden he got quite drunk. He saw the young gentleman coming down the path and spoke to him mysteriously. The young gentleman said he had not eaten but would be ready to go as soon as lunch was finished. Forty minutes or an hour.
>
> At the cantina near the bridge they trusted him for three more grappas because he was so confident and mysterious about his job for the afternoon. It was a windy day with the sun coming out from behind the clouds and then going under in sprinkles of rain. A wonderful day for trout fishing. (*IOT,* (97)

While the motifs from preceding stories and interchapters are obvious— the garden, rain, alcohol—a sense of foreboding, of unanswered questions implied by the words "mysteriously" and "mysterious," perhaps of something "out of season," give the opening of the story an uneasy quality.[21]

Following this, the three characters walk through the town, Tiny following "sullenly" behind the men with "the fishing rods, unjointed, one in each hand" (*IOT,* 97). Peduzzi greets everyone they see "elaborately," but "Nobody spoke or gave any sign to them except the town beggar, lean and old, with a spittle-thickened beard, who lifted his hat as they passed" (*IOT,* 98). The "mystery" is that Peduzzi, who is most likely known to the town for his drinking,[22] is taking the American couple fishing "out of season," and everyone realizes this. Peduzzi's secret is no mystery.

Further disharmony in the story is imparted during the confusion in the Concordia where the young gentleman and his wife try to order three marsalas. The girl behind the pastry counter, only seeing two people, says, "Two, you mean?" (*IOT,* 90). When the three drinks come, they are "muddy looking," again suggesting that all is not right, all is "out of season."

The most obvious misunderstanding in the story is the young gentleman's apology for the way he talked to Tiny at lunch: "We were both getting at the same thing from different angles," he says (*IOT,* 99). And the wife responds, "It doesn't make any difference . . . None of it makes any difference," indicating that an apology is too late, the damage is done. But the young gentleman persists in his attempt to make peace and says, "Are you too cold"—oblivious to his wife's having "on three sweaters" (*IOT*, 99). Hemingway is less concerned with recounting a completely plotted story than he is with presenting states of feeling, for here, regardless of the source of discomfort between the characters,[23] dispiritedness and disharmony are obvious. These are states of being that supercede any cause; they are tonal qualities that need no narrative framework—they simply are.

In other incidents in the story Hemingway's language further reveals moments "out of season." After the young gentleman and his wife leave Cortina, the wife thinks Peduzzi is pointing out his doctor in the doorway of a house, saying, "His doctor . . . has he got to show us his doctor?" (*IOT*, 100). But Hemingway makes clear that Peduzzi's drunkenness ("Peduzzi talked rapidly and with much winking and knowingness" [*IOT*, 100]) and his mix of dialects ("d'Ampezzo" and "tyroler German") contribute to the confusion: "the young gentleman and the wife understood nothing" (*IOT*, 100).

Hemingway even shows that the "wasteland world"[24] is "out of season." For instance, the river, like the drinks, is "brown and muddy." A "dump heap" near the river, as Dix McComas explains, is probably a "pile of war refuse" (*IOT*, 49).[25] And the cold, blustery day does not bring gentle, life-giving rain but only a few teasing sprinkles. The accumulation of these details about the environment, and the young gentleman's and Tiny's failure to understand one another, as well as Peduzzi's drunken behavior and deluded anticipation of a pleasant fishing trip provide a depressing cast to the story, bringing the sequence to its lowest point.

Near the end of "Out of Season," after Tiny has returned to town, and Peduzzi and the young gentleman give up the idea of fishing because they have no *piombo* (lead)—the young gentleman feeling relieved because "He was no longer breaking the law" (*IOT*, 102)—the two men sit and drink the marsala. Peduzzi again feels that "This was a great day. . . . A wonderful day" (*IOT*, 102); he is not willing to admit that he has no way to shore up the fragments of this fiasco. Even when Peduzzi wrangles four lire again from the young gentleman at the conclusion of the story, Hemingway again stresses Peduzzi's self-delusion: "He was through with the hotel garden, breaking up frozen manure with a dung fork. Life was opening out" (*IOT*, 13). But Peduzzi will eventually sober up and see the situation for what it is because the young gentleman says he will not, after all, be going fishing tomorrow, "very probably not" (*IOT*, 103).

In sum, Hemingway did not need to include Peduzzi's suicide, a scene he did not incorporate in the story because, as he said in a letter to Scott Fitzgerald,

At that time I was writing the In Our Time chapters and I wanted to write a tragic story *without* violence. So I didn't put in the hanging. Maybe that sounds silly. I didn't think the story needed it.[26]

Obviously, Hemingway was concerned with revealing a confluence of tonal streams rather than a narrative resolution. He did not need to include Peduzzi's suicide in the story because the language pictures the futility of existence.

In Chapter XII, following "Out of Season," the bullfighter Villalta, unlike Peduzzi, surprisingly demonstrates that everything is in season. As I noted in chapter two of this study, this interchapter marks the point in the sequence where there is no irony, where rhythm, sound, and meaning are one, just as Villalta becomes "one with the bull" (*IOT,* 105). Here man seeks and faces death with dignity and determination to triumph. Here the crowd roars, and the bull's blood roars as the bullfighter performs a self-willed act of danger and daring. This affirmative note counterpoints the tones of bitterness and degradation in the rest of the sequence, as well as provides a resting place from self-delusion and powerlessness, and thus anticipates the affirmation of "Big Two-Hearted River." Following the depressing low of "Out of Season" the sequence moves to its opposite in this bright image of Villalta's achievement.

Despite its dramatic elements, the next story, "Cross-Country Snow,"[27] is one of the most lyrical stories in the sequence in terms of the music of the language and its subtle nuances.[28] The story concerns Nick's and George's last skiing trip together in Switzerland before Nick returns to the United States. It moves from a feeling of freedom and flight as suggested by the opening ski scenes to a tone of unhappy resignation at the inn as George and Nick indirectly admit the restraints on their lives. The dynamics in the story as a whole derive from a tension between freedom and entrapment, or rather a desire to escape the feeling of entrapment, and a reluctance to accept the responsibility of commitments.[29] The story opens with this suggestion of tension between freedom and restraint:

> The funicular car bucked once more and then stopped. It could not go farther, the snow drifted solidly across the track. The gale scouring the exposed surface of the mountain had swept the snow surface into a wind-board crust. Nick, waxing his skiis in the baggage car, pushed his boots into the toe irons and shut the clamp tight. He jumped from the car sideways onto the hard wind-board, made a jump turn and crouching and trailing his sticks slipped in a rush down the slope.
> On the white below George dipped and rose and dipped out of sight. The rush and sudden swoop as he dropped down a steep undulation in the mountain side plucked Nick's mind out and left him only the wonderful flying, dropping sensation in his body. He rose to a slight up-run and then the

snow seemed to drop out from under him as he went down, down faster and faster in a rush down the last, long steep slope. Crouching so he was almost sitting back on his skis, trying to keep the center of gravity low, the snow driving like a sand-storm, he knew the pace was too much. But he held it. He would not let go and spill. Then a patch of soft snow, left a hollow by the wind, spilled him and he went over and over in a clashing of skis, feeling like a shot rabbit, then stuck, his legs crossed, his skis sticking straight up and his nose and ears jammed full of snow. (*IOT,* 107)

In the beginning of the passage the predominant soft continuous *s* sounds in "snow," "solidly," "scouring," "surface," "swept," "skis," "shut," "sideways," "sticks," and "slipped" evoke the swift movement of escape Nick finds on skis. The sensuous language renders the sensation of flight: the drifting snow is visual, the "rush" of Nick's skis auditory, and the snow "jammed" up his "nose and in his ears" tactile and gustatory. In the second paragraph of the story, the language captures—with the slow sound of "up-run"—the rhythm and speed of Nick's skiing as he goes up the slight slope; and then the language hurries forward as he goes "down, down faster and faster in a rush down the last, long steep slope." Hemingway expresses beautifully the sensation of a soul "plucked" out, a soul yearning for freedom.

Yet in contrast to this yearning for escape is a different feeling as Nick keeps his flight in check when he tries "to keep the center of gravity low." Nick's flight is not complete, and he goes "over in a clashing of skis," his attempt at freedom truncated. Nick makes a second run over the "khud," and here again the rhyme of the continuous *s* sounds makes the passage smooth and fluid, until the alliterative *t* sounds of "tight," "together," "turning," and "tightening" show that his progress is impeded and he pulls up "in a smother of snow," escape once again halted (*IOT,* 108).

Hemingway's using the name Nick again in the sequence demonstrates his effort to link tonal complexes in this story with those in the earlier stories concerned with Nick. Therefore, Nick's saying, "I can't telemark with my leg" recalls Nick's war wound in the spine in Chapter VI and his desire for "a separate peace" (*IOT,* 108). Just as in Chapter VI a separate peace means fleeing, so it does in "Cross-Country Snow." This desire for freedom from responsibility becomes clear when Nick and George stop at a Swiss house for strudel and wine and Nick notices that the waitress is pregnant. George, articulating what Nick feels, says he wishes he and Nick (whom he affectionately calls "Mike") could "just bum together" across the mountains and "put up at pubs" and "not give a damn about school or anything" (*IOT,* 110). George's comments sum up an attitude that runs throughout the sequence: a reluctance to grow up and face adult life.

In the final conversation between Nick and George a sense of numbed disappointment and entrapment at Nick's relationship with his pregnant

wife Helen is made obvious by their lamenting the poor skiing conditions
in the States. This gloominess shifts to forced hopefulness as Nick and
George insist they ski again together some day, but the passage closes with
a note of defeat as Nick decides there isn't "any good in promising":

> "Is Helen going to have a baby?" George said, coming down to the table
> from the wall.
> "Yes."
> "When?"
> "Late next summer."
> "Are you glad?"
> "Yes. Now."
> "Will you go back to the States?"
> "I guess so."
> "Do you want to?"
> "No."
> "Does Helen?"
> "No."
> George sat silent. He looked at the empty bottle and the empty glasses.
> "It's hell, isn't it?" he said.
> "No. Not exactly," Nick said.
> "Why not?"
> "I don't know," Nick said.
> "Will you ever go skiing together in the States?" George said.
> "I don't know," said Nick.
> "The mountains aren't much," George said.
> "No," said Nick. "They're too rocky. There's too much timber and they're
> too far away."
> "Yes," said George, "that's the way it is in California."
> "Yes," Nick said, "that's the way it is everywhere I've ever been."
> "Yes," said George, "that's the way it is." The Swiss got up and paid and
> went out.
> "I wish we were Swiss," George said.
> "They've all got goiter," said Nick.
> "I don't believe it," George said.
> "Neither do I," said Nick.
> They laughed.
> "Maybe we'll never go skiing again, Nick," George said.
> "We've got to," said Nick. "It isn't worth while if you can't."
> "We'll go all right," George said.
> "We've got to," Nick agreed.
> "I wish we could make a promise about it," George said.
> Nick stood up. He buckled his wind jacket tight. He leaned over George
> and picked up the two ski poles from against the wall. He stuck one of the ski
> poles into the floor.
> "There isn't any good in promising," he said. (*IOT,* 111–12)

This glum, monosyllabic dialogue and the image of the empty bottle and glasses, evoking a sense of hollowness and loss, stand in contrast to images and sounds of freedom at other points in the story. No longer capable of self-delusion and denial, Nick rests at a moment of steady acceptance of his lot. The image of his sticking one of his skis into the floor conveys anger and resentment, but also control and resoluteness. He has made up his mind to return to the States so Helen can have the baby, and that's that.[30]

As a unit, "Cross-Country Snow" and the interchapter about Villalta suggest that the sequence will move forward to a new beginning, that following the shock of initiation to death and a violent world in the first part of the sequence, it will seek relief in a more positive mingling of tonal qualities. But Hemingway undercuts this progress toward affirmation, for in Chapter XIII, which follows "Cross-Country Snow," Luis's cowardly, drunken behavior counterpoints Nick's reluctant acceptance of his responsibilities. And Maera's bitterness—"We kills the savages' bulls, and the drunkards' bulls. . . . We kill them all right. Yes. Yes. Yes" (*IOT,* 113)—shows his disgust at those who cannot kill their own bulls, those who cannot confront life with self respect. Yet, like Nick in "Cross-Country Snow," Maera tackles what he must do, even though with bitterness. This interchapter also reintroduces the motif of alcohol used by the protagonist to blunt fear, racism ("he's just an ignorant Mexican savage" [*IOT,* 113]) to intensify the feeling of hatred, and lack of accountability in the character of drunken Luis to emphasize cowardliness.

The penultimate story in the sequence, "My Old Man,"[31] like "Indian Camp," can be considered an initiation story. But unlike the third person speaker in "Indian Camp," the first person speaker, Joe, in this story interprets his experience in the self-conscious language of a young boy. This heightens the story's discordant elements, for what Joe learns, as Sidney J. Krause points out, is that Butler, Joe's father, does not fix races as his father's friends do and that he is an honest man who is in trouble with other racers rather than with the law.[32]

Butler, like the bullfighters in the interchapters, wills his own end. As Grimes explains about the story:

> It is a paradigm; therefore it repeats within the limits of a single story the patterns of the Nick Adams stories under postwar conditions and in the context of the ritual of the bulls. Joe's final thought summarizes the main discovery of the innocent in the initiation stories: "Seems like when they get started they don't leave a guy nothing."[33]

Joe, then, unlike Nick in the early *In Our Time* stories, is affected by his experience and does not delude himself.

The story opens with a mix of loss, nostalgia, and fondness as Joe recalls his father:

I guess looking at it, now, my old man was cut out for a fat guy, one of those regular little roly fat guys you see around, but he sure never got that way, except a little toward the last, and then it wasn't his fault, he was riding over the jumps only and he could afford to carry plenty of weight then. I remember the way he'd pull on a rubber shirt over a couple of jerseys and a big sweat shirt over that, and get me to run with him in the forenoon in the hot sun. (*IOT*, 115)

At other points in the story this feeling of loss is tinged with sentimentality. This occurs, for instance, in one such passage when Joe reveals his love of horses:

I was nuts about the horses, too. There's something about it, when they come out and go up the track to the post. Sort of dancy and tight looking with the jock keeping a tight hold on them and maybe easing off a little and letting them run a little going up. Then once they were at the barrier it got me worse than anything. Especially at San Siro with that big green infield and the mountains way off and the fat wop starter with his big whip and the jocks fiddling them around then the barrier snapping up and that bell going off and them all getting off in a bunch and then commencing to string out. You know the way a bunch of skins gets off. If you're up in the stand with a pair of glasses all you see is them plunging off and then the bell goes off and it seems like it rings for a thousand years and then they come sweeping round the turn. There wasn't ever anything like it for me. (*IOT*, 117)

The flowing -ing sounds, *l* and *s* sounds, and in particular the repetition of similar phrases such as "go up," "going up," "snapping up," "easing off," "way off," "going off," "getting off," "gets off," "plunging off," and "goes off" capture the sensual flowing movement of the horses and the intensity of the excitement. This passage, like many of the interchapters in between the stories, closes with an understatement—"There wasn't ever anything like it for me" (*IOT*, 117)—which clinches the tonal character of the preceding sentences. The rhythmical repetitions and the images of sensuous physicality convey the sheer thrill of the start. Joe's lyrical expression of great joy in watching a horse race, combined with his nostalgic admiration of his father, stand in contrast to the negative tonal centers at other places in the sequence and prepare for the spiritually satisfying tones in "Big Two-Hearted River."

Other slightly sentimentalized passages also deemphasize the pervasive feeling of loss in the story and the sequence as a whole. One such passage occurs when Joe describes the race in which Butler rides his own horse:

. . . I fixed the glasses on the place where they would come out back of the trees and then out they came with the old black jacket going third and they all sailing over the jump like birds. Then they went out of sight again and then they came pounding out and down the hill and all going nice and sweet and easy taking the fence smooth in a bunch, and moving away from us all solid. Looked as though you could walk across on their backs they were all so bunched and going so smooth. . . . (*IOT,* 127)

The music of the passage is conveyed in the *l* sounds in "glasses," "black," "like," "hill," "looked," and "all" (four times); and the *s* sounds in "sailing," "sight," "sweet," "easy," "fence," "solid," and "smooth." The repetition of word forms such as "come" ("came"), and the flowing -ing sounds in "going," "taking," "pounding," "sailing," and "moving" also give the passage a musical quality, a moment of hypnotic sensuousness that attempts to transcend the tonalities of submerged anger and helplessness at other points in the sequence.

At the conclusion of the story, however, the tone shifts when Butler is killed in a fall from his horse. Joe overhears a comment by an onlooker: "Well, Butler got his, all right" (*IOT,* 129). This comment recalls the savage comment in Chapter VIII when the Irish cop who murders the Hungarians says, "They're crooks, ain't they? . . . Who the hell is going to make any trouble" (*IOT,* 79). But here, unlike the Irish cop, Joe is undeceived and understands that "When they get started they don't leave a guy nothing." And unlike Nick in "Indian Camp," who feels "quite sure that he would never die" (*IOT,* 19), or Nick in "The Three-Day Blow" who feels "Still he could always go into town Saturday night" (*IOT,* 49), Joe has assimilated his experience and is able to communicate it. [34]

"My Old Man," then, like "Cross-Country Snow," brings the sequence to a point where there are no illusions, where there could be a new beginning. It goes beyond self-delusion and evasion of irrefutable truths. And although the final idea of leaving a guy "nothing" is delivered with bitterness, it is an informed bitterness.

In a number of ways, Chapter XIV, which follows "My Old Man," parallels "My Old Man" in that Maera's moral and physical strength parallels Butler's. Its mixed images of sex and death have a flat finality to them:

He felt warm and sticky from the bleeding. Each time he felt the horn coming. Sometimes the bull only bumped him with his head. Once the horn went all the way through him and he felt it go into the sand. (*IOT,* 131)

In addition, the tonality of loss pervades both story and interchapter. In "My Old Man" Joe sees the horses in the fixed race between Kircubbin and Kzar "go farther away and get smaller and smaller." But the feeling of loss in the interchapter is morbid, surreal: "Maera felt everything getting larger and larger and then smaller and smaller. . . . Then he was dead" (*IOT*, 131). This blunt end to a bullfighter who has willingly sacrificed his life for the cowardly behavior of another who cannot face up to his obligations is made doubly ironic in the context of a sequence where escape from responsibility in the former half has given way in the latter half to a diminished sense of adult duty.

In Our Time culminates in the two-part story "Big Two-Hearted River."[35] Containing almost no dialogue and revealing very little by direct statement, the story is presented in concrete, poetic images designed to convey various states of feeling. Part I moves through a series of sensory impressions that suggest a mind searching for peace. As Earl Rovit and Gerry Brenner argue, the story is an exploration of a "journey into self."[36] It is also an objective description of Nick's two days of activities in the Michigan woods. But this objective description, as Carlos Baker notes, reveals subjective centers of feeling.[37] For instance, Part I moves from a sense of ruin and collapse as Nick surveys the burnt-over countryside after he gets off the train, to a determined steadying of self as he looks into the stream at the trout and later quietly sits and smokes a cigarette. It moves to eager purpose as Nick hikes to his campsite and sets up his tent; then it shifts to a rueful moment of memory as Nick makes coffee according to Hopkins; and finally it closes with controlled equanimity as he falls asleep.

Hemingway once again uses the character Nick to embody certain sets of feeling, the tonal centers in "Big Two-Hearted River" echoing those involving Nick in other stories in the sequence. Thus, the opening of the story when Nick arrives by train in Michigan parallels Nick in "The Battler" who is riding the rails illegally and is subsequently booted off. But Nick in "Big Two-Hearted River," who no longer exists "on the outskirts of adult society," rides the train legally.[38]

The sequence as a whole thus far has presented characters incapable of adjusting to an indifferent world, although they move toward a reluctant acceptance of the nature of life, if only through escape, particularly in "Cross-Country Snow" and "My Old Man." But in "Big Two-Hearted River" Nick's removal from humanity and effort at spiritual healing through harmony with nature presents a positive note in the sequence. To suggest the need for spiritual reawakening, Hemingway opens the two-part story with images and tones that recall the wasteland landscape in "Out of Season" and the horrors of war in the interchapters:[39]

> The train went on up the track out of sight, around one of the hills of burnt timber. Nick sat down on the bundle of canvas and bedding the baggage man had pitched out of the door of the baggage car. There was no town, nothing

but the rails and the burned-over country. The thirteen saloons that had lined the one street of Seney had not left a trace. The foundations of the Mansion House hotel stuck up above the ground. The stone was chipped and split by the fire. It was all that was left of the town of Seney. Even the surface had been burned off the ground. (*IOT*, 133)

The images of destruction by fire (there are four references to fire) and the three negatives ("no," "nothing," and "not") suggest a kind of hell. Just as the old deserted mill town in "The End of Something" acts as a correlative for feelings of loss, so the wasted town and burned over countryside in this story evoke feelings of devastation. And as Flora indicates, the war and violence of the earlier pieces are a backdrop against which "Big Two-Hearted River" can be interpreted.[40]

As Nick hikes through the countryside, the emotional burden he bears is heavy, as suggested by the pack he carries which is "much too heavy" (*IOT*, 134); yet, "He felt he had left everything behind, the need for thinking, the need to write, other needs. It was all back of him" (*IOT*, 134). This sense of emotional relief is conveyed by the image of the river: "clear, brown water, colored from the pebbly bottom" where "the trout [were] keeping themselves in the current with wavering fins" (*IOT*, 133).

Nick's looking down into the water and studying the trout suggests a moment of self-reflection:[41]

Nick looked down into the pool from the bridge. It was a hot day. A kingfisher flew up the stream. It was a long time since Nick had looked into a stream and seen trout. They were very satisfactory. As the shadow of the kingfisher moved up the stream, a big trout shot upstream in a long angle, only his shadow marking the angle, then lost his shadow as he came through the surface of the water, caught the sun, and then, as he went back into the stream under the surface, his shadow seemed to float down the stream with the current, unresisting, to his post under the bridge where he tightened facing up into the current. (*IOT*, 134)

The image of the kingfisher flying up the stream, its shadow startling the trout, parallels the feelings of fear, in particular the shock of sudden death, at other points in the sequence. But the trout, which breaks "through the surface of the water," catches the sun, and then floats "unresisting" downstream, holding "his post under the bridge where he tightened facing up into the current" (*IOT*, 134) encapsulates the two-part story's central concern: the character's attempt to hold himself steady. The final long sentence of the passage, with its repetition of *s* and *sh* sounds, captures the smoothness of the kingfisher's flight, the trout's journey, and looks forward to Nick's solitary journey of self-renewal.

Nick's sitting down against a "charred stump" and smoking a cigarette,

"His legs stretched out in front of him," recalls defeated, wounded Nick in Chapter VI who sits with his back against a church wall (*IOT*, 135). Later Nick again lies on his back and looks "up into the pine trees" (*IOT*, 137). But here the images do not impart defeat, for Nick is surrounded by "heathery sweet fern" and "a long undulating country with frequent rises and descents, sandy underfoot and the country alive again" (*IOT*, 136). And when Nick reaches the spot near the river where he wants to camp, trout jump high out of the water to catch insects, and they feed "steadily all down the stream" (*IOT*, 138). These are images of a fertile, rich country, images that serve as a correlative for a mind in the process of healing.

The sensory impressions used to describe Nick setting up camp enforce a feeling of a mind searching for peace. When Nick smooths the sandy soil because he does not want any lumps, he feels the earth and smells his hands after he rips up the sweet fern by the roots. He hears the ax "slit off a bright slab of pine from one of the stumps and split it into pegs for the tent" (*IOT*, 138). He sees "the tent hung on the rope like a canvas blanket on a clothesline" (*IOT*, 138). Nick crawls into the tent, "mysterious and homelike . . . It smelled pleasantly of canvas" *IOT*, 139).

Hemingway's prose style, too, gives the sense of a mind determined to keep itself steady and unhampered:

> Nick was happy as he crawled inside the tent. He had not been unhappy all day. This was different though. Now things were done. There had been this to do. Now it was done. It had been a hard trip. He was very tired. That was done. He had made his camp. He was settled. Nothing could touch him. It was a good place. He was in his home where he had made it. Now he was hungry. (*IOT*, 139)

The paratactic sentences imply one who is unwilling or unable to cope with complexities beyond the simple tasks at hand. The repetition of the word "done" conveys the "finality of Nick's accomplishment."[42] Nick has put aside the past and he is now focusing on the present moment.

The language Hemingway uses to describe Nick preparing his meal reveals that Nick is satisfied with the simple aspects of here and now.[43] The sensations of cooking and eating—the sight, sound, feel, and smell of beans and spaghetti—express Nick's familiarity with this experience and his attempt to heighten each sensation:

> The beans and spaghetti warmed. Nick stirred them and mixed them together. They began to bubble, making little bubbles that rose with difficulty to the surface. There was a good smell. Nick got out a bottle of tomato catchup and cut four slices of bread. The little bubbles were coming faster now. Nick sat down beside the fire and lifted the frying pan off. He poured about half the contents out into the tin plate. It spread slowly on the plate. Nick knew it was

too hot. He poured on some tomato catchup. He knew the beans and spaghetti were still too hot. He looked at the fire, then at the tent, he was not going to spoil it all by burning his tongue. (*IOT*, 139–140)

The language then shifts, however, to suggest a mind aware of its fear. "Across the river in the swamp, in the almost dark, he saw a mist rising. He looked at the tent once more. All right. He took a full spoonful from the plate" (*IOT*, 140). The swamp represents here, as it does in "The Battler," a threat, a malign force that skirts the mind and forces it back to the comforting sight of the tent where it feels peace and safety. [44] But this contrast between fear and willed peace of mind is not, as Young notes, "A terrible panic," a mind "barely under control"; the story is not "a picture of a sick man"[45] who must keep physically occupied to stave off his panic. It is rather, as Carabine argues, about a man "positively enacting his ability to renew the burnt self."[46]

Thus, when Nick makes "the coffee according to Hopkins" (*IOT*, 142)—Hopkins, with whom "He had once argued about everything" (*IOT*, 141)—and the coffee is "bitter," he reveals that his mind "was starting to work" (*IOT*, 142). Nick laughs because this is "a good ending to the story" of Hopkins, a man with whom he shared a relationship "a long time ago on the Black River" (*IOT*, 141). This is not a tormented mind, but one under control; "He knew he could choke it because he was tired enough" (*IOT*, 142). Although this passage about making coffee according to Hopkins is filled with a sense of loss and the idea that a state of innocence is irretrievable—"That was a long time ago on the Black River" (*IOT*, 141)—its reference to the Four Gospels underscores the irony of the story's subtle affirmative note. [47] If the preceding stories and interchapters have emphasized the disintegration of the modern world, "Big Two-Hearted River," like the Gospels, attempts to communicate the possibility for the soul's peace in the midst of chaos.

Yet Nick learns that the coffee according to Hopkins is bitter—or rather that the conditions of life and the possibilities for the soul's peace are difficult and often unrewarding. However, Part I ends on a quiet note with a return to an emphasis on the senses, fear quieted: "The swamp was perfectly quiet," and when a mosquito hums close to Nick's ear, he puts a match to it and listens to it make "a satisfactory hiss in the flame" (*IOT*, 142). Then he curls under the blanket and falls asleep. Unlike earlier images in the sequence of prone, defeated humans, this image of Nick curled up suggests safety. Hemingway has achieved this effect by piling up a series of sensations that bring satisfaction, not emptiness and despair.

The language of Chapter XV—the interchapter sandwiched between Part I and II—comes as a shock following the simple sensory impressions of "Big Two-Hearted River: Part I." For instance, the image of the man about to be hanged lying "flat on his cot with a blanket wrapped around his head" (*IOT,* 143) is not the picture of a man at peace with himself in his tent; it is a picture of a cowardly, ruined human. Likewise, images of Sam Cardinella's legs being strapped and his losing control of his sphincter muscle as two guards approach him with a cap to go over his head, as well as one priest whispering to him to "Be a man, my son," highlight, as Sheridan Baker explains, "exactly what Nick is attempting to be on his lonely trip."[48] Following the scene of healing in the first part of the story, this interchapter reaches back to earlier stories and interchapters to fear, shame, and demoralization.

"Big Two-Hearted River: Part II" picks up where Part I left off. Nick literarily wakes up from his night of sleep. Like a lyrical poem, Part II also progresses through a series of sensory images that culminate in a single perception. The language of Part II moves from excited anticipation as Nick wakes from his sleep and prepares for his day of fishing to a wrestling with mixed feelings when he fishes in the stream. The story closes with a moment of heightened awareness as Nick admits to himself that fishing in the swamp "would be tragic" and that "There were plenty of days coming when he could fish the swamp" (*IOT,* 155, 156).

The story begins with Nick's crawling "out under the mosquito netting stretched across the mouth of the tent," the grass feeling "wet on his hands." The river looks "clear" and runs "smoothly fast." The meadow is "wet with dew" and the "medium-sized brown" grasshoppers Nick selects are also "cold and wet with the dew" (*IOT,* 145). This celebration of the senses is so strong that Nick's crawling out of the tent is like a rebirth into the sensate world.[49] Also, the prose luxuriates over the sound, sight, smell, and feel of Nick's ritualistic meal. He mixes "some buckwheat flour with water" and stirs "it smooth"; he dips "a lump of grease out of a can" and slides it "sputtering across the skillet"; on the "smoking skillet" he pours the buckwheat batter which spreads "like lard, the grease spitting sharply"; he pushes under the cake with "a fresh pine chip" and flops the cake "onto its face. It sputtered in the pan" (*IOT,* 146). This scene communicates Nick's delight in being alive.

Hemingway also conveys this sense of renewal and wonder at the physical world as Nick prepares his fishing equipment: "He put on the reel and threaded the line through the guides. He had to hold it from hand to hand, as he threaded it, or it would slip back through its own weight. It was a heavy, double tapered fly line" (*IOT,* 147). As in Part I, however, a current of unease threads through Part II. Even though Nick feels good when he feels the spring of his rod, he was "careful not to let the hook bite into his finger" (*IOT,* 147). But then the language shifts from the slight tension between satisfaction and a note of cautiousness to surprised "shock" as Nick steps into the stream:

It was a shock. His trousers clung tight to his legs. His shoes felt the gravel. The water was a rising cold shock.

Rushing, the current sucked against his legs. Where he stepped in, the water was over his knees. He waded with the current. The gravel slid under his shoes. He looked down at the swirl of water below each leg and tipped up the bottle to get a grasshopper. (*IOT,* 148)

The short punchy sentences, the repetition of the words "shock" and "current" with their implications of danger and pain, and the image of a man surrounded by a sucking, rushing body of water counterpoint the language of quiet and peace at other points in the story. And yet despite the suggestion of danger and pain here, the language subsequently imparts a sensibility under control. In particular, when Nick pulls his first fish in and releases it, the words "steady," "resting," "smooth," "cool," and "stone" characterize the emotional solidity of the experience:

Nick reached down his hand to touch him, his arm to the elbow under water. The trout was steady in the moving stream, resting on the gravel, beside a stone. As Nick's fingers touched him, touched his smooth, cool underwater feeling he was gone, gone in a shadow across the bottom of the stream. (*IOT,* 149)

But the tone shifts again when Nick hooks another fish. The language is more excited here and suggests a more intense experience: "The reel ratcheted into a mechanical shriek as the line went out in a rush." It then reveals Nick's challenge:

As he put on pressure the line tightened into sudden hardness and beyond the logs a huge trout went high out of water. As he jumped, Nick lowered the top of the rod. But he felt, as he dropped the tip to ease the strain, the moment when the strain was too great; the harness too tight. Of course, the leader had broken. There was no mistaking the feeling when all spring left the line and it became dry and hard. Then it went slack. (*IOT,* 150)

The excitement of the activity causes Nick's mouth to become dry with fear; he feels "a little sick, as though it would be better to sit down" (*IOT,* 150). But the language again shifts to impart control: "He felt like a rock, too, before he started off. By God, he was a big one. . . . He did not want to rush his sensations any" (*IOT,* 151).

Following this intense moment when the big fish gets away, the story shifts back to the quiet language of a character holding on to his calmness, the day ending with a sense of peace and potential for further tranquility:

Nick had one good trout. He did not care about getting many trout. Now

> the stream was shallow and wide. There were trees along both banks. The trees of the left bank made short shadows on the current in the forenoon sun. Nick knew there were trout in each shadow. In the afternoon, after the sun had crossed toward the hills, the trout would be in the cool shadows on the other side of the stream. (*IOT*, 152)

The repetition of "shadow," "trout," "sun," "stream," and "trees" makes for a melodic passage, one that is hypnotic in its simple echoing tones, almost Psalmlike in its vision of quiet flowing water with fish in "each shadow." These images of the natural world's offerings of physical and spiritual sustenance provide comfort and solace following a sequence of stories and interchapters that have mainly concerned themselves with spiritual barrenness, frustration, and anger resulting from fear.

Nick catches one more fish, and he does so with confidence and assurance:

> Nick worked the trout, plunging, the rod bending alive, out of the danger of the weeds into the open river. Holding the rod, pumping alive against the current, Nick brought the trout in. He rushed, but always came, the spring of the rod yielding to the rushes, sometimes jerking under water, but always bringing him in. (*IOT*, 152)

He experiences none of the emotional struggle he does with the previous fish. The words "alive" (repeated twice), "always" (repeated twice), "open river," and "spring of the rod," contrast to the words that reveal the struggle: "plunging," "danger," "pumping," "rushed," and "yielding." Following this confident catch, Nick sits and smokes a cigarette and thinks about the swamp with its low branches where "You would have to keep almost level with the ground to move at all":

> Nick did not want to go in there now. He felt a reaction against deep wading with the water deepening up under his armpits, to hook big trout in places impossible to land them. In the swamp the banks were bare, the big cedars came together overhead, the sun did not come through, except in patches; in the fast deep water, in the half light, the fishing would be tragic. In the swamp fishing was a tragic adventure. Nick did not want it. He did not want to go down the stream any further today. (*IOT*, 155)

This passage conveys an awareness of the danger in the world—"water deepening," "the sun did not come through," "the fast deep water," "the half light," "the fishing would be tragic." Unlike the movement in the former part of the sequence where characters resist acceptance of the inevitability of loss, suffering, and death, here Nick acknowledges it; and yet unlike Villalta who bravely faces the bull head on, Nick saves the more challenging confrontation with the swamp for another day. After he cleans the fish and heads back to camp, "He looked back. The river just showed through the trees. There were plenty of days coming when he could fish the swamp" (IOT, 156). Thus, the story closes with the possibility for a manly embrace with an evil force.

Hemingway omitted from his draft the final section of "Big Two-Hearted River," which concerns Nick's memories of Bill Bird, Ezra Pound, and Helen, as well as his thoughts about writing, James Joyce's writing techniques, Cezanne's painting, and fishing and bullfighting.[50] An overwhelming sense of nostalgia and loss pervade this section of the story; by eliminating it, Hemingway emphasizes an effort at transcending loss rather than loss itself.

Early drafts also indicate that Hemingway had initially conceived of two other characters—Jack and Al—accompanying Nick on his fishing trip.[51] But by focusing just on Nick as the emotive center of the two-part story, he gives the sequence coherence and integrity because the disparate elements become focused into a single tonal matrix: a complex of feelings that modify earlier tones of spiritual vacuity, helplessness, and fright. This single tonal matrix in In Our Time prepares for the more consistent tonal pattern conveyed by Frederic Henry in A Farewell to Arms.

In Our Time closes with "L'Envoi." Like the interchapters, it is short and imagistic. And like "A Very Short Story" and "Mr. and Mrs. Elliot," its satirical elements make it crackle with resentment. In the vernacular of a chipper Englishman, a speaker tells how a Greek king who led his nation into slaughter and now desires to flee says that Plastiras did the right thing in "shooting those chaps," and how "the great thing in this sort of an affair [war and revolution] is not to be shot oneself" (IOT, 157). Hemingway's parting message, in its focus on ineptitude, selfishness, and general lack of concern for fellow humans, asserts only that the conditions of life are adverse and perilous and most often confronted with cowardice and evasion.

5

A *Farewell to Arms* (1929)

Madame, all stories, if continued far enough, end in death, and he is no
true-story teller who would keep that from you.[1]

STANDING back and looking at *In Our Time* as a whole, one can see
that the book presents a precisely patterned succession of emotionally
charged units that echo, readjust, and modulate one another, all the
while moving toward an organic balance. Each segment of the book
introduces a confrontation with something shocking and horrible, creating one of the main affective currents in the sequence: psychic trauma
associated with brute terror as well as with disillusionment of every sort.
In the first half of the work, up to Chapter VI, a strong denial of this
terror begins to yield to a shattering of self-delusion. In the second half,
an attempt to come to terms with it shifts the contour of the tonal curve
toward precarious resignation.

The introduction to the stories and interchapters anticipates this lyrical
structure of the sequence as a whole. Fear and the attempt to hide the
pain associated with wartime memories of broken-legged baggage animals, corpses, and traumatized refugees establish the work's central tensions at once. "Indian Camp" is every bit as concerned with denial of fear
as is "On the Quai at Smyrna." After Nick has participated in the
jacknife delivery of an Indian baby by Caesarean section and has witnessed a suicide, he simply cannot accept that he, too, is some day going
to die in some grossly violent way.

In "The Doctor and the Doctor's Wife" the sequence gains strength
from repetition of suppressed terror and self-deceit, for the threat of an
equally savage scene lurks beneath the surface of the doctor's argument
with Dick Boulton and is reflected in his testy conversation with his
piously moralizing wife. At the end of the story Nick and his father
control their turmoil by going to the woods to shoot black squirrels rather
than confront the real source of the problem—fear of injury, possibly
death.

Sullen resentment builds in the sequence with "The End of Something," a story about Nick's fear of hurting Marjorie by telling her that their love isn't fun any more; he sulks and forces her to drag the truth from him. "The Three-Day Blow" reveals Nick's coping with his remorse over what he has done by drinking himself silly and imagining that he can always go into town to see Marjorie again on Saturday night. In "The Battler" Nick comes almost to the brink of violence himself when he confronts the former prize fighter, Ad; but he is spared a pummeling by Ad's friend Bugs, who knocks out Ad with a blackjack. Beneath the surface facade of control, forced civility, and loss in these first stories lie barely contained rage and discouragement that have been building gradually to the explosive point. Nowhere is fear confronted squarely with determination to overcome it.

Meanwhile, various disturbing war scenes in the interchapters that alternate with these stories reinforce their darker tonalities. The varied voices of the interchapters, with their experimental use of dialogue, vernacular, and satirical elements, provide strong images of death and horror that further fragment the work into increasingly volatile units. In the relationship between story and interchapter a strong suggestion of the connection between private frustration and brutality is obvious; it is often connected with unhappy sexual relationships as well as other human pressures and the parallel violence among whole peoples. An instance is the story of the married couple's suppressed fury in "The Doctor and the Doctor's Wife" and the account in Chapter III of how the soldiers shoot the Germans coming over the garden wall in Mons. That is, the soldiers have done exactly what the doctor would doubtless like to do as he cleans his shotgun: kill his enemies (in this instance, Boulton and his wife).

As I have suggested, however, a reorientation of tonal direction begins in Chapter VI. Violent confrontation is no longer just a possibility; Nick and Rinaldi are wounded physically and psychically, and the only way they know how to deal with this violation is by making "a separate peace." In "Soldier's Home," the World War I veteran, Krebs, returning from the war, is overcome by fear and inertia. Afraid of the complexities of dating, he can only watch girls walk by the house; nor can he motivate himself enough to seek employment. But after much pressure from his mother, he resolves to rouse himself from his anomie and alienation from the prewar world and to go to Kansas City to find a job.

At the very center of the book, four units—"A Very Short Story," Chapter VII, Chapter VIII, and "The Revolutionist"—serve to modify and counterpoint the affective character of Chapter VI. "A Very Short Story," with its acerbic account of a soldier's loss of love and his failure to find comfort, brings the sequence to its most cynical point and unites in one story the preoccupations of both stories and interchapters thus far: the effects of war and the failure of individuals to connect on any meaningful level. Chapter VII, the most obviously centered on fear of all the pieces, presents the voice of a terrified soldier searching for solace at a whore house. Chapter VIII focuses on murderous racism to show how some individuals contend with fear. And finally "The Revolutionist," with its tension between naive idealism and weary skepticism in the story of a young Hungarian who deals with fear by clinging to his political ideals, reorients the sequence to prepare for the muted resignation in "Big Two-Hearted River."

While the sequence suggests that there are certain ways of coping with fear, this drive toward overcoming it is continuously undermined by a very powerful and relentless current of unhappiness and demoralization. Three stories concerned with expatriates and bad marriages emphasize this persistent current. In "Mr. and Mrs. Elliot" Hubert's and Cornelia's physical failure is symptomatic of a much deeper spiritual failure. The satirical elements in the story heighten the tones of enmity and disjunction at other points in the sequence. "Cat in the Rain" shows a dissatisfied American wife in Europe trying to overcome her discontent by expressing her longings in spite of continued rebuffs from her husband. But in this story tonalities of longing and desire make ready for tones of satisfaction in "Big Two-Hearted River." "Out of Season," the gloomiest of all the stories and the lowest point in the sequence, presents not only a miserable marriage, but a deluded, drunken ex-soldier trying to convince himself of a successful fishing expedition when in fact the trip is a failure.

Interspersed among these stories of bad marriages are five interchapters centering on actions in the bullring where ritual is required to cope with fear. Although these interchapters reveal a similar preoccupation with violence and a wearing away of an attempt at dignity and courage, Chapter XII presents Villalta's success in killing a bull with grace and skill. This triumph over death, conveyed by the bright energy and fluidity of the imagery, is short lived, however, for the sequence's progress toward a fragile state of rest is continually cut away.

In "Cross-Country Snow" the tension in the language between freedom and confinement, in a story of Nick's skiing to avoid responsibility and his ultimate acceptance of his duty to his pregnant wife, takes the sequence beyond the point of self-delusion and suggests that it might level off toward a balancing of contrasting states of awareness. So does "My Old Man," a young boy's narrative of his father's death and the boy's subsequent realization that some people thought his father was a crook. But Chapters XIII and XIV (the grisly images of Maera's self-sacrifice and crude death), which alternate with these stories, underscore the futility of individual heroics and suggest that the sequence's preoccupation with fear of death has more to do with fear of dying ignobly.

Even Nick's quiet stoicism evoked in the succession of sensory impressions in "Big Two-Hearted River, Part I and II" and his deliberate camping rituals are immediately and dramatically interrupted in Chapter XV by Sam Cardinella's unmanly fear at his hanging, and the priest's senseless remarks to "be a man, my son" (*IOT,* 143).

Part II of "Big Two-Hearted River" enacts through the correlative of fishing Nick's determination to triumph over fear. His recognition of the "tragic" symbolism of the swamp is a reflex of his great change from the Nick of "Indian Camp," who is quite sure he will never die. Nick has, quite literally, grown up and faced the facts in the only way that experience has taught him—by avoiding danger because he understands his own psychic weakness.

The tranquility and peace in "Big Two-Hearted River," however, are only temporary, for "L'Envoi" is a bitter reminder that regardless of individual efforts to insure self-respect, a whole world beyond self exists where incompetence, stupidity, meaningless happenings, and demoralizing death continue to drown man's puny attempt to overcome his fear.

Hemingway continued to be preoccupied in varying degrees in his next four works—*The Torrents of Spring* (1926), *The Sun Also Rises* (1926), *Men Without Women* (1927)—with expatriated Americans in Europe following World War I, with bullfighting, with war, with miserable married and unmarried couples, with themes of initiation, death, violence, and the loss of love, honor and courage. But *A Farewell to Arms* (1929), while also concerned with some of these themes, echoes more closely than those works the lyrical structure of *In Our Time.*[2] As I have pointed out in chapter two of this study, both Chapter VI and "A Very Short Story" in *In Our Time* provide in part the "germ" for *A Farewell to Arms.* Like Chapter VI, the novel concerns a wounded young man, Frederic Henry, who becomes disillusioned with war. In addition, Nick's companion Rinaldi in Chapter VI has the same name as Frederic Henry's friend and roommate in *A Farewell to Arms.* In "A Very Short Story" and *A Farewell to Arms* a wounded soldier falls in love with a nurse; both protagonists lose their lovers but for different reasons, the unnamed soldier to another man, Frederic to death. *In Our Time* and *A Farewell to Arms* deal (*In Our Time* only in part) with expatriated persons in Europe during the time of World War I.[3] Both works struggle to find a way to deal with fear and loss; in their effort, both works imply affirmative value.

Obviously *A Farewell to Arms* has a more continuous narrative pattern and a more consistent tonal modulation than *In Our Time* because it is controlled by a single point of view: Frederic Henry's chronological reverie. Even though this single controlling point of view gives the novel cohesion, within this single voice a succession of contrasting tonal qualities proceed by juxtaposition among the novel's concerns, much the way the varied voices of the stories and interchapters in *In Our Time* proceed.

The novel is broken up into five books, the books decreasing in number of chapters from twelve each in Books I and II, to eight in Book III, five in Book IV, and four in Book V. Within these books are subjective centers of feeling which give the novel its lyrical structure. Like *In Our Time*, however, the individual segments of the novel have their own tonal characteristics, often counterpointing one another.[4] As the books become shorter and shorter, these centers gradually build in intensity and are channeled into a single tonal stream at the conclusion of the work.[5]

Briefly, *A Farewell to Arms* is a story of Frederic Henry's wounding in Italy during World War I, his subsequent falling in love with an English nurse named Catherine, their flight to Switzerland following Frederic's desertion from the Italian Army during a demoralizing military retreat from the Austrians, and finally, Catherine's death in Switzerland following the birth of their child.[6] Like *In Our Time*, the novel's various elements attempt to allay a movement toward disaster.

The novel opens in Book One with the denial of impending doom in the superficially lighthearted conversation among characters up to the point when Frederic is wounded. Book Two shifts to the playful, urgent tonalities of Catherine's and Frederic's growing love which counterpoints Frederic's loss of dignity when he is wounded. At the center of the novel, Book Three, Frederic's struggle to maintain public and private integrity amidst the wretched and frightening military retreat at Caporetto—his making "a separate peace" and desertion—reinforce on the one hand the affirmation of Catherine's and Frederic's love in Book Two with its emphasis on passion and sympathy as a way of giving meaning to existence. On the other hand, this chapter, with its images of frightened Italian civilians and soldiers mired in the mud, of terrified Italian officers assassinating other Italian officers, prefaces the dismal end of the novel. Book Four shifts to the tones of guilt and confusion as Frederic grapples with his desertion and life out of uniform; then it moves to reassertion of Catherine's and Frederic's love and the tones of spirited adventure as they escape to Switzerland; and finally it closes on a slightly comic tone in the scene of their arrest in Brissago. Book V opens on a haunting, sorrowful note as the lovers settle down in the mountains but then shifts to numbed grief when Catherine dies. The novel follows, roughly, the lyrical design of *In Our Time:* an initial reluctance to deal with fear, until abrupt confrontation with death precipitates a struggle to overcome it. Like *In Our Time*, it closes on a note of understated despair.

Book One, Chapter I, of *A Farewell to Arms* establishes the tonal character of the entire novel just as "On the Quai at Smyrna" establishes the tonal character of *In Our Time*. In *A Farewell to Arms*, however, we feel a more elegiac evocation of loss than we do in "On the Quai at Smyrna" in which fear and horror expressed in an upbeat British idiom obfuscate any tendency toward the elegiac. In *A Farewell to Arms*, however, loss is conveyed in the restrospective description of the countryside and the allusion to military maneuvers:[7]

> In the late summer of that year we lived in a house in a village that looked across the river and the plain to the mountains. In the bed of the river there were pebbles and boulders, dry and white in the sun, and the water was clear and swiftly moving and blue in the channels. Troops went by the house and down the road and the dust they raised powdered the leaves of the trees. The trunks of the trees too were dusty and the leaves fell early that year and we saw the troops marching along the road and the dust rising and leaves, stirred by the breeze, falling and the soldiers marching and afterward the road bare and white except for the leaves.[8]

One of the most closely scrutinized passages in modern American fiction,[9] this opening passage is saturated with a sense of something having passed away, something gone. Phrases such as "late summer," "pebbles and boulders dry and white," "dust rising and leaves . . . falling," "leaves fell early that year," "soldiers marching," and "bare and white" reveal a sense of painful loss and point to the catastrophic military and personal defeat that occur later in the novel. The repetition of words such as "dust," "leaves," "trees," "road," "troops," and "white" emphasize the starkly vivid images, the adjective "white" capturing the intensity of bone-deep sorrow. In addition, the echoing sounds of consonants—for instance, the *l* in "late," "lived," "village," "looked"; and *d* in "dust," "dry," "down," and "road"—give the passage a doleful quality, the lilting *l*'s underscoring poignant sorrow, the hard *d* sounds introducing a note of bitterness. Likewise, the repetition of similar phrases gives the passage a beautiful melodic echoing pattern that strongly highlights its elegiac character: "late summer of that year," "fell early that year"; "lived in a house," "went by the house"; "across the river," "in the bed of the river"; "dry and white," "bare and white"; "leaves of the trees," "trunks of the trees"; "troops marching," "soldiers marching"; "powdered the leaves," "except for the leaves."[10]

And yet very subtly, a quiet, hopeful note swirls through this passage: "the water was clear and swiftly moving and blue in the channels," and the leaves are "stirred" by a "breeze." These two images suggest rebirth and renewal and contrast to the notes of decay and loss.

The remainder of Chapter I continues this tension between painful loss and fragile respiritualization. Its recounting of troops marching in the dark, "mules on the roads with boxes of ammunition," the vineyards "thin and bare-branched," and "all the country wet and brown and dead with autumn" prepare for the retreat at Caporetto in Book Three and Catherine's death in Book Five (*FTA*, 4).[11] In addition, the image of troops muddy and wet and cartridge clips bulging under their capes "as though they were six months gone with child" anticipates not only the muddy retreat at Caporetto but Catherine's deadly pregnancy (*FTA*, 4). Even the fleeting image of the king "sitting between two generals, he himself so small that you could not see his face but only the top of his cap and his narrow back" indicates the precariousness of the military campaign and the general tenuousness of things.[12]

Yet, standing in contrast to these images of deathly forewarning are two images that look forward to Frederic's and Catherine's more blissful moments and the overall effort to resist disaster: "The plain was rich with crops" and "there were many orchards of fruit trees." The chapter closes, however, with a bitter, angry tone characteristic of the irony in *In Our Time*:

> At the start of the winter came the permanent rain and with the rain came the cholera. But it was checked and in the end only seven thousand died of it in the army. (*FTA*, 4)

These final sentences distill the novel's predominant tonal character: inconsolable heartsickness conveyed in the most understated manner. The words "winter," "permanent rain" (the motif of the rain will be discussed later in the chapter), "cholera," and "died" certainly speak of the bleakest state of being. And the word "only," in "only seven thousand died," while seeming to minimize human loss, actually calls attention to it.

This pattern in the first chapter, then, of ominousness counterpointed briefly by a suggestion of new life and prosperity is maintained throughout the novel in the dialogue between characters and in the actions between chapters and between books. An example of this tension in the dialogue occurs, for instance, in Book Three when Frederic Henry returns to the front after he is wounded and has fallen in love with Catherine. Rinaldi asks if Frederic is yet married and if Catherine is good to him, "practically speaking." Uncomfortable with Rinaldi's insensitivity, Frederic tells him to "shut up." Then Rinaldi says:

> "I am jealous maybe," Rinaldi said.
> "No, you're not."
> "I don't mean like that. I mean something else. Have you any married friends?"
> "Yes," I said.
> "I haven't," Rinaldi said. "Not if they love each other."

"Why not?"

"They don't like me."

"Why not?"

"I am the snake. I am the snake of reason."

"You're getting it mixed. The apple was reason."

"No, it was the snake." He was more cheerful. (*FTA,* 170)

Although the tone of this banter is affectionate, an uneasy undercurrent swells up in Rinaldi's denial of love and his insistence on being "the snake of reason." As an embodiment of a set of feelings, Rinaldi represents fear. [13] Unwilling to allow himself to feel vulnerable about anything, he insists, "I only like two other things [besides his work as a surgeon]; one is bad for my work and the other is over in half an hour or fifteen minutes. Sometimes less" (*FTA,* 170). When Frederic insists that Rinaldi will "get other things" (*FTA,* 171), Rinaldi says, "No. We never get anything. We are born with all we have and we never learn. We never get anything new. We all start complete" (*FTA,* 171). Rinaldi conveys hopelessness and defeat. His attitude is pessimistic, for if we cannot "get anything new," there is no point in living. And, in fact, what Rinaldi gets is syphilis. Frederic Henry, on the other hand, has discovered by accident a more meaningful way to give purpose to life: falling in love.

But Rinaldi's notion of the snake of reason—or this tonal note of fear—is embodied in other characters as well and often presents itself as helplessness borne of fear. At the end of Chapter III, Book One, when the troops are teasing the priest in the mess, the captain also conveys this pessimistic current:

"Priest not happy. Priest not happy without girls."

"I am happy," said the priest.

"Priest not happy. Priest wants Austrians to win the war," the captain said. The others listened. The priest shook his head.

"No," he said.

"Priest wants us never to attack. Don't you want us never to attack?"

"No. If there is a war I suppose we must attack."

"Must attack. Shall attack!"

The priest nodded.

"Leave him alone," the major said. "He's all right."

"He can't do anything about it anyway," the captain said. We all got up and left the table. (*FTA,* 14)

The joking and surface camaraderie among the men and their making the priest the brunt of their humor is, of course, a coverup for fear; yet their fear is justifiable given their position so close to the Austrian front. The priest, however, embodies a different complex of feelings: he is a loving individual, understanding of human nature, even of humankind's need for violence and war. Like the Magyar in Chapter XI in *In Our Time*, he is also a quiet stoic, one "who would not make war" (*FTA*, 71), and one who believes "It is never hopeless" (*FTA*, 71), one who loves and recognizes that Frederic will love. But the priest's gentleness and forgiveness are counterpointed by the captain's defeatism—"He can't do anything about it [the war] anyway."

Fear in the guise of futility is also present in much of Catherine's dialogue. For instance, in Book One, Chapter IV, when she and Frederic first meet, she communicates this feeling when speaking about her former lover:

> "I was going to cut it [her hair] all off when he died."
> "No."
> "I wanted to do something for him. You see I didn't care about the other thing and he could have had it all. He could have had anything he wanted if I would have known. I would have married him or anything. I know all about it now. But then he wanted to go to war and I didn't know."
> I did not say anything.
> "I didn't know about anything then. I thought it would be worse for him. I thought perhaps he couldn't stand it and then of course he was killed and that was the end of it." (*FTA*, 19)

On the one hand, Catherine's pessimism—"he was killed and that was the end of it"—echoes Rinaldi's and the Captain's cynicism; on the other hand, her desire to "do something for him" [her former lover] prepares for her desire to "do for" Frederic later in the novel, and this echoes the priest's notion of "When you love you wish to do things for. You wish to sacrifice for. You wish to serve" (*FTA*, 72).

Catherine's feeling of helplessness, like the captain's, however, prefigures Frederic's being "blown up . . . eating cheese" (*FTA*, 63) which is followed by a tonal shift in the novel. Up to this point fear and denial of it have been present in the dialogue among all the characters (except for the priest): between Catherine and Frederic during the "game" of their first meeting; between Frederic and Rinaldi in their talk of women and the war; and among the men in the mess. But a shift from denial of fear to finding a way to deal with it takes place when Frederic is overcome by the sensations of being wounded while he is eating a dinner of pasta and cheese with two ambulance drivers close to the Austrian front:

> . . . I heard a cough, then came the chuh-chuh-chuh-chuh—then there was a flash, as when a blast-furnace door is swung open, and a roar that started white and went red and on and on in a rushing wind. I tried to breathe but my breath would not come and I felt myself rush bodily out of myself and out and out and out and all the time bodily in the wind. I went out swiftly, all of

myself, and I knew I was dead and that it had all been a mistake to think you just died. Then I floated, and instead of going on I felt myself slide back. I breathed and I was back. The ground was torn up and in front of my head there was a splintered beam of wood. In the jolt of my head I heard somebody crying. I thought somebody was screaming. I tried to move but I could not move. I heard the machine-guns and rifles firing across the river all along the river. . . . (FTA, 54–55)

A version of what might have gone on as Nick is wounded in Chapter VI in *In Our Time*, this passage in *A Farewell to Arms* intones terrible spiritual violation conveyed by the description of a soul going, "out and out and out." Words such as "breathe," "breath," "rushing wind," "floated," "bodily in the wind," "slide back" suggest the soul's wrenching; and words such as "flash," "blast," "furnace door," "torn," "splintered beam," "screaming," and "machine-guns and rifles firing" convey the feeling of brutal physical injury and capture a sense of sudden surprise, pain, and terror.

The pattern of *A Farewell to Arms*, as Dewey Ganzel notes, "is determined by Frederic's discovery of the onslaught of death—from his assumption of invulnerability to the realization of his total loss." Catherine becomes, then, the reason for his "passionate appetite for living."[14] Thus, following this violent scene in Book One, the novel shifts in Book Two to the affirmative notes of Catherine's and Frederic's growing affection for one another. The lover's desire for physical reassurance stands in contrast to the physical and spiritual violation presented in Book One:

"You mustn't," she said. "You're not well enough."
"Yes, I am. Come on."
"No. You're not strong enough."
"Yes. I am. Yes. Please."
"You do love me?"
"I really love you. I'm crazy about you. Come on please."
"Feel our hearts beating."
"I don't care about our hearts. I want you. I'm just mad about you."
"You really love me?"
"Don't keep on saying that. Come on. Please. Please, Catherine."
"All right but only for a minute."
"All right," I said. "Shut the door."
"You can't. You shouldn't."
"Come on. Don't talk. Please come on." (FTA, 92)

The intensity of this desire, captured in the somewhat banal language of urgent love—"love," "hearts," "crazy about you," "come on please"—is a relief following Frederic's wounding. While Frederic (like Catherine,

Rinaldi, and the other characters an embodiment of a set of feelings) insists on expressing his feelings physically, Catherine insists on verbal reassurance: "You really love me?" The emotional and spiritual aspect of their desire, however, becomes more pronounced later in the novel in Book Two, Chapter XVIII, when Catherine says, "There isn't any me. I'm you. Don't make up a separate me" (FTA, 115), and "You're my religion. You're all I've got" (FTA, 116). As Edmund Wilson points out in *The Wound and the Bow*, here their relationship is "idealized," "the abstractions of a lyric emotion."[15] But this idea of human love as religion—the need to seek comfort and fulfillment in human communion—helps to offset in the novel fear of death. Although Frederic does not confess the depth of his feelings openly to Catherine, later in Book Four, Chapter XXXV, a parallel feeling is achieved in Frederic's conversation with Count Greffi. Frederic says, "My own [religious feeling] comes only at night," and Greffi says, "Then too you are in love. Do not forget that is a religious feeling" (FTA, 263).

Yet despite an effort to triumph over the movement toward defeat, Book Two (indeed the whole novel) is flooded with a current of imminent catastrophe. This is conveyed partly by the repetition of images of entrapment and allusions to feelings of imprisonment.[16] One such place occurs when Catherine tells Frederic she is pregnant:

> "You aren't angry are you, darling?"
> "No."
> "And you don't feel trapped."
> "Maybe a little. But not by you."
> "I didn't mean by me. You mustn't be stupid. I meant trapped at all."
> "You always feel trapped biologically."
> She went away a long way without stirring or removing her hand. (FTA, 139)

Coming almost half way into the novel, this passage explicitly centers on entrapment and consequent feelings of fear. The image of Catherine's emotional distancing and the stillness of her hand clearly anticipates her death. But Ray B. West argues that "the biological trap" from which Hemingway's characters cannot escape is the war, itself a symbol for the chaos of nature.[17] Thus, even though the novel seems to grope toward affirmation—in the lovers' devotion to one another and in Frederic's rejection of the meaningless violence of war—a counter current, as in *In Our Time*, most obviously present in the focus on war, continuously erodes the determination to attain dignity through love and adhering to personal ethics.

Book Three, from which Catherine is absent, zeroes in most intensely on the war and in one alarming incident after another creates an overwhelming feeling of victimization. Before Frederic is wounded, Passini's comments about war reflect this feeling of ensnarement as well as disillusionment in the war.

> There is nothing as bad as war. We in the auto-ambulance cannot even realize at all how bad it is. When people realize how bad it is they cannot do anything to stop it because they go crazy. There are some people who never realize this. There are people who are afraid of their officers. It is with them the war is made. (FTA, 50)

The repetition three times each of the words "bad," "realize," and "people," and two times "war" emphasize the evils of war and the powerlessness of individuals during war time. The generic word "people," meaning humans in general, extends the horrors of war to everyone and implies that everyone is victimized. Hemingway's allowing another character other than Frederic to speak these words stresses in the novel feelings of disgust and helplessness.

The imagery in Book Three during the retreat likewise imparts the notion of the war as biological trap. For instance, the image of the two young girls, "virgins," "like two wild birds" (FTA, 196) cornered by men who keep touching and caressing them brings to the foreground fear and unease. In addition, in Chapter XXIX images of vehicles stuck in the mud imply defenselessness and frustration. Also, the sequence of events at Udine clearly shows that war is a huge indifferent process, and its victims are gratuitously struck down. For example, one of Frederic's companions, Aymo, is shot by a countryman who is supposedly defending the town against the seemingly invincible Germans who flow "almost supernaturally" across the bridge into the town on bicycles (FTA, 211). Then Frederic, Piani, and Bonello are trapped in their hideout in a barn loft, accessible only by ladder, again conveying an image of confinement. After Bonello's desertion, Frederic himself is trapped by "Peace Brigades" shooting officers that they feel are traitors responsible for Italy's surrender. This section of the novel culminates in a frightening image of panic and pain as Frederic dives into the cold river with soldiers shooting at him. [18]

Even after Frederic has escaped assassination, the war continues to hound him. In Chapter XXXI he hides in the train with guns piled around him. And in Book Four wartime circumstances continue to pursue him and Catherine as they arrange and execute their escape to Switzerland, particularly the night they row thirty-five kilometers in storm winds and risk being caught by the Italians. Finally, in Book Five Catherine and Frederic are trapped "biologically" despite their escape from violence and their devotion to one another, for Catherine's hips are too narrow and she hemorrhages to death following a Caesarean section.

In Frederic's statements in Book Four, Chapter XXXII, Hemingway sums up the loss and horror that have been presented in images and dialogue focusing on war in Book Three:

> You saw emptily, lying on your stomach, having been present when one army moved back and another came forward. You had lost your cars and your men as a floorwalker loses the stock of his department in a fire. There was, however, no insurance. (*FTA*, 232)

Although this passage states more directly its disillusionment with an ideal than the imagistic interchapters in *In Our Time*, it nevertheless hones in on the bitter disappointment and the lack of consolation for failed ideals that *In Our Time* expresses. The analogy to economic and material destruction, however, at once minimizes the feelings of loss, but points to the issues surrounding war and the times: power and material gain. Hemingway's drawing attention to these issues calls to mind T. S. Eliot's condemnation of commercialism in "Death by Water" and Pound's condemnation of the age in *Hugh Selwyn Mauberley*.

The persistent motif of the rain is perhaps the most obvious source of feeling of doom and entrapment in the novel.[19] This motif is used for more than a backdrop against which actions and conversations are presented. It appears in the first chapter of the novel. But in Book Two, Chapter XVIII, it is used to emphasize Catherine's emotional makeup and to convey a state of mind—fear:

> "I like to walk in it. But it's very hard on loving."
> "I'll love you always."
> "I'll love you in the rain and in the snow and in the hail and—what else is there?"
> "I don't know. I guess I'm sleepy."
> "Go to sleep, darling, and I'll love you no matter how it is."
> "You're not really afraid of the rain are you?"
> "Not when I'm with you."
> "Why are you afraid of it?"
> "I don't know."
> "Tell me."
> "Don't make me."
> "Tell me."
> "No."
> "Tell me."
> "All right. I'm afraid of the rain because sometimes I see me dead in it."
> "No."
> "And sometimes I see you dead in it."
> "That's more likely."
> "No, it's not, darling. Because I can keep you safe. I know I can. But nobody can help themselves." (*FTA*, 126)

Catherine's fears and Frederic's reassurance encapsulate the curve of feeling in the entire novel: a reluctance to concede to fear which yields to confrontation with it, and then to utter defeat—"But nobody can help themselves" (*FTA*, 126). The back and forth rhythm of the dialogue— "Tell me," "Don't make me," "No," "Tell me"—is a microcosm of the larger tensions in the novel between the effort to give life meaning and the tidal wave of ugly happenings that drown this effort.

The motif of the rain also creates a dreary note in Book Two when Catherine and Frederic are at the hotel in Milan the night Frederic has to return to the front following his convalescence. This dreariness offsets the delicately joyful tonalities of Catherine's and Frederic's love. At first Catherine and Frederic ask one another if they have fathers, both indicating, "You won't have to meet him," as if they know that they won't have to concern themselves with the complexities of in-law relationships (*FTA*, 154). Then Frederic's hearing the rain outside reminds him of Marvell: "But at my back I always hear / Time's wingèd Chariot hurrying near" (*FTA*, 154). Hemingway's allusion to Marvell emphasizes the sense of time's running out and the pressure Frederic feels of some external force bearing down on them. It also aligns Frederic's sensibility with the lyric tradition (thus emphasizing states of awareness) and the *carpe diem* tradition—the lover exhorting his mistress to make love while they have time—a tradition that was the result, in part, of the discovery that humankind was no longer at the center of the universe. Frederic's discovery is not that he is no longer the center of the universe, but that he is trapped by the conditions of existence and has very little control over what may happen to him. In addition, the allusion to Marvell's poem— with its technique of hyperbole and understatement—enriches the ironic elements in *A Farewell to Arms*: Catherine and Frederic do "sport" while they "may," or rather live intensely, and though they make their sun run, they cannot make their "sun / stand still." As Bernard Oldsley points out, Hemingway, like Pound and Eliot, used allusion not simply for decoration but "as a means of achieving resonance, depth, layers of sometimes contradictory meaning."[20]

Within the passage, however, the allusion to Marvell strongly counterpoints Catherine's and Frederic's talk of the baby, the tangible expression of their love, for Frederic keeps emphasizing that they must hurry:

> "How will you arrange it?"
> "The best way I can. Don't worry, darling. We may have several babies before the war is over."
> "It's nearly time to go."
> "I know. You can make it time if you want."
> "No."
> "Then don't worry, darling. You were fine until now and now you're worrying."

"I won't. How often will you write."
"Every day. Do they read your letters?"
"They can't read English enough to hurt any."
"I'll make them very confusing," Catherine said.
"But not too confusing."
"I'll just make them a little confusing."
"I'm afraid we have to start to go."
"All right, darling."
"I hate to leave our fine house."
"So do I."
"But we have to go."
"All right. But we're never settled in our home very long."
"We will be."
"I'll have a fine home for you when you come back." (*FTA*, 155)

Their uncertainty about where to have the baby, Frederic's uninterest in participation in the birth ("How will you arrange it"), his reminding her that they have to leave ("I'm afraid we have to start to go," and "But we have to go"), as well as their commenting on the possibility of his being wounded again ("Perhaps you'll be hurt just a little in the foot"), echo once again the tension in the novel between a drive toward fulfillment (here embodied in Catherine) and the undermining of it (embodied in Frederic). And all of this is placed against the backdrop of the insistent rain which drives home the pathos of the scene and forebodes the unhappy outcome of the novel.

The motif of the rain is also sustained throughout Book Three when Frederic is separated from Catherine and he grapples with his feelings about the war, desertion, and his longing for his love. Hemingway uses the word rain twenty-four times in Chapter XXVI, as Schneider notices, just before the retreat and seventeen times in Chapter XXVII during the retreat.[21]

In addition, in Chapter XXVII, while it is again raining, Frederic confesses during the retreat that he is

> embarrassed by the words sacred, glorious, and sacrifice and the expression in vain. . . . I had seen nothing sacred, and the things that were glorious had no glory and the sacrifices were like the stockyards at Chicago if nothing was done with the meat except to bury it. . . . finally only the names of places had dignity. . . . Abstract words such as glory, honor, courage, or hallow were obscene beside the concrete names of villages, the numbers of roads, the names of rivers, the numbers of regiments and the dates. (*FTA*, 185)

This passage helps explain not only Frederic's, but Rinaldi's and the Captain's, cynicism about the war. Far from the delicate lyricism of the passages involving Catherine and Frederic, it emphasizes the need for

Frederic's "separate peace." Recalling Pound's attack on the rhetoric of the age in *Sextus Propertius,* its tonality of outrage is made more depressing by the presence of the "permanent" rain and its placement in the context of the Italian military retreat.

Unlike *In Our Time* where most of the material is rendered and not directly stated, *A Farewell to Arms* contains a number of passages such as the one above where direct statement either precedes or follows an image to reenforce the tonal character of the work. Another such passage occurs (again during the rain) when Frederic and Catherine have decided to flee to Switzerland and Frederic speculates about his night fears:

> I know that the night is not the same as the day: that all things are different, that the things of the night cannot be explained in the day, because they do not then exist, and the night can be a dreadful time for lonely people once their loneliness has started. But with Catherine there was almost no difference in the night except that it was an even better time. If people bring so much courage to this world the world has to kill them to break them, so of course it kills them. The world breaks every one and afterward many are strong at the broken places. But those that will not break it kills. It kills the very good and the very gentle and the very brave impartially. If you are none of these you can be sure it will kill you too but there will be no special hurry. (FTA, 249)

In addition to preparing for Catherine's death in its focus on breaking courageous people by killing them, this passage emphasizes complete resentment of life as a trap. The "world," some undefined force, is responsible for victimizing individuals and creating in them fear of the "night" and an undignified death. The repetition of "kill" and "kills" (five times), and the echoing sounds of "lonely," "loneliness," "break," "breaks," and "broken," make apparent Frederic's anger about the unfairness of life and its lack of reward, a preoccupation in both *In Our Time* and *A Farewell to Arms.*

Still in Book Three during the retreat the motif of the rain also reenforces Frederic's feelings of longing for Catherine. The sight of the two young "virgins" in Aymo's truck reminds Frederic of the fifteenth century anonymous lyric:

> Blow, blow, ye western wind. Well, it blew and it wasn't the small rain but the big rain down that rained. It rained all night. You knew it rained down that rained. Look at it. Christ, that my love were in my arms and I in my bed again. (FTA, 197)

But Frederic's misery is more pronounced than the prayerlike longing of the speaker in the anonymous lyric:[22]

Western wind, when wilt thou blow,
The small rain down can rain?
Christ, if my love were in my arms,
And I in my bed again!

As with the allusion to Marvell, so with this allusion Hemingway links the novel to lyrical poetry with its emphasis on states of feeling. And by incorporating lyric poetry into the novel, Hemingway achieves the kind of compression and intensity that lyric poetry achieves. In A *Farewell to Arms*, however, the motif of rain suggests not a "small" renewing spring rain, but rather nightmare torrents that wash away hope of new life.

These western winds and torrential rains in Book Three anticipate the storm winds in Book Four that help Frederic row to Switzerland; but even though he escapes without being harmed and his lover is in his arms once again, she is not there for long. For in Book Five, Chapter XL, the rains come again "for three days" after the snows of winter, and then Catherine and Frederic go into town for the birth of the baby. The rain then persists throughout Chapter XLI during Catherine's and Frederic's final ordeal. Indeed, the novel closes with the word "rain": "After a while I went out and left the hospital and walked back to the hotel in the rain" (*FTA*, 332). Considered by some critics one of the great endings in American literature, this line is a masterpiece of understatement. The divergent elements in the novel—the affirmative assertion of love and independent ethics regarding the war contrasted to the desolation of war and death—are funneled into this single note of suffering and lament.[23] As in *In Our Time*, the respite of peace and tranquillity in A *Farewell to Arms* is short lived. Figuratively speaking, Frederic has fished in the swamp, and he pays the "tragic" consequences—losing his loved one.

Prior to Catherine's death, however, when Frederic learns that their baby is dead, the language in the novel presents a sour, but stoical, acceptance of the injustice of an indifferent universe. In this scene, too, the presence of the rain contributes to the tone of wretchedness:

> Now Catherine would die. That was what you did. You died. You did not know what it was about. You never had time to learn. They threw you in and told you the rules and the first time they caught you off base they killed you. Or they killed you gratuitously like Aymo. Or gave you the syphilis like Rinaldi. But they killed you in the end. You could count on that. Stay around and they would kill you. (*FTA*, 327)

Recalling Frederic's earlier fears in the night concerning the world's having "to kill them to break them," this passage is written in short, stiff sentences that repeat key words—"die" and "kill"—to strengthen the feeling of gall (*FTA*, 249). And the notion of there being an impersonal "they" who is responsible for human misery once again emphasizes the feeling of victimization. Reminiscent of Maera's bitterness in *In Our Time* about having to kill others' bulls (and then getting gored to death himself)—and the many other examples of unnecessary death and suffering in *In Our Time*—this articulation in *A Farewell to Arms* of the way things are precisely sums up the feelings communicated in *In Our Time*.

Immediately following this passage Frederic recalls an incident that occurred when he was once camping. This section parallels imagistically the above statements:[24]

> Once in camp I put a log on top of the fire and it was full of ants. As it commenced to burn, the ants swarmed out and went first toward the centre where the fire was; then turned back and ran toward the end. When there were enough on the end they fell off into the fire. Some got out, their bodies burnt and flattened, and went off not knowing where they were going. But most of them went toward the fire and then back toward the end and swarmed on the cool end and finally fell off into the fire. I remember thinking at the time that it was the end of the world and a splendid chance to be messiah and lift the log off the fire and throw it out where the ants could get off onto the ground. But I did not do anything but throw a tin cup of water onto the log, so that I would have the cup empty to put whiskey in before I added water to it. I think the cup of water on the burning log only steamed the ants. (FTA, 327–28)

This "parable" mirrors the action in the novel: the ants, like Frederic and Catherine and the soldiers at the Italian front, move toward death; when they realize they are endangered, they turn the opposite direction and flee; and although the opposite direction offers a brief alleviation, it too leads to death. Frederic's indifference toward the ants, his not acting as a "messiah"—a sympathetic savior, symbol of love and mercy—is analogous to his powerlessness at Catherine's bedside; this helplessness undermines the "religion" of their love. The feeling at the end of the novel certainly suggests that "it was the end of the world."

The unrelieved oppressiveness in the novel indicated by the almost continuous presence of the rain, by the all-consuming nightmare of war, by the cynicism of Rinaldi, the captain, and the discouraged Italians is faintly and very briefly—like Villalta's victory over the bull in *In Our Time* and Nick's fishing in "Big Two-Hearted River"—counterpointed in the passages in which Catherine and Frederic proclaim their love, and in some subtly comic scenes such as when Frederic is being operated on, and when they are arrested in Switzerland. In addition to the passage quoted earlier from Book Two regarding Catherine's and Frederic's love, Frederic's description of three doctors who examine his leg and his response to them is comic relief following his shocking psychic and physical wounding:

> "Six months for what?" I asked.
> "Six months for the projectile to encyst before the knee can be opened safely."
> "I don't believe it," I said.
> "Do you want to keep your knee, young man?"
> "No," I said.
> "What?"
> "I want it cut off," I said, "so I can wear a hook on it."
> "What do you mean? A hook?"
> "He is joking," said the house doctor. He patted my shoulder very delicately. "He wants to keep his knee. This is a very brave young man. He has been proposed for the silver medal of valor." (FTA, 97)

Frederic is expressing his dissatisfaction with the doctors because he feels a higher ranking doctor won't require him to wait six months before he is operated on. Dr. Valentini, however, unlike the three stuffy doctors who initially examine him—and who tells Frederic he will have "ten drinks" and thinks Miss Barkley "a lovely girl"—thinks Frederic should have his leg operated on immediately. Although this major has "the star in a box on his sleeve," he appears almost a buffoon with his moon face and "mustaches" that go "straight up" (FTA, 100). The surface texture of this passage is humorous, even absurd, but it also underscores Frederic's stoicism and his urgency to get on with life, an effort that complements Frederic's and Catherine's intense desire for one another.

This comic relief in Book Two is balanced in Book Four by the scene in which Frederic and Catherine are arrested and insist they are cousins wanting to do the "winter sport" (FTA, 280). When the Swiss lieutenant finds out they have money, he mentions his father's hotel at Wengen as a possibility for vacation. The following section counterpoints the first part of Chapter XXXVII involving the escape, which is suspenseful and fast moving:

> "There is no winter sport at Montreux."
> "I beg your pardon," the other official said.
> "I come from Montreux. There is very certainly winter sport on the Montreux Oberland Bernois railway. It would be false for you to deny that."
> "I do not deny it. I simply said there is no winter sport at Montreux."
> "I question that," the other official said. "I question that statement."
> "I hold to that statement."
> "I question that statement. I myself have *luge-ed* into the streets of Montreux. I have done it not once but several times. Luge-ing is certainly winter sport."

The other official turned to me.

"Is luge-ing your idea of winter sport, sir? I tell you you would be very comfortable here in Locarno. You would find the climate healthy, you would find the environs attractive. You would like it very much."

"The gentleman has expressed a wish to go to Montreux."

"What is luge-ing?" I asked.

"You see he has never even heard of luge-ing!"

That meant a great deal to the second official. He was pleased by that.

"Luge-ing," said the first official, "is tobogganing."

"I beg to differ," the other official shook his head. "I must differ again. The toboggan is very different from the luge. The toboggan is constructed in Canada of flat laths. The luge is a common sled with runners. Accuracy means something."

"Couldn't we toboggan?" I asked.

"Of course you could toboggan," the first official said. "You could toboggan very well. Excellent Canadian toboggans are sold in Montreux. Ochs Brothers sell toboggans. They import their own toboggans."

The second official turned away. "Tobogganing," he said "requires a special *piste*. You could not toboggan into the streets of Montreux. Where are you stopping here?"

"We don't know," I said. "We just drove in from Brissago. The carriage is outside."

"You make no mistake in going to Montreux," the first official said. "You will find the climate delightful and beautiful. You will have no distance to go for winter sport."

"If you really want winter sport," the second official said, "you will go to the Engadine or to Mürren. I must protest against your being advised to go to Montreux for the winter sport."

"At Les Avants above Montreux there is excellent winter sport of every sort." The champion of Montreux flared at his colleague.

"Gentleman," I said, "I am afraid we must go. My cousin is very tired. We will go tentatively to Montreux." (*FTA*, 283)

Once again the novel has sought release from the movement toward catastrophe. The officials' silly disagreement about recreation coming immediately after Catherine's and Frederic's dangerous escape gives a false sense of security and freedom to the work. The seemingly minor distinctions the officials make between lugeing and tobogganing, and their superficially civil handling of disagreements—"I beg to differ" and "I must differ again"—are great contrasts to earlier preoccupations in the novel with physical and spiritual violation. Nevertheless, the officials' pettiness about such trivial concerns and their inability to come to congenial concensus about "winter sport" ("The champion of Montreux glared at his opponent") point up, as in *In Our Time*, the difficulty of human compatibility.

But Book Five shifts quickly from this lighter note to an elegiac tone that immediately recalls the somber, depressing character of Chapter One:

> That fall the snow came very late. We lived in a brown wooden house in the pine trees on the side of the mountain and at night there was frost so that there was thin ice over the water in the two pitchers on the dresser in the morning. . . .
> Outside, in front of the chalet a road went up the mountain. The wheel ruts and ridges were iron hard with the frost, and the road climbed steadily through the forest and up and around the mountain to where there were meadows, and barns and cabins in the meadows at the edge of the woods looking across the valley. The valley was deep and there was a stream at the bottom that flowed down into the lake and when the wind blew across the valley you could hear the stream in the rocks. (FTA, 289–90)

As I have suggested throughout this study, Hemingway's style is the correlative for "despair and bitterness."[25] Simple syntactical rhythms, the heavy use of nouns and weak verbs emphasize individual images and give the passage a strong visual quality. The image of the frost and ice over the water on the two pitchers forebodes an end to Catherine's and Frederic's affair; but that "you could hear the stream in the rocks" in the "deep" valley suggests the depth and everlastingness of their feelings for one another.

Although this final book, consisting of only four chapters, centers on Catherine's and Frederic's quiet happiness in the mountains, and "the war seemed as far away as the football games of some one else's college," it continues to plunge forward to a grim end (FTA, 291). The "object of their romantic love," as Gerry Brenner notes, "is to fend off reality, replete as it is with suffering and irrationality."[26] Thus, in Chapter XXXVIII Catherine's desire "to be all mixed up" conveys this sense of retreat into obsessive love (FTA, 300):

> "I'd rather look at you. Darling, why don't you let your hair grow?"
> "How grow?"
> "Just a little longer."
> "It's long enough now."
> "No, let it grow a little longer and I could cut mine and we'd be just alike only one of us blonde and one of us dark."
> "I wouldn't let you cut yours."
> "It would be fun. I'm tired of it. It's an awful nuisance in the bed at night."
> "I like it."
> "Wouldn't you like it short?"
> "I might. I like it the way it is."

"It might be nice short. Then we'd both be alike. Oh, darling, I want you so much I want to be you too."

"You are. We're the same one." (FTA, 299)

Catherine's desire to change hairstyles so they can be closer underscores her courage and strength and emphasizes in the novel that drive to escape fear; Frederic, on the other hand, betrays his uneasiness with change ("I like it the way it is"), thus representing a countercurrent. But despite the chapter's impulse toward affirmation, reflected in part by Catherine's preoccupation with hair, subtle hints such as Catherine's being "rather narrow in the hips" hold the prose to a deadly course (FTA, 294). Indeed, the chapter closes with a chilling image of imprisonment as "the moon was shining in the window and made shadows on the bed from bars on the windowpanes" (FTA, 300).

The brevity and intensity of the next chapter, Chapter XXXIX, help to speed the novel toward a miserable end. The subject of hair again comes up, on the one hand to show how time has passed ("By the middle of January I had a beard" [FTA, 302]), and on the other to highlight the irony of Catherine's death, for she decides that she does not want to cut her hair until after the baby is born so she can be "a fine and different girl for you [Frederic]" (FTA, 304); but, of course, she never has this opportunity. In addition, the image of Catherine and Frederic sitting together on the logs along the edge of a road that "went down through the forest" explicitly connects Catherine and Frederic to Frederic's story about the doomed ants on the log in the final chapter. As they sit on the log, however, Catherine says, "She [the baby] won't come between us, will she? The little brat." And Frederic says, "No. We won't let her" (FTA, 304). The baby does come between them, but not in the way they expect. Like the preceding chapter, this one closes on a note of foreboding. Catherine says that after the baby is born, she will be thin again and Frederic can fall in love with her all over; Frederic says, "I love you enough now. What do you want to do? Ruin me?" And she says, "Yes. I want to ruin you." Then Frederic says, "Good . . . that's what I want too" (FTA, 305). Ultimately Frederic is "ruined," but not in the way they hope.

Chapter XL, as I noted earlier, is made more grim by the motif of the rain: "In the night it started raining. It rained on all morning and turned the snow to slush and made the mountain-side dismal" (FTA, 306). This chapter, too, is brief and spare and closes with a clear indication that time is running out for the lovers: "the baby was very close now and it gave us both a feeling as though something were hurrying us and we could not lose any time together" (FTA, 311).

The final chapter has a deadened, stunned quality to it. It opens with

Frederic's noticing Catherine's "stirring in the bed" with her labor pains and closes with his "saying good-by to a statue" and walking back to the hotel in the rain (*FTA*, 312, 332). Catherine begins labor bravely saying, "I won't die darling," but worn down by pain and exhaustion she becomes fearful and says, "I won't die, will I. . . . Because I don't want to die and leave you, but I get so tired of it and I feel I'm going to die" (*FTA*, 319, 323). While Catherine determinedly fights her fear, saying she's not "a bit afraid," and that "It's just a dirty trick" (*FTA*, 331), Frederic sees that even before she dies Catherine looks "gray" and "dead." Then in fear he puts himself through this agony:

> Poor, poor dear Cat. And this was the price you paid for sleeping together. This was the end of the trap. This was what people got for loving each other. . . . So now they got her in the end. You never got away with anything. Get away hell! It would have been the same if we had been married fifty times. And what if she should die? She won't die. . . . She's just having a bad time. . . . But what if she should die? She can't die. Yes, but what if she should die? She can't die. Yes, but what if she should die? She can't, I tell you. Don't be a fool. It's just a bad time. It's just nature giving her hell. . . . She can't die. Why would she die? What reason is there for her to die? There's just a child that has to be born, the by-product of good nights in Milan. . . . But what if she should die? She won't die. But what if she should die? She won't. She's all right. But what if she should die? She can't die. But what if she should die? Hey, what about that? What if she should die? (*FTA*, 320–21)

Blanche Gelfant argues that the language in this passage:

> is trite and repetitious to the point of compulsion; the sentences are distressingly simple; and the movement is erratic, syncopated by the nervous rushes and ebbs of fear. But closer study of the monologue reveals the marvelous economy of Hemingway's art as well as a highly creative use of the cliche. Through the very banalities of the passage, the repetitions, the erratic tempo and dialectic structure, Hemingway expresses simultaneously several levels of experience—Frederic's surface panic and the scurry of his immediate thoughts, the underlying depths of his anxiety, and the total moral integrity of his character. [27]

At first, Frederic tries to tell himself, as Gelfant suggests, that Catherine is just having a bad time; then he tries to fit himself into the stereotype of "the nervous husband"; then, since he can find no logic for her death, he settles for a simple assertion: "She can't die." Then he is "flung back again and again to the initial and still unanswered question, 'But what if she should die'?"

The bewilderment and shock that Frederick feels are reflected in the helpless repetition of this question and in the accelerated pace with which it comes as his futile monologue draws to an end. He has found no way out of the trap. But by refusing to capitulate to the easy cliche and the sentimental illusions, he has maintained intellectual and moral integrity. He has done this, however, at the expense of all hope. At the conclusion of the monologue both he and the reader have the clear foreknowledge of doom. . . . The alternative to escape, which Frederic takes, is to acknowledge the truth of the situation, and this acknowledgement is signified by the change of style, back to his clipped and precise everyday speech.[28]

The "precise everyday speech" Frederic shifts to is this simple, flat sentence: "The Doctor came into the room" (*FTA*, 321). Then following a brief conversation with the doctor, Frederic approves of the doctor's performing an operation, but he is "afraid to go in" to the operating room. Afterwards, when the doctor holds up the baby, which looks "like a freshly skinned rabbit" (*FTA*, 324), Frederic has "no feeling of fatherhood" (*FTA*, 325); even before he knows the baby is dead, his lack of parental feeling suggests the loss he is already beginning to suffer. But like Nick in *In Our Time*, he is a survivor even though his loss is flooded with bitterness and anger. At the very end when he knows Catherine is dead, and the nurses tell him he can't go into the room, he says to them, dully, "You get out. . . . The other one too" (*FTA*, 332). His feeling that he is saying goodbye to a statue conveys the absolute finality of Catherine's death and the complete sense of abandonment he experiences. As in *In Our Time*, love ultimately brings pain, not happiness, and childbirth brings death, not fulfillment.[29]

In both *In Our Time* and *A Farewell to Arms* the sensibilities are burdened by a past. In *In Our Time* communion with nature and ritualistic behavior provide a brief relief from the psychic trauma the past has created. In *A Farewell to Arms* a celebration of human love provides a fragile and fleeting ease from similar trauma.[30]

But both works in their attempts to triumph over fear are, finally, affirmative. Even though Catherine's death closes the work in the most depressing key,[31] just as "L'Envoi" closes *In Our Time* on a distressing note, Frederic's suffering is not meaningless; he is not a complete victim, for with awareness of death has come an intense desire to live fully.[32] This effort to triumph with dignity and understanding over fear of a hideous death is a preoccupation that Hemingway continued to struggle with in subsequent novels with varying degrees of success.

Notes

Introduction

1. Ernest Hemingway quoted in Mary Hemingway, *How It Was* (New York: Knopf, 1976), 305.

2. In 1923 Hemingway contributed six prose pieces, each a paragraph long, entitled "In Our Time" to the "Exiles" edition of Margaret Anderson's and Jane Heap's the *Little Review*. These pieces, according to Carlos Baker and E. R. Hagemann, were based on a series of six sentences in *Paris, 1922*, a draft of a work thought to be stolen from Hemingway's first wife Hadley at the Gare de Lyon in December 1922 (Baker, *Ernest Hemingway: A Life Story* [New York: Scribner's, 1969], 108; Hageman, "A Collation, with Commentary, of the Five Texts of the Chapters in Hemingway's *In Our Time*, 1923–28," *The Papers of the Bibliographical Society of America* 73 [1979]: 443; reprinted in *Critical Essays on Ernest Hemingway's In Our Time*, ed. Michael S. Reynolds [Boston: G. K. Hall, 1983], 38), but later discovered in a notebook and copied over on telegraph forms (Kenneth S. Lynn, *Hemingway* [New York: Simon and Schuster, 1987], 188n). At the suggestion of William Bird, Hemingway's friend and publisher, Hemingway wrote twelve additional pieces (which he called "chapters") and added them to the six that appeared in the *Little Review* (Baker, *A Life Story*, 112; Lynn, *Hemingway*, 193). In March 1924 the eighteen "chapters" were published as *in our time* by Bird's The Three Mountains Press. Sixteen of the "chapters" in *in our time* later became the interchapters placed between the fourteen stories in *In Our Time*, first published by Boni and Liveright in 1925 and subsequently by Scribner's in 1930, to which Hemingway added an introduction, "On the Quai at Smyrna." The other two "chapters" in *in our time* were titled and typeset as stories, "A Very Short Story" and "The Revolutionist," and included with the stories in *In Our Time*.

For a thorough essay about the publication of the "chapters," see Hagemann, "A Collation," 38–51.

3. *Ernest Hemingway: Selected Letters 1917–61*, ed. Carlos Baker (New York: Scribner's, 1981), 128.

4. Hemingway, *Selected Letters*, 157.

5. Jackson L. Benson, "Patterns of Connection and Their Development in Hemingway's *In Our Time*," *Rendezvous* 5 (1970): 37–52; Clinton S. Burhans, Jr., "The Complex Unity of *In Our Time*," *Modern Fiction Studies* 14 (Fall 1968): 313–28; E. M. Halliday, "Hemingway's *In Our Time*," *Explicator* 7 (1949): item 35; Robert M. Slabey, "The Structure of *In Our Time*," *South Dakota Review* (1965): 38–52 (reprinted in *Critical Essays*, ed. Reynolds, 76–87); Philip Young, "Adventures of Nick Adams," in *Hemingway: A Collection of Critical Essays*, ed. Robert P. Weeks (Englewood Cliffs, N.J.: Prentice-Hall, 1962), 95–112.

For further discussions of the genre, unity, structure, and form of *In Our Time* (1925), see Sheridan Baker, *Ernest Hemingway: An Introduction and Interpretation* (New York: Holt, 1967); Keith Carabine, "Hemingway's *In Our Time*: An Appreciation," *Fitzgerald/Hemingway Annual* (1979): 301–26, and "'A Pretty Good Unity': A Study of Sherwood

Anderson's 'Winesburg, Ohio' and Ernest Hemingway's 'In Our Time'" (Ph.D. diss., Yale University, 1978); James M. Cox, "*In Our Time*: The Essential Hemingway," *Southern Humanities Review* 22, no. 4 (Fall 1988): 305–20; Larry E. Grimes, *The Religious Design of Hemingway's Early Fiction* (Ann Arbor, Mich.: UMI Research Press, 1985); Richard Hasbany, "The Shock of Vision: An Imagist Reading of *In Our Time*," in *Ernest Hemingway: Five Decades of Criticism*, ed. Linda W. Wagner (Ann Arbor, Mich.: University of Michigan Press, 1973), 224–40; D. H. Lawrence, "*In Our Time*: A Review," in *Hemingway: A Collection*, ed. Robert P. Weeks (Englewood Cliffs, N.J.: Prentice-Hall, 1962), 93–94; David J. Leigh, "*In Our Time*: The Interchapters As Structural Guides to a Psychological Pattern," *Studies in Short Fiction* 12 (1975): 1–8; E. D. Lowry, "Chaos and Cosmos in *In Our Time*," *Literature and Psychology* 26, no. 3 (1976): 108–17; Robert M. Luscher, "The Short Story Sequence: An Open Book," *Short Story Theory at a Crossroads*, ed. Susan Lohafer and Jo Ellyn Clarey (Baton Rouge: Louisiana State University Press, 1989), 148–67; Susan Garland Mann, *The Short Story Cycle: A Genre Companion and Reference Guide* (New York: Greenwood Press, 1989), 71–91; Debra A. Moddelmog, "The Unifying Consciousness of a Divided Conscience: Nick Adams as Author of *In Our Time*," *American Literature* 60, no. 4 (1989): 591–610; Gilbert H. Muller, "*In Our Time*: Hemingway and the Discontents of Civilization," *Renascence* 29 (1977): 185–92; James Nagel, "Literary Impressionism and *In Our Time*," *Hemingway Review* 1 (Spring 1987): 17–26; David Seed, "'The Picture of the Whole': *In Our Time*," in *Ernest Hemingway: New Critical Essays*, ed. Robert A. Lee (Totowa, N.J.: Barnes, 1983), 13–35; Elizabeth D. Vaugn, "*In Our Time* As Self-Begetting Fiction," *Modern Fiction Studies* 35 (Winter 1989): 707–16; Linda W. Wagner, "Juxtaposition in Hemingway's *In Our Time*," *Studies in Short Fiction* 12 (1975): 243–52; Wirt Williams, *The Tragic Art of Ernest Hemingway* (Baton Rouge: Louisiana State University Press, 1981); Harlan Harbour Winn, "Short Story Cycles of Hemingway, Steinbeck, Faulkner, O'Connor" (Ph.D. diss., University of Oregon, 1975); Carl Wood, "Hemingway's Fragmentary Novel," *Neuphilologische Mitteilungen* 74, no. 4 (1974): 716–26.

6. To avoid confusion, the fictional pieces in the *Little Review*, as well as the "chapters" in *in our time* and *In Our Time*, will be called interchapters.

7. Rosenthal and Gall, *The Modern Poetic Sequence: The Genius of Modern Poetry* (New York: Oxford University Press, 1978), 9.

8. Rosenthal and Gall, *The Modern Poetic Sequence*, 15.

Although my study uses the method of analysis employed by Rosenthal and Gall in *The Modern Poetic Sequence*, it is also indebted to the many studies that discuss the work's thematic and narrative elements. This debt will be obvious in the following pages.

Other commentators who suggest Hemingway's work has lyrical elements are, among others, Keith Carabine, "Hemingway's *In Our Time*: An Appreciation," 301–26; Daniel J. Schneider, "Hemingway's A Farewell to Arms: The Novel as Pure Poetry," *Modern Fiction Studies* 14 (1968): 283–96; Linda W. Wagner, *Hemingway and Faulkner: inventors/masters* (Metuchen, N.J.: Scarecrow, 1975), and "Juxtaposition in Hemingway's *In Our Time*," and "The Poetry in American Fiction," in *American Modern: Essays in Fiction and Poetry* (Port Washington, N.Y.: National, 1980); and Robert Penn Warren, "Ernest Hemingway," *Kenyon Review* 9 (1947): 1–28 (reprinted in *Five Decades*, ed. Wagner, 75–102).

In *Hemingway: Expressionist Artist* Raymond S. Nelson relates *In Our Time* to the works of the Expressionists; that is, Hemingway, like the Expressionists, is concerned with evoking states of feeling in his writing. See also James Nagel's "Literary Impressionism and *In Our Time*" for a discussion about the connections between the characteristics of the Impressionists and the Imagists.

9. M. L. Rosenthal, *The Poet's Art* (New York: Norton, 1987), 97. Rosenthal points out that these "affects" are not "themes" or "concepts or ideas."

10. For discussions of *Hugh Selwyn Mauberley*, see M. L. Rosenthal, *A Primer of Ezra Pound* (New York: Grosset, 1960), 29–41; Rosenthal and Gall, *The Modern Poetic Sequence*, 196–203. For discussions of *The Waste Land* see M. L. Rosenthal, *The Modern Poets: A Critical Introduction* (New York: Oxford University Press, 1960), 81–94; M. L. Rosenthal, *Sailing into the Unknown: Yeats, Pound, Eliot* (New York: Oxford University Press, 1978), 162–79; and Rosenthal and Gall, *The Modern Poetic Sequence*, 153–64.

Keith Carabine argues that *In Our Time* is "a volume of interrelated chapters comparable in structure and purpose, if not quality, to his sponsor's *Hugh Selwyn Mauberley* and T. S. Eliot's *The Waste Land*," ("Hemingway's *In Our Time*: An Appreciation," 306). Carabine does not, however, discuss the work as a modern poetic sequence.

Using Pound's expression "organ base," Wagner points out that "The book is unified, finally by its organ base of tone—a mood of unrelieved somberness if not outright horror" (*Hemingway and Faulkner*, 57).

11. Wagner notes that George Wickes quotes John Peale Bishop as saying, "In Paris, Hemingway submitted much of his apprentice work in fiction to Pound. It came back to him blue-penciled, most of the adjectives gone. The comments were unsparing" (*Hemingway and Faulkner*, 31).

Other studies focusing specifically on Pound's influence on Hemingway include Richard Hasbany, "The Shock of Vision: An Imagist Reading of *In Our Time*," in *Five Decades*, ed. Wagner, 224–40; Harold M. Hurwitz, "Hemingway's Tutor, Ezra Pound," *Modern Fiction Studies* 17 (1971–72): 469–82 (reprinted in *Five Decades*, ed. Wagner, 8–21); Jacqueline Tavernier-Courbin, "Ernest Hemingway and Ezra Pound," in *Ernest Hemingway: The Writer in Context*, ed. James Nagel (Madison: University of Wisconsin Press, 1984), 179–200; and Linda W. Wagner, "Juxtaposition in Hemingway's *In Our Time*," and "The Poetry in American Fiction," in *American Modern*.

12. Hemingway, *Selected Letters*, 384.

13. Hemingway Collection, John F. Kennedy Library, Boston, Massachusetts.

14. Hemingway, *Selected Letters*, 113; see also 649–50, 544–46, 548–51, 603–5, 739–41.

15. *Literary Essays of Ezra Pound*, ed. T. S. Eliot (New York: New Directions, 1954), 3, 9.

16. Hemingway, *Selected Letters*, 383.

17. Rosenthal, *A Primer*, 42.

18. Lynn, *Hemingway*, 246; on the other hand, in *Hemingway: The Paris Years* Michael S. Reynolds says that Hemingway deliberately mispelled Eliot's name (Cambridge: Basil Blackwell, 1989), 366 n. 24.

19. *By-Line: Ernest Hemingway. Selected Articles and Dispatches of Four Decades*, ed. William White (New York: Scribner's, 1967), 133.

20. Hemingway, *Selected Letters*, 701.

21. See Nicholas Joost and Alan Brown, "T. S. Eliot and Ernest Hemingway: A Literary Relationship," *Papers on Language and Literature* 14, no. 4 (1978): 425–49.

22. See for instance Bickford Sylvester's essay "Hemingway's Italian *Waste Land*: The Complex Unity of 'Out of Season,'" in *Hemingway's Neglected Short Fiction: New Perspectives*, ed. Susan Beegel (Ann Arbor, Mich.: UMI Research Press, 1989), 75–98.

Philip Young points out that in *The Sun Also Rises* Jake is Hemingway's Fisher King (*Ernest Hemingway: A Reconsideration* [University Park: Pennsylvania State University Press, 1966], 87).

For a discussion of the Grail Quest motif in *The Sun Also Rises*, see Charles B. Newman, "Hemingway's Grail Quest," *University of Kansas Review* 28 (1961–62): 295–303.

A number of critics recognize that the despair communicated in *A Farewell to Arms* is similar to that in *The Waste Land*. Donna Gerstenberger in "*The Waste Land* in A

Farewell to Arms" (*Modern Language Notes* 76 [1961]: 24–25) maintains that Hemingway, like T. S. Eliot in *The Waste Land*, alludes to Marvell's poem—direct evidence of Hemingway's inability to escape Eliot's influence.

23. "A set of objects, a situation, a chain of events which shall be the formula of that *particular* emotion; such that when the external facts, which must terminate in sensory experience, are given, the emotion is immediately evoked" (*Selected Essays* [New York: Harcourt, 1932], 124–25).

24. See, for instance, Carlos Baker, *Hemingway: The Writer as Artist*, 4th ed. (Princeton: Princeton University Press, 1972), 56; Earl Rovit and Gerry Brenner, *Ernest Hemingway* (Boston: G. K. Hall, 1986), 28; Philip Young, *Reconsideration*, 183.

25. In "Toward a Formalist Criticism of Fiction," William J. Handy discusses how Hemingway's fictional scenes function as images, and that Hemingway learned to achieve this poetic technique from Pound who encompassed in his definition of the image the entire poem (*Four Modes: A Rhetoric of Modern Fiction*, ed. James M. Mellard [New York: Macmillan, 1973], 306).

In his letter to Edmund Wilson (quoted at the beginning of this introduction), Hemingway emphasizes in his image of a passing coastline the importance for him of making his writing visual, of evoking states of feeling through sensuous language. Thus, his scenes (or images) can be viewed, first from afar, then up close, first in a "chapter," then in a story.

26. Hemingway, *By-Line*, 219.

27. Hemingway, *Death in the Afternoon*, (New York: Scribner's, 1933), 2.

28. Hemingway, *Selected Letters*, 153.

Chapter 1. "In Our Time" (1923)

1. Hemingway, *By-Line*, 219.

2. "In Our Time," *Little Review*, Exiles Number (Spring 1923), 3–5, appeared in the fall of 1923.

In October 1923 Robert McAlmon's Contact Publishing Company published Hemingway's *Three Stories and Ten Poems*. Two of the stories in this volume, "My Old Man" and "Out of Season," were later included in *In Our Time*. These stories are considered by a number of commentators to be apprenticeship stories influenced by Sherwood Anderson and Gertrude Stein (see Arthur Waldhorn, *A Reader's Guide to Ernest Hemingway* [New York: Farrar, Straus and Giroux, 1972], 43–45; Rovit and Brenner, *Ernest Hemingway*, 26–27). The third story, "Up in Michigan," considered one of Hemingway's best, was rejected by the publisher of *In Our Time* because of its frank dealing with sex (*Selected Letters*, 157). The poems in *Three Stories and Ten Poems*, on the other hand, are considered by many critics, in particular Edmund Wilson ("Dry Points," *Dial* 77 [1924]: 340–41), to be unimportant, although they reflect Hemingway's familiarity with imagism and an attempt to break with the previous century's poetic diction. The volume of poems and stories does not, however, appear to be a deliberately ordered sequence of tonally-interrelated works.

3. Charles A. Fenton, *The Apprenticeship of Ernest Hemingway: The Early Years* (New York: Farrar, 1954), 229.

4. Lynn, *Hemingway*, 197.

5. Fenton, *The Apprenticeship*, 238; Carlos Baker, *A Life Story*, 108.

6. Fenton, *The Apprenticeship*, 237–38; Lynn, *Hemingway*, 197.

7. On the other hand, Reynolds notes that "the first six [interchapters] he gave Jane Heap had no governing scheme," and "they did not hang together" (*The Paris Years*, 123, 114).

8. "In Our Time," *The Little Review* (1923): 3. Subsequent references to this particular version will appear in the text as *LR* with the appropriate page number. Quotations from *in our time*, facsimile (Paris: The Three Mountains Press, 1924) will be indicated by the abbreviation *iot* and the appropriate page number.

9. "Only Let the Story End as Soon as Possible: Time-and-History in Ernest Hemingway's *In Our Time*," in Reynolds, *Critical Essays*, 53.

10. Peter L. Hays' *A Concordance to Hemingway's* In Our Time (Boston: G. K. Hall, 1990), published after this study was written, gives a computer analysis of the text and proves what scholars have indicated: Hemingway's wide use of repetition throughout *In Our Time*.

11. "An 'image' is that which presents an intellectual and emotional complex in an instant of time" (Pound, *Literary Essays*, 4).

Richard Hasbany notes that in Hemingway's use of first and third person point of view in the interchapters he is trying

> to create an expanded image of some kind. In the first person interchapters and stories he presents the subjective emotions of the narrator—an image of an emotion created by presenting what the narrator perceives, those actions that have combined to create the emotion. In presenting the thing, the motion, Hemingway has exercised an imagist poet's discriminating selectivity. He must lay bare only the objects and actions that cause an intuitive perception in the reader. ("The Shock of Vision: An Imagist Reading of *In Our Time*," 231–32).

12. Robert O. Stephens gives a correlated nonfiction source: "World Series of Bull Fighting a Mad, Whirling Carnival," *Toronto Star Weekly*, 27 October 1923, p. 33 (*Hemingway's Nonfiction: The Public Voice* [Chapel Hill: The University of North Carolina Press, 1968], 364).

Both Lynn and Reynolds point out that the second interchapter was inspired by Mike Strater (Lynn, *Hemingway*, 197; Reynolds, *The Paris Years*, 114); Fenton says that Hemingway wrote the interchapter in the voice of an American who was with him during the bullfighting (*The Apprenticeship*, 238).

13. See *Selected Letters*, 189, for Hemingway's comments about *Huckleberry Finn*.

Philip Young, among others, indicates that Hemingway's style was influenced by Mark Twain's (*Reconsideration*, 211–40).

See Richard Bridgman for a discussion of Hemingway's use of the colloquial style (*The Colloquial Style in America* [New York: Oxford University Press, 1966], 195–230).

14. Hemingway explains that the bullfight was a "tragedy," and the tragedy "all centered in the bull and in the man" (*Death in the Afternoon*, 6, 20). He also notes that "the matador, if he knows his profession, can increase the amount of the danger of death that he runs exactly as much as he wishes" (21). Hemingway notes that the bullfight is "strongly disciplined by ritual," and a good bullfighter must be "skillful, knowing, brave, and competent" (1–25). A good bullfighter like Joselito, Hemingway says,

> is performing a work of art and he is playing with death, bringing it closer, closer, closer, to himself, a death that you know is in the horns because you have the canvas-covered bodies of the horses on the sand to prove it. He gives the feeling of immortality, and, as you watch it, it becomes yours. Then when it belongs to both of you, he proves it with the sword. (*Death in the Afternoon*, 213)

15. Item 94a, Hemingway Collection, John F. Kennedy Library, Boston, Massachusetts.

16. Hemingway, *Selected Letters*, 91–92.

17. Fenton, *The Apprenticeship*, 229.

18. Ibid., 229.

19. Ibid., 233.

20. Waldhorn, A Reader's Guide, 47.

21. Ibid., 48.

22. Malcolm Cowley in "Nightmare and Ritual in Hemingway" (in Hemingway: A Collection of Critical Essays, ed. Weeks, 46) explains that the rain in In Our Time is a conscious symbol of disaster.

In "Hemingway's A Farewell to Arms: The Novel as Pure Poetry" (Modern Fiction Studies 14 [1968]: 283–96) Daniel J. Schneider discusses the poetic effect of the repetition of the word "rain" in A Farewell to Arms. See chapter five of this study for additional comments about Hemingway's use of this word.

23. See Paul Smith for a discussion of an "unpublished and unrecorded chapter" recounting the beginning of the British retreat from Mons, a chapter Smith calls "Mons Three" ("'Mons [Three]': An Unpublished In Our Time Chapter," Hemingway in Italy and Other Essays, ed. Robert W. Lewis [New York: Praeger, 1990], 107–12).

24. T. S. Eliot, Collected Poems: 1909–1962 (New York: Harcourt, 1930), 55.

25. Cowley notes that "the wall itself is so vivid that, for the reader, it tends to become a sort of metaphor for all the impassable obstacles we see in nightmares: the swamps in which our feet are mired, the endless steps, the river that must, and cannot be crossed" ("Nightmare and Ritual in Hemingway," 45).

26. Item 94a, Hemingway Collection, John F. Kennedy Library, Boston Massachusetts.

27. Hagemann, "Only Let the Story End as Soon as Possible," 53.

28. Ibid., 53.

29. Cowley feels that in "Hemingway's unconscious mind, all these walls may have been the images of death" ("Nightmare and Ritual," 46).

30. See Reynolds, "Two Hemingway Sources for in our time," in Critical Essays, ed. Reynolds, 31–37; see also Stephens, Hemingway's Nonfiction, 365.

31. New York Times, 1 Dec. 1922, p. 1, col. 1 (quoted in Reynolds, "Two Hemingway Sources," 32–33).

32. Reynolds, "Two Sources," 33; Lynn, Hemingway, 198; Meyers, Hemingway: A Biography (New York: Harper, 1985), 105.

33. Bruce Fogelman pointed out to me the similarities in images. The complete poem is as follows:

THE rustling of the silk is discontinued,
    Dust drifts over the court-yard,
        There is no sound of foot-fall, and the leaves
Scurry into heaps and lie still,
And she the rejoicer of the heart is beneath them:

A wet leaf that clings to the threshold.

(Personae [New York: New Directions, 1926], 108).

David Seed also notes the similarity in images (18): "The wet dead leaves on the courtyard anticipate the death of the ministers, help to establish a sombre tone, and in fact are probably borrowed from one of Pound's imagist poems—'Liu Ch'e, which evokes absence through the image of a deserted courtyard" ("'The Picture of the Whole': In Our Time," in Ernest Hemingway: New Critical Essays, ed. Lee, 13–35).

Similar images appear in "Ts'ai Chi'h":

THE petals fall in the fountain,
        the orange-coloured rose-leaves,
    Their ochre clings to the stone.

(Personae, 108)

and "In a Station of the Metro":

> T HE apparition of these faces in the crowd;
> Petals on a wet, black bough.

(Personae, 109)

34. Pound, *Literary Essays*, 4.
35. Item 94a, Hemingway Collection, John F. Kennedy Library, Boston, Massachusetts.
36. Cf. Rovit and Brenner, *Ernest Hemingway*, 31–32.
37. Pound, *Personae*, 191.

Chapter 2. *in our time* (1924)

1. Hemingway, *Selected Letters*, 408.
2. By August 1923 Hemingway had completed the additional twelve interchapters to make up *in our time*.
3. This was suggested by Rosenthal's and Gall's comment about *The Waste Land*: T. S. Eliot "used language, not for narrative or dramatic purposes of character illustration or suspense and resolution, but first and foremost to build the poem's tonal centers" (*The Modern Poetic Sequence*, 160).
4. This idea was suggested by Rosenthal's idea that Eliot's two major works (*The Waste Land* and *The Four Quartets*) "are not so much direct religious expressions as journeys of a sensibility over the landscape of its own condition. This sensibility, the 'hero' of the poems, goes through many adventures, not in a narrative sequence but in a montage of images, memories, portraits and caricatures, dramatic scenes, and musings" (*The Modern Poets*, 89).
5. Stephens gives the *Toronto Daily Star*, 22 July 1922, as the source for this interchapter (*Hemingway's Nonfiction*, 7).
6. The stories and interchapters in *In Our Time* are available from Scribner's in two versions: *In Our Time* (1925, 1930), and *The Short Stories of Ernest Hemingway* (1966). This study uses *In Our Time* (1925, 1930). References to *in our time* are taken from a facsimile of the edition printed in Paris by The Three Mountains Press, 1924. Subsequent references to *In Our Time* will appear in the text as *IOT* with the appropriate page number; references to *in our time* will appear in the text as *iot* with the appropriate page number.
7. Item 94a, Hemingway Collection, John F. Kennedy Library, Boston, Massachusetts.
8. E. R. Hagemann explains that this incident is fictional, but that the battle was actual. Two hundred thousand Austrians were killed and wounded; twenty-five thousand taken prisoner. The "victorious" Italians had ninety thousand losses. Hemingway served at Fosalta di Piave, and on the night of 8 July 1918, he was badly wounded ("Only Let the Story End as Soon as Possible," 55).
   The name Nick, Reynolds reveals, was inspired by Nick Nerone, a "much-decorated and three times wounded Italian officer in the war" (*The Paris Years*, 127).
9. As a number of commentators suggest, this "chapter" is the germ of the idea for Frederic Henry's making a separate peace in *A Farewell to Arms*.
10. Item 94a, Hemingway Collection, John F. Kennedy Library, Boston, Massachusetts.
11. Ibid. Frederick J. Hoffman in "No Beginning and No End: Hemingway and Death" notes that all of *In Our Time* is "an early testimony to the powerful influence of

'the unreasonable wound.' The most important meaning of that book is not its portrayal of a placid boyhood but the exercise of a sensibility profoundly changed by violence" (*Essays in Criticism* 3 [1953]: 73–84).

Malcolm Cowley was the first to suggest the significance of "the wound" in Hemingway's work; see *The Portable Hemingway* (New York: Viking, 1944) and "Hemingway's Wound—And Its Consequences for American Literature" (*Georgia Review* 38, no. 2 [1984]: 223–39). See also Young, *Reconsideration*, 40–48; cf. Lynn, *Hemingway*, 103–4.

Chapter four of this study, in a discussion of "Big Two-Hearted River," makes further reference to the impact of physical violence upon the sensibility.

12. Bridgman demonstrates the "verbal and syntactic" care that Hemingway uses to describe Nick's head taking three different positions, each showing the pained movement of an injured man in shock. Between each description of Nick's head movement, Hemingway renders Nick's thoughts and his remarks to Rinaldi (*The Colloquial Style in America*, 218–19).

13. Item 94a, Hemingway Collection, John F. Kennedy Library, Boston, Massachusetts.

14. Ibid. Kathryn Zabelle Derounian discusses in detail the three typescripts of the seventh interchapter, available at the John F. Kennedy Library in Boston, noting that Hemingway's revisions show how "he gradually omitted irrelevant details and succeeded in expressing an exact sequence of events in simple yet forceful language. Even more impressively, he accurately showed Nick's view of his situation; and through restricted style and sentence structure (subject-verb-object), he conveyed Nick's shocked reaction to it. That is no small achievement in a piece of writing only two hundred words long" (in *Critical Essays*, ed. Reynolds, 75).

15. Slabey notes that Chapter VI is the symbolic center of *In Our Time* ("The Structure of *In Our Time*," in *Critical Essays*, ed. Reynolds, 77).

16. Item 94a, Hemingway Collection, John F. Kennedy Library, Boston Massachusetts.

17. Bridgman argues that Hemingway capitalizes "Jesus" in the last sentence of the interchapter to indicate "economically, that there the name occurs outside the essentially disbelieving mind of the soldier who prays 'please please dear jesus.' Also, by technical means he has contrasted the frenetic, jammed tumbling words of prayer under fire: 'Oh jesus christ get me out of here. Dear jesus get me out. Christ please please please christ' with the relaxed and syntactically expansive details of the day following the shelling: 'hot and muggy and cheerful and quiet.' Both procedures force the reader to proceed as deliberately as a motorist on an unfamiliar detour" (*The Colloquial Style in America*, 217).

18. Item 94a, Hemingway Collection, John F. Kennedy Library, Boston, Massachusetts.

19. Ibid.

20. Reynolds, "Two Hemingway Sources for *in our time*," in *Critical Essays*, ed. Reynolds, 34–35.

21. In the *in our time* version Drevitts is spelled both Drevetts and Drevitts, most likely because of a typesetting error. In the drafts and in *In Our Time* the name is spelled Drevitts (Item 94a, Hemingway Collection, John F. Kennedy Library, Boston, Massachusetts).

22. Item 94a, Hemingway Collection, John F. Kennedy Library, Boston, Massachusetts. Coming as it does following two interchapters having to do with the Italian counterattack against the Austrians in World War I, this interchapter suggests on first reading that perhaps Hemingway is slandering Italians, but as Reynolds points out, Hemingway's own experience with Italians during the war and after was positive, and he

therefore does not sympathize with his fictional characters' attitude that it is acceptable to kill Italians ("Two Hemingway Sources for *in our time*," 36).

23. Hemingway was wounded in July 1918 at the Austrian front, and while recovering from his leg injuries in Milan, fell in love with a Red Cross nurse named Agnes Von Kurowsky. When he recovered, he returned to Oak Park, Illinois, to earn the two hundred dollars a month Agnes required of him before she would join him and marry him. But in March 1919 Hemingway received a letter from her saying their love was only a "boy and girl affair," and she announced her plans to marry an Italian duke. Devastated, Hemingway fled to the family cottage in the woods and for months he could not write at all. When he did begin to write, his sentences "were short and simple, the irony bitter and harsh, each word like his first steps without crutches or his cane" (Peter Griffin, "The Young Hemingway: Three Unpublished Stories," *The New York Times Magazine*, 18 August 1985, sec. 6, p. 15; see especially Agnes' letters in *Hemingway in Love and War*, ed. Henry S. Villard and James Nagel [Boston: Northeastern University Press, 1989]).

Robert E. Scholes notes that despite Hemingway's changing the pronoun "I" to "he" in the *In Our Time* version, the interchapter still reads as though it were first person ("Decoding Papa: 'A Very Short Story' as Word and Text," in *Semiotics and Interpretation* [New Haven: Yale University Press, 1982], 111). See Paul Smith, *A Reader's Guide to the Short Stories of Ernest Hemingway* (Boston: G. K. Hall, 1989), 25–29, for the compositional history of this story. This interchapter, then, provides the background for the bitterness of the sequence, and gives it a confessional note; and while not detracting from the other interchapters in its cynicism, it is perhaps the weakest link in terms of brevity and compression of language.

24. Item 94a, Hemingway Collection, John F. Kennedy Library, Boston, Massachusetts.

25. Hemingway renames Ag Luz in *In Our Time* for fear of libel (*Selected Letters*, 469). He also changes Torre di Mosta to Pordenone. Perhaps Hemingway chose the name Luz (love) to heighten the irony in the interchapter.

In "'A Very Short Story' as Therapy" Scott Donaldson discusses the three versions of "A Very Short Story" and notes that "Behind a pretense of objectivity, it [the story] excoriates the faithless Agnes" (in *Hemingway's Neglected Short Fiction: New Perspectives*, ed. Susan F. Beegel [Ann Arbor, Mich.: UMI Research Press, 1989], 99–105.

26. Carabine, "Hemingway's *In Our Time*: An Appreciation," 314.

27. Hemphill, "Hemingway and James," *The Kenyon Review* 11 (1949), 53.

28. Item 94a, Hemingway Collection, John F. Kennedy Library, Boston, Massachusetts.

29. Donaldson notes that in the *In Our Time* version Hemingway adds the words "to the front" in the fourth paragraph to suggest "a picture of a harried soldier perusing the letters from his loved one during respite from combat. . . . The attempt here is obviously to arouse sympathy for the male narrator . . . that is what is wrong with 'A Very Short Story.' The narrator is too good, too noble, too unfairly wronged," ("'A Very Short Story' as Therapy," 105).

30. Paul Smith emphasizes this story's important place in the progression from Hemingway's Chicago manuscripts on the war, through the Nick Adams chapters in *In Our Time* to *A Farewell to Arms* (*A Reader's Guide*, 27).

31. Hemingway also considered the following titles, "An Even Shorter Story," "The Wounded Revolutionist," and "The Worried Revolutionist" (Smith, *A Reader's Guide*, 31).

32. Jim Steinke, "The Two Shortest Stories of Hemingway's *In Our Time*," *Critical Essays*, ed. Reynolds, 223.

33. Hemingway's well known "iceberg technique" is at work here, the word "torture"

being that part of the iceberg that is submerged. In an often-quoted passage from an interview with George Plimpton, Hemingway says, " . . . I always try to write on the principle of the iceberg. There is seven eighths of it under water for every part that shows. Anything you know you can eliminate and it strengthens your iceberg. It is the part that doesn't show. If a writer omits something because he does not know it then there is a hole in the story" (*Writers at Work*, ed. George Plimpton [New York: Penguin Books, 1963], 235). In a discussion about "Out of Season," Hemingway also says that " . . . you could omit anything if you knew that you omitted and the omitted part would strengthen the story and make people feel something more than they understood" (*A Moveable Feast* [New York: Scribner's, 1964], 75).

For a discussion of Hemingway's omissions and concealments, see Gerry Brenner, *Concealments in Hemingway's Works* (Columbus: Ohio State University Press, 1983), 27–41; Julian Smith, "Hemingway and the Thing Left Out," in *Five Decades*, ed. Wagner, 188–200; and Paul Smith, "Hemingway's Early Manuscripts: The Theory and Practice of Omission," *Journal of Modern Literature* 10, no. 2 (1983): 268–88; for a book-length discussion of Hemingway's "craft of omission" in four manuscripts, see Susan F. Beegel, *Hemingway's Craft of Omission* (Ann Arbor, Mich.: UMI Research Press, 1988).

34. Burhans, "The Complex Unity of *In Our Time*," 323.

35. Hunt, "Another Turn for Hemingway's 'The Revolutionist': Sources and Meanings,'" *Fitzgerald/Hemingway Annual* (1977): 212; reprinted in *Critical Essays*, ed. Reynolds, 203–17.

36. Benson, "Patterns of Connection and Their Development in Hemingway's *In Our Time*," 50.

37. Carabine, "Hemingway's *In Our Time*," 314–15.

38. Johnston, "Hemingway and Mantegna: The Bitter Nail Holes," *The Journal of Narrative Technique* 1 (1979), 89.

39. Ibid., 89.

40. In "Hemingway's 'Revolutionist': An Aid to Interpretation" Barbara S. Grosclose argues that the Mantegna painting the speaker is referring to is *The Dead Christ* in Milan (circa 1501). This painting is "atypical of contemporary productions" (such as Giotto's, Masaccio's, and Piero della Francesca's), according to Grosclose, "in its extremely foreshortened view of the body of Christ and in the intense realism of the wounds he received during the crucifixion. It is a tour-de-force of perspective occuring late in the artist's career, and in the depiction of the figure of Christ, the painter emphasizes the finality of death" (*Modern Fiction Studies* 17 [1971]: 568). Grosclose's point is that if we know something about Mantegna, Giotto, Piero della Francesca, and Masaccio, we will put into contrast the Magyar's optimism in rejecting Mantegna and the earthbound qualities of the painter's Christ, and the skepticism of the speaker for embracing Mantegna's vision of a dead, tortured human.

Anthony Hunt, however, argues that we don't need to know the origin of the artist's paintings to understand this story. In a discussion of the story as it appears in *In Our Time*, he says we should examine it in a matrix of *in our time* and with geographical and political backgrounds implied. Hunt notes that the young revolutionist prefers country over city, or the sunny hills of Tuscany and Romagna over the city, Milan, of the northern Italian painter, Mantegna. Also, the young revolutionist wants to pass through Milan quickly because "his mind was already looking forward to walking over the pass" (*iot*, 21). Biographically speaking, Milan was the city of Hemingway's disappointments, for in Milan Agnes von Kurowsky said she would not be able to celebrate her first Christmas with Hemingway (and in Chapter X it is in Milan where the soldier and Luz part still quarreling). Besides geography as one touchstone for interpretation of the story, Hunt also argues for politics as another, for the young Communist not only rejects painters recommended by the party, but he wraps up his reproductions of the Renaissance painters in a copy of *Avanti*, the paper of the Italian socialist party, edited by Mussolini, future dictator of the Fascists; Hemingway is thus underscoring the political confusion in the country at the time ("Another Turn for Hemingway's Revolutionist': Sources and Meanings," in *Critical Essays*, ed. Reynolds, 209, 214).

41. Grimes, *The Religious Design*, 45.

42. Young discusses Hemingway's code at length; he says that it is made of "the controls of honor and courage which in a life of tension and pain make a man a man and distinguish him from the people who follow random impulses, let down their hair, and are generally messy, perhaps cowardly, and without inviolable rules for how to live holding tight," (*Reconsideration*, 63).

See also Rovit and Brenner for a discussion of the tutor and tutor-tyro stories (*Ernest Hemingway*, 77–82, 39–40, 49–50, 63–67).

43. Burhans, "The Complex Unity of *In Our Time*," 318.

44. See M. L. Rosenthal for a discussion of "Envoi" (*A Primer*, 29–41).

45. Hemingway, *Death in the Afternoon*, 6.

46. Item 94a, Hemingway Collection, John F. Kennedy Library, Boston, Massachusetts.

47. Ibid.

48. Pound, *Literary Essays*, 4.

49. Ibid., 401.

50. Lynn notes the sexual imagery in the bullfighting interchapters, as does Jackson J. Benson (*Hemingway*, 213; "Patterns of Connection and Their Development in Hemingway's *In Our Time*," 51).

51. M. L. Rosenthal, *A Primer*, 41.

52. Hemingway did not witness the execution, but he could have if he had wanted to, for he had passed by the jail in Chicago only a few hours earlier (Lynn, *Hemingway*, 211).

53. Hemingway, *Selected Letters*, 91–92.

54. Fenton, *The Apprenticeship*, 241.

55. Bridgman, *The Colloquial Style in America*, 218.

56. E. D. Lowry, "Chaos and Cosmos in *In Our Time*," 117.

57. As Hemingway wrote to Pound on August 5, 1923:

The whole thing closes with the talk with the King of Greece and his Queen in their garden, (just written), which shows the king all right. The last sentence in it is———Like all Greeks what he really wanted was to get to America.———My pal Shorty [Wornall], movie director with me in Thrace, just brings the dope on the King. Edifying.
The king closes it in swell shape. Oh that king. (*Selected Letters*, 91–92)

58. Pound was the first to notice the source for the title (Hemingway, *Selected Letters*, 378).
David Seed explains that the title

comes from the Episcopalian Order for Morning Prayer—'Give peace in our time, O Lord.' Hemingway ironically implies a general sense of peace as well as a specific contrast with warfare here. The response to this prayer is also directly relevant to Hemingway's work: 'Because there is none other that fighteth for us, but only thou, O God.' Here man's helplessness is stressed in order to make him put more trust in God. Hemingway keeps the first emphasis but blocks his characters' access to any spiritual consolation. ("'The Picture of the Whole': *In Our Time*," 15.)

59. Halliday, "Hemingway's *In Our Time*," item 35.

Chapter 3. *In Our Time* (1925): Before a Separate Peace

1. Hemingway, *Selected Letters*, 113, 154.
2. Ibid., 123.
3. "Indian Camp," "Big Two-Hearted River, Part I and II," "The Doctor and the Doctor's Wife," "The End of Something," "The Three-Day Blow," "Soldier's Home," "Mr. and Mrs. Elliot," "Cat in the Rain," and "Cross-Country Snow."
4. Hemingway, *Selected Letters*, 123.
5. Ibid., 157.
6. Ibid., 154–55.
7. Ibid., 470.
8. Young, *Reconsideration*, 34.
9. Wirt Williams explains that, "The interchapters are part of the book's intricate melody-harmony-counterpoint schema: they are harmony and counterpoint to the main line the stories represent, and within their own sequence they show several smaller melody-harmony-counterpoint arrangements. The first interchapter points the course of the book; the last serves to summarize it. The first suggests that life is a journey in the dark; the last declares that the great necessity is to survive" (*The Tragic Art*, 34).
10. Hemingway, *Selected Letters*, 157–58.
11. Eliot, *Selected Essays*, 124–25; Pound, *Literary Essays*, 401.
12. The Nick Adams stories are collected in *Ernest Hemingway: The Nick Adams Stories*, preface by Philip Young (New York: Scribner's, 1972).
13. For instance, Philip Young argues that *In Our Time* is "a book of short stories that is nearly a novel about him [Nick]" (*Reconsideration*, 32). But less than half of the Nick Adams stories appear in *In Our Time*, five in the first half of the book; Nick also appears in Chapter VI and in "Big Two-Hearted River, Part One and Two."

   Carlos Baker, (in *The Writer as Artist*, 125–31), Joseph DeFalco (in *The Hero in Hemingway's Short Stories* [Pittsburgh: University of Pittsburgh Press, 1963], 14–20), and others claim that the sequence is more a bildungsroman, a novel of a maturing young man, than a collection of stories. More recently Debra A. Moddelmog argues that *In Our Time* is a novel "unified by the consciousness of Nick Adams as he attempts to come to terms through his fiction with his involvement in World War I and, more recently, with the problems of marriage and his fear of fatherhood" ("The Unifying Consciousness of a Divided Nick Adams as Author of *In Our Time*," 608).
14. See Paul Smith for the composition history of the Introduction (*A Reader's Guide*, 189–90).
15. Leiter, "Neurol Projections in Hemingway's 'On the Quai at Smyrna,'" *Studies in Short Fiction* 5 (1968): 384–86.
16. For example, to mention only a few, G. Thomas Tanselle discusses "Indian Camp" as a "parable of the gradual supplanting of one culture by another" ("Hemingway's 'Indian Camp,'" *Explicator* 20 [1962]: item 53); Kenneth G. Johnston discusses the story as "the abortive initiation of a sensitive boy who is not able to cope with, nor to learn from, the violent lessons of the night" ("In the Beginning: Hemingway's 'Indian Camp,' *Studies in Short Fiction* 15 [1978]: 102–4); Dick Penner emphasizes the relationship between father and son and Nick's initiation to death ("The First Nick Adams Story," *Fitzgerald/Hemingway Annual* [1977]: 192–202); Kenneth Bernard introduces the idea that George is the father of the Indian baby ("Hemingway's 'Indian Camp,' *Studies in Short Fiction*, 2, no. 1 [1965]: 291).
17. Smith, *A Reader's Guide*, 35.
18. Hemingway, *The Nick Adams Stories*, 13–15.
19. Ibid., 14.

20. Lynn suggests that "Indian Camp" was inspired by emotions surrounding the birth of John Hadley Nicanor (*Hemingway*, 229). Cf. Paul Smith, *A Reader's Guide*, 36–38.

21. Cf. DeFalco, *The Hero*, 25–39.

22. Hays points out that Hemingway's use of the word "know" amounts to "a pattern of incremental repetition: Nick thinks he knows what the Indian woman is undergoing; his father corrects him, telling him he doesn't know; and at story's end Dr. Adams has to confess that he doesn't know why the Indian husband committed suicide" (*A Concordance*, ix).

23. Flora, *Hemingway's Nick Adams* (Baton Rouge: Louisiana State University Press, 1982), 22.

24. The following critics feel that Nick observed the incident and is humiliated by it: Baker, *The Writer as Artist*, 129; Leo Gurko, *Ernest Hemingway and the Pursuit of Heroism* (New York: Crowell, 1968), 176; Constance Montgomery, *Hemingway in Michigan* (New York: Fleet, 1966), 65.

Philip Young implies that Nick overhears the conversation between his mother and father. This is an upsetting experience for him, and he takes his father's side and rejects his mother (*Reconsideration*, 33). Young also notes that Hemingway once said that "this story was about the time he discovered his father was a coward" (*Reconsideration*, 33n).

See Paul Smith, for a detailed discussion of the critical approaches to this story (*A Reader's Guide*, 61–67).

25. Hays notices that "Dick Boulton calls him the unfamiliar and somewhat demeaning 'Doc' (7 times), which echoes 'the little dock,' as well as rhyming internally with 'half cock' and 'knock (your eye teeth down your throat),' each of the latter occurring in a line with 'Doc,'" (*A Concordance*, ix).

26. R. M. Davis insists that the gun "is at least a substitute for vital communication with his wife," and that the doctor's pumping the shells onto the bed is a sexual and even onanistic fantasy ("Hemingway's 'The Doctor and the Doctor's Wife,'" *Explicator* 23 [Sept. 1966]: item 1).

27. Horst H. Kruse argues that the cycle of the mill is an analogue for the end of Nick's and Marjorie's relationship. The second growth is a symbol of Marjorie's future, and the schooner is a symbol for Nick ("Ernest Hemingway's 'The End of Something': Its Independence as a Short Story and Its Place in the 'Education of Nick Adams,'" *Studies in Short Fiction* 4 [Winter 1967]: 152–66).

Harry Barba notes that the tone in reference to the mill anticipates Marjorie's and Nick's breakup ("The Three Levels of 'The End of Something,'" *Philological Papers* 17 [June 1970]: 76–80).

See Paul Smith for additional critical approaches (*A Reader's Guide*, 50–55).

28. Kruse, "Hemingway's 'The End of Something,'" 161.

29. Welland, "Idiom in Hemingway: A Footnote," *Journal of American Studies* 18, no. 3 (1984): 449–51.

30. Lynn sees Marjorie as a "younger incarnation of Hadley" (Hemingway's first wife). He thus sees "The End of Something" as a "veiled expression of Hemingway's feelings about his marriage—with a dash of wish fulfillment thrown in. For in real life the rejected woman would not depart without setting a difficult condition" (*Hemingway*, 254–55).

Carlos Baker and Jeffrey Meyers, on the other hand, feel that Marjorie is modeled on Marjorie Bump of Petoskey, the daughter of a hardware dealer (Baker, *A Life Story*, 757; Meyers, *A Biography*, 49). Meyers points out, however, that a crucial passage in the story—"It isn't fun any more"—written in 1925 is more related to the end of Hemingway's marriage to Hadley.

Reynolds implies that Hemingway once said to Hadley, "You know too much," which she subsequently responds to in a letter. Reynold's point is that Hadley provided material for Hemingway's fiction (*The Young Hemingway*, 148).

31. Kruse, "Hemingway's 'The End of Something,'" 162.

32. Whitt, "Hemingway's 'The End of Something,'" *Explicator* 9 (June 1950): item 58. Cf. Gerry Brenner, *Concealments*, 20–21, 242, n. 38.

33. See Kruse for a discussion of the analog of fishing as portent to the end of the affair, "Hemingway's 'The End of Something,'" 164–66.

34. In "The Biographical Fallacy and 'The Doctor and the Doctor's Wife'" (*Studies in Short Fiction* 16 [1979]: 61–65) Richard Fulkerson argues that "The End of Something" is an independent story. On the other hand, Philip Young says that "The End of Something" is like a chapter in a novel in that it by no means has all of its meaning when taken in isolation" (*Reconsideration*, 34).

35. On the contrary, James M. Mellard argues that there are seven scenes within the story as in a one-act drama, "all contained within the ceremonial pattern of the drinks Nick and Bill take" (*Four Modes*, 287).

36. "The Three-Day Blow," Philip Young points out, relates among other things how "The End of Something" felt to Nick: "the end of the affair with Marjorie felt like the autumnal three-day wind storm that is blowing . . ." (*Reconsideration*, 34–35).

37. Kenneth Johnston, however, says that "the fact that he has not yet eaten of the forbidden fruit suggests the essential innocence of his affair of the heart." Johnston supports this in a note saying, "A scene set in the same orchard in 'Summer People' lends support to this interpretation. An hour before Nick has physical relations with Kate, he takes a bite from a green apple" (" 'Three-Day Blow': Tragicomic Aftermath of a Summer Romance," *Hemingway Review* 2 [Fall 1982]: 21–25), 22.

38. Cf. Mellard, *Four Modes*, 285–89.

39. For a discussion about Hemingway's reference to these particular baseball teams, novels, and authors, see Kenneth G. Johnston, "Tragicomic Aftermath," 21–25.

40. Kruse notes that it is improbable "that the interpretation [Bill's reasons for Nick's breaking up with Marjorie] furnishes the true motive for Nick's behavior in 'The End of Something.' It is more likely that Hemingway is exploiting a favorite theme of his, that of failure of communication" (152–66).

41. Initially called "The Great Man" (Item 269, Hemingway Collection, John F. Kennedy Library), this story was later more appropriately renamed "The Battler" to convey more incisively the irony of the former prize fighter's dehumanization. This title—with its play on the word "battler"—also links the stories about Nick as a youth to the stories about adulthood, war, and postwar Europe.

See Paul Smith for the composition history of this story (*A Reader's Guide*, 115–21).

Hemingway wrote this story to replace "Up in Michigan," a story his publishers would not include in the sequence. Even though "Up in Michigan" is written from a woman's point of view, unlike the other stories in the sequence, it is an initiation story that captures the tonalities of bitter loss and pain, and it would have echoed and balanced other works in the sequence.

42. Hemingway's addition to the manuscript of the sentence about the swamp being on both sides of the track suggests that he wanted to show a connection between "The Battler" and "The Big Two-Hearted River" (Item 269, Hemingway Collection, John F. Kennedy Library, Boston, Massachusetts). For a discussion about the parallels between "The Battler" and "Big Two-Hearted River," see Frank B. Kyle, "Parallel and Complementary Themes in Hemingway's 'Big Two-Hearted River' Stories and 'The Battler,'" *Studies in Short Fiction* 16 (1979): 295–300.

Chapter 4. *In Our Time,* Part Two: After a Separate Peace

1. "An Interview with Ernest Hemingway," George Plimpton, *The Paris Review* 18 (1958): 60–89; reprinted in *Writers at Work: The Paris Review Interviews,* ed. Plimpton, 233.

2. Burhans notes that "The world as it actually is 'in our time' set against man's expectations and hopes; and his consequent problems and difficulties in trying to live in it with meaning and order—these, then, are the central themes which Hemingway explores 'in detail' in the stories as he had made them 'the picture of the whole' in the vignettes" ("The Complex Unity," 326).

3. Hemingway was pleased with this story; as he wrote to Robert McAlmon on 10 December 1924, "This is the best short story I ever wrote so am sending it" (*Selected Letters,* 139). Some critics suggest that Hemingway's own experiences in the war in 1914 are the source for the story; see Peter Griffin's and Michael Reynolds' biographies for this period of Hemingway's life.

4. Like Krebs, Hemingway also lied about his experiences in the war, as his biographers and other commentators point out; see, for instance, Reynolds, *The Paris Years,* 189ff.

5. Wagner notes that this passage is Hemingway's "ethic of virtue." "So long as man had choice, his heroism had to depend on his resolution of that choice . . ." (*Hemingway and Faulkner,* 57).

6. Roberts, "In Defense of Krebs," *Studies in Short Fiction* 13 (1976–77): 517.

7. Grimes argues that "Now the truth of war remembered, rather than anticipated, leads these soldiers to expect nothing" (*The Religious Design,* 45).

8. Hays notes that the "narrative voice in 'Soldier's Home' says 11 times 'He did not want,' 6 times, with part of a seventh, on one page; 'he liked' occurs 13 times in 3 pages, with the pattern 'he liked' 6 times on one page, one 'he . . . liked' on the next, followed 4 times by 'he liked' and twice by 'he . . . liked' on the third" (*A Concordance,* ix). Paul Smith feels that Hemingway's style regresses here "to the styles of Gertrude Stein and Sherwood Anderson—almost as if he had not yet written 'Indian Camp'" (*A Reader's Guide,* 71).

9. See Paul Smith for sources of this image (*A Reader's Guide,* 70).

10. DeFalco feels that this is not an initiation story, but one in which the character attempts to sever all ties with the past (*The Hero,* 142). See also John J. Roberts, "In Defense of Krebs," 515–18; cf. Robert W. Lewis, Jr., "Hemingway's Concept of Sport in 'Soldier's Home,'" *Rendezvous* 5 (Winter 1970): 19–27.

11. Louis Broussard sees "Mr. and Mrs. Elliot" as a satire on *The Waste Land,* "and as such a rejection of the despair prevalent in contemporary art and epitomized in the early poetry of Eliot." Just as the fisher-king of Eliot's dead land is sterile, so the husband and wife in Hemingway's are unable to procreate. Broussard characterizes this story as "a vindictive piece" ("Hemingway as a Literary Critic," *The Arizona Quarterly* 20 [1964]: 197, 198).

As I noted in the introduction to this study, Lynn argues that Hemingway's changing the title of the story from "Mr. and Mrs. Smith" to "Mr. and Mrs. Elliot" "did not, once again, have anything to do with mercy, but stemmed rather from his habitual uncertainty about how to spell T. S. Eliot's name" (*Hemingway,* 246). In this story, Lynn points out, Hemingway was able to mock two poets, not only T. S. Eliot, but also Chard Powers Smith.

Paul Smith feels that "Mr. and Mrs. Elliot" has been ignored, and as "one of the best most sophisticated satires, in that it transcends its seminal gossip," it "deserves another reading" (*A Reader's Guide,* 79); see also Smith's "From the Waste Land to the Garden with the Elliots" in Beegel, *Neglected Short Fiction,* 123–29.

12. See for instance Carlos Baker (*The Writer as Artist*, 135–36), Sheridan Baker (*An Introduction and Interpretation*, 26), and Philip Young (*Reconsideration*, 178). For more detailed considerations of the story's symbology and for discussions of the wife's longing for motherhood and her husband's denial, see Hagopian, Holmsland, Lodge, Magee, Miller, Steinke, and Gertrude White. Joost and Brown draw parallels between the American wife in "Cat in the Rain" and the typist in Eliot's "Fire Sermon."

13. Item 320, Hemingway Collection, John F. Kennedy Library, Boston, Massachusetts.

14. On the other hand, Holmsland sees the cat as a "symbol around which the whole story centers. . . . Seen against the background of marital triteness and quest for a cat to compensate needs, it looms as a metaphor of the wife's deep, unfulfilled desires" ("Structuralism and Interpretation: Ernest Hemingway's 'Cat in the Rain,'" *English Studies* 67 [1986]: 223–24). DeFalco argues that Hemingway uses the cat as a "springboard for the expression of the basic needs of individuals" (*The Hero*, 158). Magee notes that the cat is a child surrogate ("Hemingway's 'Cat in the Rain,'" *Explicator* 26 [September 1967]: item 8); and Hagopian says the cat is a symbol of the child the wife wants ("Symmetry in 'Cat in the Rain,'" *College English* 24 [1962]: 232). Miller and Gertrude White, on the other hand, feel that the cat is more than a symbol of the child the wife wants—it is a symbol of the wife herself ("'Cat in the rain,'" *Linguistics in Literature* 1, no. 2 [1976]: 33; "We're All 'Cats in the Rain,'" *Fitzgerald/Hemingway Annual* [1978], 243). But Steinke insists that critics' "assertions about the cat not being a cat simply aren't convincing" ("Hemingway's 'Cat in the Rain,'" *Spectrum* 25, nos. 1, 2 [1983]: 39).

15. Bennett, "The Poor Kitty and the Padrone and the Tortoise-shell Cat in 'Cat in the Rain,'" *Hemingway Review* 8 (Fall 1988): 31.

16. Paul Smith notes the parallels between the American wife and the woman in Eliot's "The Game of Chess" who brushes out her hair ("Some Misconceptions of 'Out of Season,'" in *Critical Essays*, ed. Reynolds, 237). So does Grimes (*The Religious Design*, 8).

17. For discussions about point of view and structure in "Out of Season" see Paul R. Jackson, "Hemingway's 'Out of Season,'" *Hemingway Review* 1 (Fall 1981): 12–13; and Paul Smith, "Some Misconceptions of 'Out of Season.'"

Hemingway initially entitled the story "Before the Season," which suggests that a more favorable season has yet to come. Perhaps he changed the title to "Out of Season" to emphasize the feeling of displacement and alienation at this particularly low point in the sequence (Item 644, Hemingway Collection, John F. Kennedy Library, Boston, Massachusetts).

Both "Out of Season" and "My Old Man" were published in *Three Stories and Ten Poems* in 1923 and later incorporated into *In Our Time* in 1925. Since the stories in *In Our Time* do not appear in the order they were written, I again point out Hemingway's deliberate placement of them.

18. In a discussion of point of view, Paul R. Jackson explains that by repeating "young gentleman" throughout the story, Hemingway achieves satiric distancing and stresses Peduzzi's expectations ("Hemingway's 'Out of Season,'" 12–13). On the other hand, Paul Smith notes that "In the setting copy and the 1923 edition of *Three Stories and Ten Poems* 'young gentleman' is abbreviated to 'y.g.' randomly in 14 of 23 instances from the beginning of the Concordia scene to the story's end. Hemingway's abbreviation of the young gentleman was a deliberate satiric device, for at the point in the typescript when the young gentleman orders the three marsalas at the Concordia the typescript reads, '"Three marsalas,"' said the ~~young gentle~~ y.g. to the girl . . ." ("Some Misconceptions," 251 n. 13).

19. See Giovanni Cecchin for Peduzzi's identity ("Peduzzi Prototype," *Hemingway Review* 4 (Fall 1985): 54.

20. Paul Smith points out that "In nearly every passage something is misspoken or misunderstood" ("Some Misconceptions," 248).

21. Hemingway's typed addition of the word "mysteriously" to the typescript entitled "Before the Season" suggests his intent to emphasize an enigmatic tone at the beginning of the story. Also, his handwritten addition at the end of the typescript of the sentences, "It was wonderful. This was a great day after all. A wonderful day," echoes the line at the beginning of the story, "A wonderful day for trout," and intensifies the irony in the story: it is literarily a great day for trout fishing, but fishing is illegal on this day, and the circumstances involved in this outing—Peduzzi's need for money for alcohol, the young gentleman's and Tiny's argument—reveal that it's a terrible day to do anything; in fact, the outing is a disaster (Item 644, Hemingway Collection, John F. Kennedy Library, Boston, Massachusetts).

22. Dix McComas notes that through the character of Peduzzi, "The recent war is present . . . Drunken and garbed in his dirty uniform now reduced to selling frogs, spreading manure, and preying on tourists, he is the prototypical veteran, and victim of the war" ("The Geography of Ernest Hemingway's 'Out of Season,'" *Hemingway Review* 3 [Fall 1984]: 49, n. 8).

23. Kenneth G. Johnston, among other critics, argues that the young gentleman's and Tiny's discussion at lunch had to do with abortion ("Hemingway's 'Out of Season' and the Psychology of Errors," *Literature and Psychology* [1971]: 41–46).

24. Grimes, *The Religious Design*, 27.

25. McComas, "The Geography of Ernest Hemingway's 'Out of Season,'" 49.

Hemingway added by hand on the typescript ("Before the Season"): "It was brown and muddy. Off on the right there was a dump heap." By doing so, he emphasizes the feeling of desolation and disaster in the story (Item 644, Hemingway Collection, John F. Kennedy Library, Boston, Massachusetts).

26. Hemingway, *Selected Letters*, 181.

On the other hand, Paul Smith argues that "Hemingway remembered Peduzzi's suicide as 'the real end of the story' which he deliberately left out in obedience to his new-found theory" [the theory of omission] ("Some Misconceptions," 238).

See *A Moveable Feast*, 74–75, for Hemingway's reference to his omitting the "real end of the story" of "Out of Season." Carlos Baker was the first to note Hemingway's new narrative technique in this story (*A Life Story*, 109).

For discussions about Hemingway's omissions in other works, see Paul Smith, "Hemingway's Early Manuscripts: The Theory and Practice of Omission," *Journal of Modern Literature* 10 (Fall 1983): 268–88, and Julian Smith, "Hemingway and the Thing Left Out," *Journal of Modern Literature* 1 (Fall 1970–71): 169–82; reprinted in *Five Decades*, ed. Wagner, 188–200. See also Susan F. Beegel, *Hemingway's Craft of Omission*. For a study of Hemingway's "concealments," see Gerry Brenner, *Concealments*.

27. Stephens gives "Christmas on the Roof of the World" (*Toronto Star Weekly*, December 1922, p. 19) as a nonfiction correlative (*Hemingway's Nonfiction*, 365).

28. Barbara Sanders' linguistical examination of "Cross-Country Snow" looks closely at the language and certain patterns the language reveals, but does not discuss its poetic technique ("Linguistic analysis of 'Cross-Country Snow,'" *Linguistics and Literature* 1, no. 2 [1978]: 43–52).

Paul Smith notes that "the story's structure—a significant scene or event, a dialogue between two friends drinking, an implicit subject rather abruptly introduced and then not quite dismissed with a variety of vinous wit—is one Hemingway had recently followed in greater detail in 'The Three-Day Blow' and used again in the Burguete fishing scene in *The Sun Also Rises*" (*A Reader's Guide*, 83).

29. See Kenneth G. Johnston, "'Cross-Country Snow': Freedom and Responsibility"

(*The Tip of the Iceberg: Hemingway and the Short Story* [Greenwood, Fl.: Penkevill, 1987], 63–68) for further discussion of the themes of freedom and responsibility.

30. As Flora argues, Nick and George are "bidding adieu to the period of youth and irresponsibility that skiing partly symbolizes, and both of them know it" (*Hemingway's Nick Adams*, 195).

31. Reynolds points out that "My Old Man" is Hemingway's "first story in which the father disappoints the son," ("Hemingway's 'My Old Man': Turf Days in Paris," in *Hemingway in Italy*, ed. Lewis, 102).

Hemingway responded to Fitzgerald's rating of "My Old Man":

> Why did you leave out My Old Man? That's a good story, always seemed to me, though not the thing I'm shooting for. It belongs to another categorie [sic] along with the full fight story and the 50 Grand. The kind that are easy for me to write. (*Selected Letters*, 180)

"My Old Man" has often been regarded as an imitation of Sherwood Anderson's "I Want to Know Why." See Paul P. Somers, Jr., "The Mark of Sherwood Anderson on Hemingway: A Look at the Text" for a discussion of Anderson's influence on Hemingway (*South Atlantic Quarterly* 73 [1974]: 487–503). See Paul Smith for the dissimilarities in the stories (*A Reader's Guide*, 12).

32. Krause, "Hemingway's 'My Old Man,'" *Explicator* 1962, Item 39; reprinted in *Critical Essays*, ed. Reynolds, 252–53.

33. Grimes, *The Religious Design*, 49.

34. Cf. Gerry Brenner, *Concealments*, 9ff.

35. Hemingway wrote to Edward J. O'Brien on September 12, 1924 that "Big Two-Hearted River"

> is much better than anything I've done. What I've been doing is trying to do country so you don't remember the words after you read it but actually have the country. It is hard because to do it you have to see the country all complete all the time you write and not just have a romantic feeling about it. (*Selected Letters*, 123)

Once again, Hemingway writes about his preoccupation with conveying states of feeling.

36. Rovit and Brenner, *Ernest Hemingway*, 66.

One of the most closely examined of all Hemingway's stories, "Big Two-Hearted River" has received numerous interpretations. The following are perhaps the most noted: Cowley and Carlos Baker focus on the ritualistic concerns of the story; Young (*Reconsideration*), Rovit and Brenner, and DeFalco give psychological interpretations of the story; Adair compares the story's "interior landscape and symbolic action" with other Hemingway works to show that "Nick is trying to get the past 'straight' in his head, but in disguised terms" ("Landscapes of the Mind: 'Big Two-Hearted River,'" *College Literature* 4 [1977]: 144–45); P. V. Anderson deals with Nick's loss of confidence; Sheridan Baker sees it as an indirect acknowledgement of Hemingway's wounding at Fossalta; Flora (*Hemingway's Nick Adams*, 179–80) and Debra A. Moddelmog ("The Unifying Consciousness of a Divided Nick Adams as Author of *In Our Time*," 591–610) point out that "Big Two-Hearted River" is as much a "marriage" story as it is a "war" story; James L. Green examines Hemingway's style and says it parallels the idea of emotional control of pain; Howard L. Hannum notes the parallels between the story and an ode ("Soldier's Home: Immersion Therapy"); Korn argues that the prose movement in the story parallels Nick's emotional movement; Stein says that Hemingway writes in the tradition of Eliot's *Four Quartets* and focuses on the cycle of exile and return ("Ritual in Hemingway's 'Big Two-Hearted River,'" 561); and Wirt Williams sees "Big Two-Hearted River" as "the cumulative statement of the young-man chronicle, and it is thus crucial within the apparatus of *In Our Time.*" Williams further sees it as an "imagistic parable of a spiritual journey from desolation to renewal," rising from "the thematic and tonal low of 'My Old Man' to a reconciliation between man and the world." Williams sees several modes in the story: the literal account of the fishing trip; a communion fable of reaffirmation of personal faith in life; and "the provisional ordering of the demi-tragic experience of the book" (*The Tragic Art*, 37).

Jackson J. Benson sums up criticism about the story by pointing out two themes around which critics focus their discussions: "the repudiation of Malcolm Cowley's 'nightmare at noonday' and Philip Young's 'a terrible panic just under control' "; and "a growing interest in the influence on Hemingway of Cezanne's paintings. These two themes come together in the assertion in several articles that the story is essentially a nature story after all, a sharply realized aesthetic experience" ("Criticism of the Short Stories: The Neglected and the Oversaturated—An Editorial," *The Hemingway Review* 8 [Spring 1989]: 32).

37. Baker, *The Writer as Artist*, 122.

38. Frank B. Kyle, "Parallel and Complementary Themes in Hemingway's Big Two-Hearted River Stories and 'The Battler,' " 299.

39. Hemingway says, "The story was about coming back from the war but there was no mention of war in it" (*A Moveable Feast*, 76).

The most popular version of the war trauma theory in "Big Two-Hearted River" is Philip Young's (*Reconsideration*, 43–48). See note 37 for other interpretations.

40. Flora, *Hemingway's Nick Adams*, 147.

41. See Sheridan Baker, *An Introduction and Interpretation*, 152.

42. Elizabeth J. Wells, "A Statistical Analysis of the Prose Style of Ernest Hemingway: 'Big Two-Hearted River,' " in *The Short Stories of Ernest Hemingway: Critical Essays*, ed. Jackson L. Benson [Durham, N.C.: Duke University Press, 1975], 134.

43. Keith Carabine notes that Hemingway emphasizes satisfaction in the story, not panic (" 'Big Two-Hearted River': A Reinterpretation," *Hemingway Review* 1 [Fall 1982]: 44).

44. The swamp like the story itself has received a number of interpretations: Adair notes that it is "emblematic of the lower depths of Nick's conscious mind, which he is not ready to fish" ("Landscapes," 144); Sheridan Baker argues that the swamp represents the darkness of death (*An Introduction and Interpretation*, 154); Frank B. Kyle sees the swamp as chaos, but combined with the safety the camp fire represents, the two represent the reality of human existence ("Parallel and Complementary Themes in Hemingway's Big Two-Hearted River Stories and 'The Battler,' " 300); a number of critics, among them Richard B. Hovey (*Hemingway: The Inward Terrain*), see the swamp as having sexual and female associations; James Twitchell ("The Swamp in Hemingway's 'Big Two-Hearted River' ") says there is no swamp, not outside Nick's imagination, that is; and, finally, Philip Young feels that the swamp represents the "bad place," the recurring memory of Fossalta and Nick must not go there (*Reconsideration*, 47).

45. Young, *Reconsideration*, 46–47.

46. Carabine, " 'Big Two-Hearted River': A Reinterpretation," 42.

47. See Jack F. Stewart for a discussion of the Christian allusions in "Big Two-Hearted River" ("Christian Allusions in 'Big Two-Hearted River,' " *Studies in Short Fiction* 15 [1978]: 194–96). Flora also notes the reference to the Four Gospels, but he sees the story having the rhythm of Genesis (*Hemingway's Nick Adams*, 164).

48. Sheridan Baker, *An Introduction and Interpretation*, 153.

49. Flora also sees Nick's crawling out of the tent as birth (*Hemingway's Nick Adams*, 164).

50. See Items 96 (typescript) and 274 (manuscript), Hemingway Collection, John F. Kennedy Library, Boston, Massachusetts. See Bernard Oldsley for a discussion of these

drafts (*Ernest Hemingway: The Papers of a Writer*, ed. Bernard Oldsley [New York: Garland, 1981], 37–62).

As Hemingway wrote to Robert McAlmon on 15 November 1924,

> I have decided that all that mental converstion in the long fishing story is the shit and have cut it all out. The last nine pages. The story was interrupted you know just when I was going good and I could never get back into it and finish it. I got a hell of a shock when I realized how bad it was and that shocked me back into the river again and I've finished it off the way it ought to have been all along. Just the straight fishing. (*Selected Letters*, 133)

51. See Item 279, Hemingway Collection, John F. Kennedy Library, Boston, Massachusetts.

Chapter 5. *A Farewell to Arms* (1929)

1. Hemingway, *Death in the Afternoon*, 122.

2. While *The Sun Also Rises*, like *In Our Time*, is concerned in part with violence and bullfighting, post war expatriates, loss of love, honor, and courage, its bitter detached narrator and its focus on "the cultural crisis of its time" (Rovit and Brenner, *Ernest Hemingway*, 139) make its lyrical structure less dynamic than A *Farewell to Arms* and even less like *In Our Time* than A *Farewell to Arms*.

3. Bernard Oldsley discusses the elements Hemingway used from "Chapter VI," "Chapter VII," "A Very Short Story," "Now I Lay Me," and "In Another Country" to develop the novel:

> (1) the initial wounding of the protagonist (who is then neurotic, insomniac, and in need of therapy), (2) the sacred-profane theme centering on prayer and the priest, as well as true love and whorehouses; (3) the trio of characters consisting of an American officer, a girl (American, British, Italian), and an Italian officer; (4) the question of marriage; and (5) the ironic theme of "a separate peace" (*Hemingway's Hidden Craft: The Writing of A Farewell to Arms* [University Park: Pennsylvania State University Press, 1979], 54).

4. Schneider notes that, "the typical procedure, as in lyric poetry, is to intensify the dominant emotion by means of a simple contrast of emotions" ("Hemingway's A *Farewell to Arms*: The Novel as Pure Poetry," 256).

While Oldsley does not discuss tonal contrasts in A *Farewell to Arms*, he does discuss the "tone" as "that of the disappointed, or 'ruined,' romantic." Oldsley further notes that this tone is appropriate "for a book that is presented as a battleground where we are privileged to view the immemorial struggle between man's idealization of the world and his reluctant acceptance of brute fact." Oldsley then discusses how that struggle is presented through "oppositional pairs" (*Hidden Craft*, 30).

5. A number of commentators identify the lyrical character of A *Farewell to Arms*. Among them, Schneider discusses A *Farewell to Arms* as "pure poetry" ("The Novel as Pure Poetry," 283–96). Charles R. Anderson examines a number of lyric passages that are submerged beneath what he calls a tough, spare, secular prose. These passages, according to Anderson, reveal the spiritual dimension of Hemingway's prose ("Hemingway's Other Style," in *Ernest Hemingway: Critiques of Four Major Novels*, ed. Carlos Baker [New York: Scribner's, 1962], 41–46).

Other discussions of the structure of the novel include H. K. Russell's which discusses the novel's structure as that of a five-act Elizabethan tragedy ("The Catharsis in A *Farewell to Arms*," *Modern Fiction Studies* 1 [1955]: 25–30). R. W. West argues that the form of the novel resembles a drama, each book "composed of five separate series of scenes, and each scene is broken into sections which might be likened to stage directions and dialogue" ("A Farewell to Arms," in *The Art of Modern Fiction*, ed. R. W. Stallman and Ray B. West [New York: Holt, 1949], 622–33). More recently Michael S. Reynolds notes a pattern of the "seasonal cycle of the land and the seasonal cycle of war" (*Hemingway's First War: The Making of A Farewell to Arms* [Princeton: Princeton University Press, 1976], 263).

6. Using Baker's biography of Hemingway, Oldsley distills Hemingway's involvement in World War I and draws parallels to the situation in A *Farewell to Arms*. Oldsley concludes his brief account of Hemingway's involvement in the war by saying that

> Hemingway did *not* have the love-of-his-life affair that Lieutenant Henry does. He was *not* a combat hero, and did *not* shoot anyone. He was *not* involved in the Caporetto retreat. He did *not* desert criminally, if justifiably; and he did *not* flee to Switzerland. He was *not* the common law husband of a beautiful Scotch woman, was *not* the father of her stillborn child. (*Hidden Craft*, 45)

7. For a discussion of Frederic Henry's memories of Catherine, see James Nagel, "Catherine Barkley and Retrospective Narration in a *Farewell to Arms*," in *Six Decades*, ed. Wagner, 171–85. In "The Dantean Perspective in Hemingway's A *Farewell to Arms*," Arnold E. Davidson notes that there are two varieties of retrospective narration in A *Farewell to Arms*: "first person retrospective clear," in which the narrator understands what he has experienced; and "first person retrospective confused," in which the narrator tells his story in an attempt to clarify his own understanding of what has happened. Davidson further notes that a combination of these two varieties of narration results in a "complex double vision," in which experiences are "emotionally relived but objectively related" (*The Journal of Narrative Technique* 3 [1973]: 123–24).

8. Hemingway, A *Farewell to Arms* (New York: Scribner's, 1929). Subsequent references to this edition will appear in the text as *FTA* with the appropriate page number.

9. Among the many discussions of this passage are Carlos Baker, *The Writer as Artist* ("The Mountain and the Plain"); Walker Gibson, *Tough, Sweet, and Stuffy: An Essay on Modern American Prose Style*, 28–42; Oldsley, *Hidden Craft*, 63–68; and Reynolds, *Hemingway's First War*, 55–57.

10. Reynolds argues that Hemingway's revisions to this passage add rhythm rather than introduce new detail. This supports the idea that Hemingway was striving to create strong images (*Hemingway's First War*, 57).

11. See Reynolds for the history of the real military campaign (*Hemingway's First War*, 87–135).

12. According to Reynolds, King Victor Emmanuel lived in Udine in 1915 and made daily visits to the front to encourage the troops (*Hemingway's First War*, 91).

13. Schneider notes that in this novel "characters exist for the sake of the emotion and, as in lyric poems, need not be three-dimensional. Indeed, any full and vivid particularization of characters is likely to work against the dominant emotion, for when a character is complex and fully realized, he is scarcely able to maintain a single, fixed emotion or state of mind" ("The Novel as Pure Poetry," 254).

See Carlos Baker, *The Writer as Artist*, "The Mountain and the Plain," for the "emblematic people" which give the novel symbolic effects.

14. Ganzel, "A *Farewell to Arms*: The Danger of Imagination," *Sewanee Review* 79 (1971): 590.

15. Wilson, *The Wound and the Bow* (New York: Farrar, 1947), 222.

16. Numerous commentators have noted the idea of entrapment in the novel, in particular, Ray B. West, "A Farewell to Arms."

17. West, "The Biological Trap," in *Critiques of Four Major Novels*, ed. Carlos Baker, 33.

18. Malcolm Cowley, on the other hand, characterizes Frederic's plunge into the river as a baptism, following which Frederic sees more clearly the realities of war.

19. For discussions about doom and entrapment and the motif of rain, see especially Carlos Baker, *The Writer as Artist*, 8; Grimes, *The Religious Design*, 104; Young, *Reconsideration*, 92; and James F. Light, "The Religion of Death in *A Farewell to Arms*," in *Critiques of Four Major Novels*, 43–44.

20. Oldsley, *Hidden Craft*, 26.

21. Schneider, "The Novel as Pure Poetry," 264.

22. See Oldsley for a discussion of Hemingway's use of this lyric and Peele's "A Farewell to Arms," (*Hidden Craft*, 33).

23. In an interview with George Plimpton Hemingway indicated that he revised the end of the novel thirty-nine times; there are, however, forty-one revisions of the end of the novel in the Hemingway Collection at the John F. Kennedy Library.

24. Flora compares Frederic's recollection of the ants on the log to Nick's recalling Hopkins in "Big Two-Hearted River" (*Hemingway's Nick Adams*, 166n).

Ray B. West points out that, "The relationship of this parable to Catherine's predicament is unmistakable. For her there is likewise no messiah to come to the rescue. Death is the end of it, and the only value in death is man's knowledge of it" ("The Biological Trap," 35).

James Nagel writes:

> The famous "ants" passage, in which, in the past, Frederic observed ants coming out of a burning log and dropping off into the fire, most likely represents thinking at the time of the action when he would long for the ability to be a "messiah" and control death, thus saving Catherine. Frederic relates the events of this final episode without interpretation, suggesting that the facts speak for themselves and also, perhaps, that the recapitulation of the most painful episode of his life is almost too much for him, that his emotions can be controlled only in restraint. In this sense he is much less moved by his own physical wounding, about which he seems free to assess and evaluate without fear of the feelings involved; it is Catherine's death that he handles with emotional caution. ("Catherine Barkley and Retrospective Narration in *A Farewell to Arms*," 182)

25. Schneider, "The Novel as Pure Poetry," 253–54.

26. Brenner, *Concealments*, 41.

27. Gelfant, "Language as a Moral Code in *A Farewell to Arms*," *Modern Fiction Studies* (1975): 174.

28. Gelfant, "Language as a Moral Code," 175.

29. "If two people love each other there can be no happy end to it" (Hemingway, *Death in the Afternoon*, 122).

30. Stanley Cooperman points out that the

> Technological warfare eliminated the battlefield as a resource for ritual, while flabby rhetoric and political opportunism eliminated the temple. Only love remained, but very briefly and very deceptively: Catherine, after all, shattered Frederic Henry's ritual by dying quite without his consent. ("Death and Cojones: Hemingway's *A Farewell to Arms*," *The South Atlantic Quarterly* 63 [1964]: 88)

31. Among those who feel that there is little hope at the end of the novel are Brenner who feels that Frederic has little reason to live once he has written his story (*Concealments*, 41) and William A. Glasser, who insists Frederic is defeated ("A Farewell to Arms," *Sewanee Review* 74 [1966]: 465).

32. Davidson, among others, shares this point of view.

Works Cited

Adair, William. "Ernest Hemingway and the Poetics of Loss." *College Literature* 10 (1983): 294–306.

———. "Landscapes of the Mind: 'Big Two-Hearted River.'" *College Literature* 4 (1977): 144–51. Reprint. *Critical Essays on Hemingway's In Our Time*, edited by Michael S. Reynolds, 260–67. Boston: G. K. Hall, 1983.

Anderson, Charles R. "Hemingway's Other Style." In *Ernest Hemingway: Critiques of Four Major Novels*, edited by Carlos Baker, 41–46. New York: Scribner's, 1962.

Anderson, Paul Victor. "Nick's Story in Hemingway's 'Big Two-Hearted River.'" *Studies in Short Fiction* 7 (Fall 1970): 564–72.

Arnold, Matthew. "Dover Beach." In *The New Oxford Book of English Verse 1250–1950*, edited by Helen Gardner. New York: Oxford University Press, 1972.

Astro, Richard and Jackson J. Benson. *Hemingway: In Our Time*. Corvallis: Oregon State University Press, 1974.

Baker, Carlos. *Ernest Hemingway: A Life Story*. 1969. Reprint. New York: Scribner's, 1988.

———, ed. *Ernest Hemingway: Critiques of Four Major Novels*. New York: Scribner's, 1962.

———, ed. *Ernest Hemingway: Selected Letters 1917–1961*. New York: Scribner's, 1981.

———, ed. *Hemingway and His Critics: An International Anthology*. New York: Hill, 1961.

———. *Hemingway: The Writer as Artist*. 4th ed. Princeton: Princeton University Press, 1972.

Baker, Sheridan. *Ernest Hemingway: An Introduction and Interpretation*. New York: Holt, 1967.

Baldeshwiler, Eileen. "The Lyric Short Story: The Sketch of a History." *Studies in Short Fiction* 6 (1969): 443–53.

Barba, Harry. "The Three Levels of 'The End of Something.'" *West Virginia Philological Papers* 7 (June 1970): 76–80.

Bardacke, Theodore. "Hemingway's Women." In *Ernest Hemingway: The Man and His Work*, edited by John K. M. McCaffrey, 340–51. New York: World, 1950.

Beegel, Susan F., ed. *Hemingway's Craft of Omission: Four Manuscript Examples*. Ann Arbor, Mich.: UMI Research Press, 1988.

———, ed. *Hemingway's Neglected Short Fiction: New Perspectives*. Ann Arbor, Mich.: UMI Research Press, 1989.

Bennett, Warren. "The Poor Kitty and the Padrone and the Tortoise-shell Cat in 'Cat in the Rain.'" *Hemingway Review* 8 (1988): 26–36.

Benson, Jackson L. "Criticism of the Short Stories: The Neglected and the Oversaturated—An Editorial." *The Hemingway Review* 8 (Spring 1989): 30–35.

————. *Hemingway: The Writer's Art of Self-Defense*. Minneapolis: University of Minnesota Press, 1969.

————. "Patterns of Connection and Their Development in Hemingway's *In Our Time*." *Rendezvous* 5 (1970): 37–52.

————, ed. *The Short Stories of Ernest Hemingway: Critical Essays*. Durham, N.C.: Duke University Press, 1975.

Bernard, Kenneth. "Hemingway's 'Indian Camp.'" *Studies in Short Fiction* 2, no. 1 (1965): 291.

Bigsby, C. W. E. "Hemingway: The Recoil from History." In *The Twenties: Fiction, Poetry, Drama*, edited by Warren French, 203–213. Deland, Fla.: Everett/Edwards, 1975.

Brasch, James D. and Joseph Sigman. *Hemingway's Library: A Composite Record*. New York: Garland, 1981.

Brenner, Gerry. *Concealments in Hemingway's Works*. Columbus: Ohio State University Press, 1983.

Bridgman, Richard. "Ernest Hemingway." From *The Colloquial Style in America*, 195–230. New York: Oxford University Press, 1966.

Broussard, Louis. "Hemingway as a Literary Critic." *The Arizona Quarterly* 20 (1964), 197–204.

Bruccoli, Matthew J. *Ernest Hemingway's Apprenticeship. Oak Park: 1916–17*. Washington, D.C.: Microcard Editions, 1971.

Burhans, Clinton S., Jr. "The Complex Unity of *In Our Time*." *Modern Fiction Studies* 14 (Fall 1968): 313–28.

Carabine, Keith. "'Big Two-Hearted River': A Re-interpretation." *Hemingway Review* 1 (Fall 1982): 39–44.

————. "Hemingway's *In Our Time*: An Appreciation." *Fitzgerald/Hemingway Annual* (1979): 301–26.

————. "A Pretty Good Unity": A Study of Sherwood Anderson's 'Winesburg, Ohio' and Ernest Hemingway's *In Our Time*. Diss. Yale University, 1978.

Carter, Ronald. "Style and Interpretation in Hemingway's 'Cat in the Rain.'" In *Language and Literature*, edited by Ronald Carter, 65–80. Boston: Allen and Unwin, 1982.

Cecchin, Giovanni. "Peduzzi Prototype." *Hemingway Review* 4 (Fall 1985): 54.

Colvert, James B. "Ernest Hemingway's Morality in Action." *American Literature* 27 (1955): 372–85.

Cooperman, Stanley. "Death and *Cojones*: Hemingway's *A Farewell to Arms*." *The South Atlantic Quarterly* 63 (1964): 85–92.

Cowley, Malcolm. "Hemingway at Midnight," *New Republic*, 14 Aug. 1944: 190–95. Reprint. *Portable Hemingway*, edited by Malcolm Cowley, vii–xxiv. New York: Viking, 1945.

————. "Hemingway's Wound—And Its Consequences for American Literature." *Georgia Review* 38, no. 2 (1984): 223–39.

————. *A Second Flowering: Works and Days of the Lost Generation*. New York: Viking, 1956.

Cox, James M. "*In Our Time*: The Essential Hemingway." *Southern Humanities Review* 22 (Fall 1988): 305–20.

Davidson, Arnold E. "The Dantean Perspective in Hemingway's A *Farewell to Arms.*" *The Journal of Narrative Technique* 3 (1973): 121–30.

Davis, Robert Murray. "Hemingway's 'The Doctor and the Doctor's Wife.' " *Explicator* 23 (September 1966): item 1.

———. " 'If You Did Not Go Forward': Process and Stasis in A *Farewell to Arms.*" *Studies in the Novel* 2 (1970): 305–11.

DeFalco, Joseph. *The Hero in Hemingway's Short Stories.* Pittsburgh: University of Pittsburgh Press, 1963.

Derounian, Kathryn Zabelle. *Papers of the Bibliographic Society of America* 1982. Reprint. *Critical Essays on Ernest Hemingway's In Our Time,* edited by Michael S. Reynolds, 61–65. Boston: G. K. Hall, 1983.

Donaldson, Scott. " 'A Very Short Story' as Therapy." In *Hemingway's Neglected Short Fiction: New Perspectives,* edited by Susan F. Beegel, 99–105. Ann Arbor, Mich.: UMI Research Press, 1989.

Dupre, Roger. "Hemingway's *In Our Time.*" Diss. St. John's University, 1979.

Eliot, T. S. *Collected Poems: 1909–1962.* New York: Harcourt, 1930.

———. *Selected Essays.* New York: Harcourt, 1932.

Evans, Robert. "Hemingway and the Pale Cast of Thought." *American Literature* 38 (May 1966): 161–76.

Fenton, Charles A. *The Apprenticeship of Ernest Hemingway: The Early Years.* New York: Farrar, 1954. Reprint. New York: Viking, 1958; New York: Octagon, 1975.

Fitts, Bill D. " 'The Battler': Lexical Foregrounding in Hemingway." *Language and Literature* 7, nos. 1–3 (1982): 81–92.

Flora, Joseph M. *Hemingway's Nick Adams.* Baton Rouge: Louisiana State University Press, 1982.

Fox, Stephen D. "Hemingway's 'The Doctor and the Doctor's Wife.' " *The Arizona Quarterly* 29 (1973): 19–25.

Freedman, Ralph. "Nature and Forms of the Lyrical Novel." In *Four Modes: A Rhetoric of Modern Fiction,* edited by James M. Mellard, 372–83. New York: Macmillan, 1973.

Fulkerson, Richard. "The Biographical Fallacy and 'The Doctor and the Doctor's Wife.' " *Studies in Short Fiction* 16 (Winter 1971): 61–65.

Gajdusek, Robert E. "Dubliners in Michigan: Joyce's Presence in Hemingway's *In Our Time.*" *Hemingway Review* 2 (1982): 48–61.

Ganzel, Dewey. "A *Farewell to Arms:* The Danger of Imagination." *Sewanee Review* 79 (1971): 576–97.

Gelfant, Blanche. "Language as a Moral Code in A *Farewell to Arms.*" *Modern Fiction Studies* (1975): 173–76.

Georgiannis, Nicholas. "Nick Adams on the Road: 'The Battler' as Hemingway's Man On the Hill." In *Critical Essays on Ernest Hemingway's In Our Time,* edited by Michael S. Reynolds, 176–88. Boston: G. K. Hall, 1983.

Gerstenberger, Donna. "The Waste Land in A *Farewell to Arms.*" *Modern Language Notes* 76 (1961): 24–25.

Gibb, Robert. "He Made Him Up: 'Big Two-Hearted River' as Doppelganger." *Hemingway Notes* (Fall 1979): 20–24. Reprint. *Critical Essays on Ernest Hemingway's In Our Time,* edited by Michael S. Reynolds, 254–59. Boston: G. K. Hall, 1983.

Gibson, Walker. *Tough, Sweet, and Stuffy: An Essay on Modern American Prose Style.* Bloomington: Indiana University Press, 1966.

Glasser, William A. "A Farewell to Arms." *Sewanee Review* 74 (1966): 453–59.

Goodman, Paul. "The Sweet Style of Ernest Hemingway." *The New York Review of Books* 17 (11), 30 Dec. 1971, 27–28. Reprint. *Ernest Hemingway: Five Decades of Criticism*, edited by Linda W. Wagner, 153–60. Port Washington, N.Y.: National, 1980.

Graham, John. "Ernest Hemingway: The Meaning of Style." *Modern Fiction Studies* 6 (1960–61): 298–313. Reprint. *Studies in A Farewell to Arms*, compiled by John Graham, 88–105. Charles E. Merrill Studies. Columbus, Ohio: Merrill, 1971.

Grebstein, Sheldon Norman. *Hemingway's Craft*. Carbondale & Edwardsville, Ill.: Southern Illinois University Press, 1973.

Green, James L. "Symbolic Sentences in 'Big Two-Hearted River.'" *Modern Fiction Studies* 14 (1968): 307–12.

Griffin, Peter. *Along with Youth: Hemingway the Early Years*. New York: Oxford University Press, 1985.

———. "The Young Hemingway: Three Unpublished Stories." *The New York Times Magazine*, 18 August 1985, Sec. 6, 15.

Grimes, Larry E. *The Religious Design of Hemingway's Early Fiction*. Ann Arbor, Mich.: UMI Research Press, 1985.

Groseclose, Barbara S. "Hemingway's 'The Revolutionist': An Aid to Interpretation." *Modern Fiction Studies* 17 (1971): 565–70.

Gurko, Leo. *Ernest Hemingway and the Pursuit of Heroism*. New York: Crowell, 1968.

Hagemann, E. R. "A Collation, with Commentary, of the Five Texts of the Chapters in Hemingway's *In Our Time*, 1923–28." *The Papers of the Bibliographical Society of America* 73 (1979): 443–58. Reprint. *Critical Essays on Ernest Hemingway's In Our Time*, edited by Michael S. Reynolds, 38–51. Boston: G. K. Hall, 1983.

———. "Only Let the Story End as Soon as Possible": Time-and-History in Ernest Hemingway's *In Our Time*." *Modern Fiction Studies* (1980): 255–62. Reprint. *Critical Essays on Ernest Hemingway's In Our Time*, edited by Michael S. Reynolds, 52–60. Boston: G. K. Hall, 1983.

———. "Word-Count and Statistical Survey of the Chapters in Ernest Hemingway's *In Our Time*." *Literary Research Newsletter* 5 (1980): 21–30.

Hagopian, John V. "Symmetry in 'Cat in the Rain.'" *College English* 24 (Dec. 1962): 220–22. Reprint. *Short Stories of Ernest Hemingway: Critical Essays*, edited by Jackson L. Benson, 230–32. Durham, N.C.: Duke University Press, 1975.

Halliday, E. M. "Hemingway's Ambiguity: Symbolism and Irony." *American Literature* 28 (1956): 1–22. Reprint. *Hemingway: A Collection of Critical Essays*, edited by Robert P. Weeks, 52–71. Englewood Cliffs, N.J.: Prentice-Hall, 1962.

———. "Hemingway's *In Our Time*." *Explicator* 7 (1949): item 35.

Handy, William J. *Modern Fiction: A Formalist Approach*. London: Feffer & Simons, 1971.

———. "Toward a Formalist Criticism of Fiction." In *Four Modes: A Rhetoric of Modern Fiction*, edited by James M. Mellard, 303–9. New York: Macmillan, 1973.

Hanneman, Audre. *Ernest Hemingway: A Comprehensive Bibliography*. Princeton: Princeton University Press, 1967.

Hannum, Howard L. "Nick Adams and the Search for Light." *Studies in Short Fiction* 23 (1986): 9–18.

———. "Soldier's Home: Immersion Therapy and Lyric Pattern in 'Big Two-Hearted River.'" *Hemingway Review* 3 (Spring 1984): 2–13.

Hanrahan, Gene Z., ed. *The Wild Years: Ernest Hemingway.* New York: Dell, 1962.

Hasbany, Richard. "The Shock of Vision: An Imagist Reading of *In Our Time.*" In *Ernest Hemingway: Five Decades of Criticism*, edited by Linda W. Wagner, 224–40. Ann Arbor: Michigan University Press, 1973.

Hays, Peter L. *A Concordance to Hemingway's In Our Time* Boston: G. K. Hall, 1990.

———. "Hemingway and the Fisher King." *University Review* 32 (1966): 225–28.

Hemingway, Ernest. "The Art of the Short Story." *The Paris Review* 23 (1981): 85–102.

———. *By-Line: Ernest Hemingway. Selected Articles and Dispatches of Four Decades.* Edited by William White. New York: Scribner's, 1967.

———. *Death in the Afternoon.* New York: Scribner's, 1933.

———. *Ernest Hemingway: Selected Letters, 1917–1961.* Edited by Carlos Baker. New York: Scribner's, 1981.

———. *Ernest Hemingway's Apprenticeship.* Edited by Matthew J. Bruccoli. Washington, D.C.: Microcard, 1971.

———. *A Farewell to Arms.* New York: Scribner's, 1929.

———. "Homage to Ezra." *This Quarter* 1, no. 1 (1925): 221–25.

———. "In Our Time." *Little Review* 1923.

———. *in our time.* Paris: The Three Mountains Press, 1924.

———. *In Our Time.* New York: Scribner's, 1925.

———. "An Interview with Ernest Hemingway." With George Plimpton. *The Paris Review* 18 (1958): 60–89. Reprint. *Writers at Work: The Paris Review Interviews.* 2nd Series. Edited by George Plimpton. New York: Penguin, 1963.

———. *Men Without Women.* New York: Scribner's, 1927.

———. *A Moveable Feast.* New York: Scribner's, 1964.

———. *The Nick Adams Stories.* Preface by Philip Young. New York: Scribner's, 1972.

———. *The Short Stories of Ernest Hemingway.* New York: Scribner's, 1966.

———. *The Sun Also Rises.* New York: Scribner's, 1926.

———. *Three Stories and Ten Poems.* Paris: Contact Publishing Company, 1923.

———. *The Torrents of Spring.* New York: Scribner's, 1926.

———. Unpublished Manuscripts held at the John F. Kennedy Library in Boston, Massachusetts.

Hemingway, Mary. *How It Was.* New York: Knopf, 1976.

Hemphill, George. "Hemingway and James." *The Kenyon Review* 11 (1949): 50–60. Reprint. *Ernest Hemingway: The Man and His Work*, edited by John K. M. McCaffery, 329–39. New York: World, 1950.

Hoffman, Frederick J. "No Beginning and No End: Hemingway and Death." *Essays in Criticism* 3 (1953): 73–84.

Holmsland, Oddar. "Structuralism and Interpretation: Ernest Hemingway's 'Cat in the Rain.'" *English Studies* 67 (1986): 221–33.

Hotchner, A. E. *Papa Hemingway: A Personal Memoir by A. E. Hotchner.* New York: Random, 1966.

Hovey, Richard B. *Hemingway: The Inward Terrain.* Seattle: University of Washington Press, 1968.

Hunt, Anthony. "Another Turn for Hemingway's 'The Revolutionist': Sources and Meanings.'" *Fitzgerald/Hemingway Annual* (1977) 119–35. Reprint. *Critical Essays on*

Ernest Hemingway's In Our Time, edited by Michael S. Reynolds, 203–17. Boston: G. K. Hall, 1983.

Hurwitz, Harold M. "Hemingway's Tutor, Ezra Pound." *Modern Fiction Studies* 17 (1971–72): 469–82. Reprint. *Ernest Hemingway: Five Decades of Criticism,* edited by Linda W. Wagner, *Five Decades,* 8–21. Port Washington, N.Y.: National, 1980.

Jackson, Paul R. "Hemingway's 'Out of Season.'" *Hemingway Review* 1 (Fall 1981): 11–17.

Jain, S. P. *Hemingway: A Study of his Short Stories.* New Delhi: Arnold-Heinemann, 1985.

Johnson, David R. "'The Last Good Country': Again the End of Something." *Fitzgerald/ Hemingway Annual* (1979): 363–70.

Johnston, Kenneth G. "Hemingway and Mantegna: The Bitter Nail Holes." *The Journal of Narrative Technique* 1 (1971): 86–94.

———. "Hemingway's 'Out of Season' and the Psychology of Errors." *Literature and Psychology* 21 (November 1971): 41–46. Reprint. *Critical Essays on Ernest Hemingway's In Our Time,* edited by Michael S. Reynolds, 227–34. Boston: G. K. Hall, 1983.

———. "In the Beginning: Hemingway's 'Indian Camp.'" *Studies in Short Fiction* 15 (1978): 102–4.

———. "'Three-Day Blow': Tragicomic Aftermath of a Summer Romance." *Hemingway Review* 2 (Fall 1982): 21–25.

———. *The Tip of the Iceberg: Hemingway and the Short Story.* Greenwood, Fla.: Penkevill, 1987.

Joost, Nicholas and Alan Brown. "T. S. Eliot and Ernest Hemingway: A Literary Relationship." *Papers on Language and Literature* 14, no. 4 (1978): 425–49.

Junkins, Donald. "Hemingway's Contribution to American Poetry." *Hemingway Notes* 4 (Fall 1985): 18–23.

Kazin, Alfred. *On Native Grounds.* New York: Doubleday, 1942.

Killinger, John. *Hemingway and the Dead Gods: A Study in Existentialism.* Lexington: University of Kentucky Press, 1960.

Korn, Barbara. "Form and Idea in Hemingway's 'Big Two-Hearted River.'" *English Journal* 56 (1967): 979–81, 1014.

Krause, Sidney J. "Hemingway's 'My Old Man.'" *Explicator* (January 1962): item 39. Reprint. *Critical Essays on Ernest Hemingway's In Our Time,* edited by Michael S. Reynolds, 252–53. Boston: G. K. Hall, 1983.

Kruse, Horst H. "Ernest Hemingway's 'The End of Something': Its Independence As a Short Story And Its Place in the 'Education of Nick Adams.'" *Studies in Short Fiction* 4 (1967): 152–66.

Kyle, Frank B. "Parallel and Complementary Themes in Hemingway's Big Two-Hearted River Stories and 'The Battler." *Studies in Short Fiction* 16 (1979): 295–300.

Lawrence, D. H. *"In Our Time: A Review."* In *Phoenix.* New York: Viking, 1936.

Lebowitz, Alan. "Hemingway in Our Time." *Yale Review* 58 (1969): 321–41.

Lee, A. Robert, ed. *Ernest Hemingway: New Critical Essays.* Totowa, N.J.: Barnes, 1983.

Leigh, David J. *"In Our Time:* The Interchapters As Structural Guides to a Psychological Pattern." *Studies in Short Fiction* 12 (1975): 1–8.

Leiter, Louis H. "Neurol Projections in Hemingway's 'On the Quai at Smyrna.'" *Studies in Short Fiction* 5 (1968): 384–86.

Levin, Harry. "Observations on the Style of Ernest Hemingway." *Kenyon Review* 13 (1951): 581–609.

Lewis, Robert W., Jr. "Hemingway's Concept of Sport and 'Soldier's Home.'" *Rendezvous* 5 (Winter 1970): 19–27.

———, ed. *Hemingway in Italy and Other Essays*. New York: Praeger, 1990.

Light, James F. "The Religion of Death in *A Farewell to Arms*." *Modern Fiction Studies* 7 (1961) 169–73. Reprint. *Ernest Hemingway: Critiques of Four Major Novels*, edited by Carlos Baker, 39–40. New York: Scribner's, 1988.

Lodge, David. "Analysis and Interpretation of the Realist Text: A Pluralistic Approach to Ernest Hemingway's 'Cat in the Rain,'" *Poetics Today* 1 (1980): 5–19.

Lohani, Shreedhar Prasad. "The Narrator in Fiction: A Study of the Narrator's Presence in Joyce's *Dubliners* and Hemingway's *In Our Time*. Diss. Southern Illinois University, 1984.

Lowry, E. D. "Chaos and Cosmos in *In Our Time*." *Literature and Psychology* 26, no. 3 (1976): 108–17.

Luscher, Robert M. "The Short Story Sequence: An Open Book." In *Short Story Theory at a Crossroads*, edited by Susan Lohafer and Jo Ellyn Clarey, 148–167. Baton Rouge: Louisiana State University Press, 1989.

Lynn, Kenneth S. *Hemingway*. New York: Simon and Schuster, 1987.

Magee, John D. "Hemingway's 'Cat in the Rain.'" *Explicator* 26 (September 1967): item 8.

Mann, Susan Garland. *The Short Story Cycle: A Genre Companion and Reference Guide*. New York: Greenwood Press, 1989.

McCaffery, John K. M., ed. *Ernest Hemingway: The Man and His Work*. New York: World, 1950.

McComas, Dix. "The Geography of Ernest Hemingway's 'Out of Season.'" *Hemingway Review* 3 (Fall 1984): 46–49.

Mellard, James M., ed. *Four Modes: A Rhetoric of Modern Fiction*. New York: Macmillan, 1973.

Meyers, Jeffrey. *Hemingway: A Biography*. New York: Harper, 1985.

Miller, Leslie. "'Cat in the Rain.'" *Linguistics in Literature* 1, no. 2 (1976): 29–34.

Moddelmog, Debra A. "The Unifying Consciousness of a Divided Nick Adams as Author of *In Our Time*." *American Literature* 60, no. 4 (1989): 591–610.

Monteiro, George. "This is Pal Bugs: Ernest Hemingway's 'The Battler.'" *Studies in Short Fiction* 23 (1986): 179–83.

Montgomery, Constance. *Hemingway in Michigan*. New York: Fleet, 1966.

Muller, Gilbert H. "*In Our Time*: Hemingway and the Discontents of Civilization." *Renascence* 29 (1977): 185–92.

Nagel, Gwen L. "A Tessera for Frederic Henry: Imagery and Recurrence in *A Farewell to Arms*." In *Ernest Hemingway: Six Decades of Criticism*, edited by Linda W. Wagner, 187–93. Ann Arbor: University of Michigan Press, 1973.

Nagel, James. "Catherine Barkley and Retrospective Narration in *A Farewell to Arms*." In *Ernest Hemingway: Six Decades of Criticism*, edited by Linda W. Wagner, 171–85. Ann Arbor: University of Michigan Press, 1973.

———. *Ernest Hemingway: The Writer in Context*. Madison: University of Wisconsin Press, 1984.

————. "Literary Impressionism and *In Our Time*." *Hemingway Review* 1 (Spring 1987): 17–26.

Nahal, Chaman. *The Narrative Pattern in Ernest Hemingway's Fiction.* Rutherford, N.J.: Fairleigh Dickinson University Press, 1971.

Nelson, Raymond S. *Hemingway: Expressionist Artist.* Ames: Iowa State University Press, 1979.

Newman, Charles B. "Hemingway's Grail Quest." *University of Kansas Review* 28 (1961–62): 295–303.

Oldsley, Bernard, ed. *Ernest Hemingway: The Papers of a Writer.* New York: Garland, 1981.

————. *Hemingway's Hidden Craft: The Writing of A Farewell to Arms.* University Park: Pennsylvania State University Press, 1979.

Parker, Alice. "Hemingway's 'The End of Something.'" *Explicator* 10 (1951–52): item 36.

Penner, Dick. "The First Nick Adams Story." *Fitzgerald/Hemingway Annual* (1977): 195–202.

Petrarca, Anthony J. "Irony of Situation in Ernest Hemingway's 'Soldier's Home.'" *English Journal* 58 (1969): 664–67.

Plimpton, George, ed. *Writers at Work.* The Paris Interviews. Second Series. New York: Penguin, 1985.

Pound, Ezra. *Literary Essays of Ezra Pound.* New York: New Directions, 1935.

————. *Personae: The Collected Shorter Poems of Ezra Pound.* New York: New Directions, 1926.

Reynolds, Michael S., ed. *Critical Essays on Ernest Hemingway's In Our Time.* Boston: G. K. Hall, 1983.

————. *Hemingway: The Paris Years.* New York: Blackwell, 1989.

————. *Hemingway's First War: The Making of A Farewell to Arms.* Princeton: Princeton University Press, 1976.

————. "Hemingway's 'My Old Man': Turf Days in Paris." In *Hemingway in Italy and Other Essays*, edited by Robert W. Lewis, 101–6. New York: Praeger, 1990.

————. *The Young Hemingway.* New York: Blackwell, 1986.

Roberts, John J. "In Defense of Krebs." *Studies in Short Fiction* 13 (1976–77): 515–18.

Rosenthal, M. L. *The Modern Poets: A Critical Introduction.* New York: Oxford University Press, 1960.

————. *The New Poets: American and British Poetry Since World War II.* New York: Oxford University Press, 1967.

————. *The Poet's Art.* New York: Norton, 1987.

————. *A Primer of Ezra Pound.* New York: Grosset, 1960.

————. *Sailing Into the Unknown: Yeats, Pound, Eliot.* New York: Oxford University Press, 1978.

Rosenthal, M. L. and Sally M. Gall. *The Modern Poetic Sequence: The Genius of Modern Poetry.* New York: Oxford University Press, 1983.

Rovit, Earl and Gerry Brenner. *Ernest Hemingway.* Boston: Hall, 1986.

Russell, H. K. "The Catharsis in A *Farewell to Arms*." *Modern Fiction Studies* 1 (1955): 25–30.

Sanders, Barbara. "Linguistic Analysis of 'Cross-Country Snow.'" *Linguistics and Literature* 1, no. 2 (1978): 43–52.

Schneider, Daniel J. "Hemingway's A *Farewell to Arms:* The Novel as Pure Poetry." *Modern Fiction Studies* 14 (1968): 283–96. Reprint. *Ernest Hemingway: Five Decades of Criticism,* edited by Linda W. Wagner, 252–66. Ann Arbor: University of Michigan Press, 1973.

Scholes, Robert. "Decoding Papa: 'A Very Short Story' as Word and Text." In *Semiotics and Interpretation.* New Haven: Yale University Press, 1982.

Seed, David. "'The Picture of the Whole': *In Our Time.*" In *Ernest Hemingway: New Critical Essays,* edited by A. Robert Lee, 13–35. Totowa, N.J.: Barnes, 1983.

Slabey, Robert M. "The Structure of *In Our Time.*" *South Dakota Review* (1965): 38–52. Reprint. *Critical Essays on Ernest Hemingway's In Our Time,* edited by Michael S. Reynolds, 76–87. Boston: G. K. Hall, 1983.

Smith, Julian. "Hemingway and the Thing Left Out." *Journal of Modern Literature* 1, no. 2 (1970–71): 169–82. Reprint. *Ernest Hemingway: Five Decades of Criticism,* edited by Linda W. Wagner, 188–200. Ann Arbor: University of Michigan Press, 1973.

Smith, Paul. "From the Waste Land to the Garden with the Elliots." In *Hemingway's Neglected Short Fiction,* edited by Susan F. Beegel, 123–29. Ann Arbor, Mich.: UMI Research Press, 1988.

———. "Hemingway's Early Manuscripts: The Theory and Practice of Omission." *Journal of Modern Literature* 10 (July 1983): 268–88.

———. "'Mons (Three)': An Unpublished *In Our Time* Chapter." In *Hemingway in Italy and Other Essays,* edited by Robert W. Lewis, 107–12. New York: Praeger, 1990.

———. A *Reader's Guide to the Short Stories of Ernest Hemingway.* Boston: G. K. Hall, 1989.

———. "Some Misconceptions of 'Out of Season.'" In *Critical Essays on Ernest Hemingway's In Our Time,* edited by Michael S. Reynolds, 235–51. Boston: G. K. Hall, 1983.

Smith, Peter A. "Hemingway's 'On the Quai at Smyrna' and the Universe of *In Our Time.*" *Studies in Short Fiction* 24, no. 2 (1987): 159–62.

Sojka, Gregory S. "Who is Sam Cardinella, and Why Is He Hanging Between Two Sunny Days at Seney?" *Fitzgerald/Hemingway Annual* (1976): 217–23.

Somers, Paul P., Jr. "The Mark of Sherwood Anderson on Hemingway: A Look at the Texts." *South Atlantic Quarterly* 73 (Autumn 1974): 487–503.

Stein, William Bysshe. "Love and Lust in Hemingway's Short Stories." *Texas Studies in Literature and Language* 3 (1961): 234–42.

———. "Ritual in Hemingway's 'Big Two-Hearted River.'" *Texas Studies in Literature and Language* 1 (1960): 55–61.

Steinke, Jim. "Hemingway's 'Cat in the Rain.'" *Spectrum* 25, nos. 1 and 2 (1983): 36–44.

———. "The Two Shortest Stories of Hemingway's *In Our Time.*" In *Critical Essays on Ernest Hemingway's In Our Time,* edited by Michael S. Reynolds, 218–26. Boston: G. K. Hall, 1983.

Stephens, Robert O. *Hemingway's Nonfiction: The Public Voice.* Chapel Hill: University of North Carolina Press, 1968.

Stewart, Jack F. "Christian Allusions in 'Big Two-Hearted River.'" *Studies in Short Fiction* 15 (1978): 194–96.

Strandberg, Victor H. "Eliot's Insomniacs." *South Atlantic Quarterly* 58 (1969): 67–73.

Sylvester, Bickford. "Hemingway's Italian *Waste Land*: The Complex Unity of 'Out of Season.'" In *Hemingway's Neglected Short Fiction*, edited by Susan F. Beegel, 75–98. Ann Arbor, Mich.: UMI Research Press, 1988.

Tanselle, G. Thomas. "Hemingway's 'Indian Camp.'" *Explicator* 20 (February 1962): item 53.

Tavernier-Courbin, Jacqueline. "Ernest Hemingway and Ezra Pound." In *Ernest Hemingway, The Writer in Context*, edited by James Nagel, 179–200. Madison: University of Wisconsin Press, 1984.

Twitchell, James. "The Swamp in Hemingway's 'Big Two-Hearted River.'" *Studies in Short Fiction* 9 (1972): 275–76.

Vandersee, Charles. "The Stopped Worlds of Frederic Henry." In *Studies in a Farewell to Arms*, compiled by John Graham, 55–65. Columbus, Ohio: Merrill, 1971.

Vaugn, Elizabeth D. "*In Our Time* as Self-Begetting Fiction." *Modern Fiction Studies* 35 (Winter 1989): 707–16.

Villard, Henry Serrano and James Nagel. *Hemingway in Love and War.* Boston: Northeastern University Press, 1989.

Waggoner, Hyatt. "Hemingway and Faulkner: 'The End of Something.'" *Southern Review* 4 (1968): 458–66.

Wagner, Linda W. *American Modern: Essays in Fiction and Poetry.* Port Washington, N.Y.: National, 1980.

———, ed. *Ernest Hemingway: Five Decades of Criticism.* Ann Arbor: University of Michigan Press, 1973.

———, ed. *Ernest Hemingway: Six Decades of Criticism.* Ann Arbor: University of Michigan Press, 1987.

———. *Hemingway and Faulkner: inventors/masters.* Metuchen, N.J.: Scarecrow, 1975.

———. "Juxtaposition in Hemingway's *In Our Time*." *Studies in Short Fiction* 12 (1975): 243–52.

———. "*The Sun Also Rises*: One Debt to Imagism." *Journal of Narrative Technique* 11 (1972): 88–98.

Waldhorn, Arthur. *A Reader's Guide to Ernest Hemingway.* New York: Octagon, 1983.

Warren, Robert Penn. "Ernest Hemingway." *Kenyon Review* 9 (1947): 1–28. Reprint. *Ernest Hemingway: Five Decades of Criticism*, edited by Linda W. Wagner, 75–102. Ann Arbor: University of Michigan Press, 1973.

Watts, Emily Stipes. *Ernest Hemingway and the Arts.* Urbana: University of Illinois Press, 1971.

Weber, Brom. "Ernest Hemingway's Genteel Bullfight." In *The American Novel and the Nineteen Twenties*, edited by Malcolm Bradbury and David Palmer, 151–63. New York and London: Arnold, 1971.

Weeks, Robert P., ed. *Hemingway: A Collection of Critical Essays.* Englewood Cliffs, N.J.: Prentice-Hall, 1962.

Welland, Dennis. "Idiom in Hemingway: A Footnote." *Journal of American Studies* 18, no. 3 (1984): 449–51.

Wells, Elizabeth J. "A Statistical Analysis of the Prose Style of Ernest Hemingway: 'Big Two-Hearted River.'" *Fitzgerald/Hemingway Annual* (1969): 47–69. Reprint. *The Short Stories of Ernest Hemingway: Critical Essays*, edited by Jackson L. Benson, 129–35. Durham, N.C.: Duke University Press, 1975.

West, Ray B. "A Farewell to Arms." *Sewanee Review* 55 (1945): 120–35. Reprint. *The Art of Modern Fiction*, edited by R. W. Stallman and Ray B. West, 622–33. New York: Holt, 1949.

"Western Wind." Anonymous. In *The New Oxford Book of English Verse 1250–1950*, edited by Helen Gardner, 20. New York: Oxford University Press, 1972.

White, Gertrude M. "We're All 'Cats in the Rain.'" *Fitzgerald/Hemingway Annual* (1978): 241–46.

White, William, ed. *By-Line: Ernest Hemingway: Selected Articles and Dispatches of Four Decades*. New York: Scribner's, 1967.

Whitt, Joseph. "Hemingway's 'The End of Something.'" *Explicator* 9 (1950–51): item 58.

Williams, Wirt. *The Tragic Art of Ernest Hemingway*. Baton Rouge: Louisiana State University Press, 1981.

Wilson, Edmund. "Dry Points." *Dial* 77 (1924): 340–41.

———. *The Shores of Light: A Chronical of the Twenties to Thirties*. New York: Farrar, 1952.

———. *The Wound and the Bow*. New York: Farrar, 1947.

Winchell, Mark Royden. "Fishing the Swamp: 'Big Two-Hearted River' and the Unity of *In Our Time*." *South Carolina Review* 18, no. 2 (1986): 18–29.

Winn, Harlan Harbour III. "Short Story Cycles of Hemingway, Steinbeck, Faulkner, O'Connor." Diss. University of Oregon. 1975.

Wood, Carl. "Hemingway's Fragmentary Novel." *Neuphilologische Mitteilungen* 74, no. 4 (1974): 716–26.

Woodward, Robert H. "Hemingway's 'On the Quai at Smyrna': An exercise in Irony." *Exercise Exchange* 10 (1963): 11–12.

Wylder, Delbert E. *Hemingway's Heroes*. Albuquerque: University of New Mexico Press, 1969.

Young, Philip. "Adventures of Nick Adams." In *Hemingway: A Collection of Critical Essays*, edited by Robert P. Weeks, 95–112. Englewood Cliffs, N.J.: Prentice-Hall, 1962.

———. *Ernest Hemingway: A Reconsideration*. 1952. Reprint. University Park: Pennsylvania State University Press, 1966.

Young, Philip, and W. C. Mann, eds. *The Hemingway Manuscripts: An Inventory*. University Park: Pennsylvania State University Press, 1969.

Index